"I know who did it!"

"Ruth, what are you doing here? It's six o'clock in the morning."

"I know who broke in and ripped off my paintings. They were stolen, remember? Dead guys and all that. I can't believe you could dismiss a felony like it was an overdue book."

"Ruth, you're distraught," Helma said. She took a glass from her cupboard. "Have a glass of orange juice."

"Do you have coffee?"

"Research has shown that fruit juice can be as stimulating as coffee."

"Except it tastes funny. Besides, I have every reason to be, as you say, distraught. Art theft is a crime. Look at Munch's *The Scream*. It disappears every time you turn around."

"It was stolen for ransom money," Helma pointed out.

"My thief doesn't want money. That strip of slashed art left on my bed wasn't just a threat to my life. I know what it was: the rat wants to stop my show."

"And your suspect is?"

Ruth emoted as if announcing a vaudeville act. "The only person who makes sense!"

By Jo Dereske

INDEX TO MURDER
CATALOGUE OF DEATH
BOOKMARKED TO DIE
FINAL NOTICE
MISS ZUKAS AND THE STROKE OF DEATH
MISS ZUKAS AND THE ISLAND MURDERS
MISS ZUKAS AND THE LIBRARY MURDERS

INDEX TO MURDER

JO DERESKE

A V O N

An Imprint of HarperCollinsPublishers

This is a work of fiction. Names, characters, places, and incidents are products of the author's imagination or are used fictitiously and are not to be construed as real. Any resemblance to actual events, locales, organizations, or persons, living or dead, is entirely coincidental.

AVON BOOKS
An Imprint of HarperCollins*Publishers*
10 East 53rd Street
New York, New York 10022-5299

Copyright © 2008 by Jo Dereske
ISBN: 978-0-06-079086-8
www.avonmystery.com

First Avon Books paperback printing: May 2008

Avon Trademark Reg. U.S. Pat. Off. and in Other Countries, Marca Registrada, Hecho en U.S.A.
HarperCollins® is a registered trademark of HarperCollins Publishers.

Printed in the U.S.A.

10 9 8 7 6 5 4 3 2 1

For Carolyn Hart and Mary Daheim,
women of great generosity and humor

Contents

INDEX TO MURDER

Chapter 1

A Calamitous Suggestion

On a cold Tuesday evening in October, Miss Helma Zukas finally realized her friend Ruth Winthrop was unlikely to recover. Because, in fact, Ruth Winthrop had no intention of recovering.

"My life is over," Ruth announced in despondency so deep it bordered on gratification. "My heart has been shredded to Parmesan."

Ruth sprawled on the sofa in Helma's apartment, her long legs stretched beyond the coffee table where Helma had just returned Ruth's whiskey glass to the safety of a coaster. No denying she *looked* as if her life were over: bagged eyes, slumped shoulders, garbed in the same paint-stained jeans and sweater she'd been wearing for a week.

Helma Zukas rarely interrupted people in the throes of passionate emotion unless there was imminent danger. In her experience, unnaturally agitated states were exhausting to maintain and wore down quickest when unencouraged.

But Ruth might be the exception. The situation had

been deteriorating and Ruth's obsession escalating for a month. The time had come to do something. *Anything.* Little did Helma suspect that her innocent suggestion would result in deception, destruction, and death.

"I have no illusions this time," Ruth continued, running her hands through her hair until it sprang out in a wild nimbus. "None. What's over is over and the curtain has hit the stage. The lights are out, the mop has flopped. The balcony is closed."

Despite the melodrama, Ruth's lament rang with truth. Helma herself suspected the permanency of the situation, but she hadn't believed Ruth would. Not after all these years. Not *really.*

Helma had seen Paul's face, had heard the finality in his voice when he stopped by her apartment to say goodbye before he caught his flight back to Minnesota, his shoulders weighted by sorrow and, yes, resignation. "I'm glad you're Ruth's friend, Helma," he'd said, and Helma hadn't responded to his implied hope that she'd stand by Ruth. It wasn't necessary.

She'd watched him descend the staircase of the Bayside Arms, and as soon as his foot touched the sidewalk, she closed her door and telephoned Ruth.

For three days Helma had received no answer at Ruth's studio/house that nestled against the alley a half mile away, neither to phone calls made every three hours or by knocking at the locked door each morning and night on her drive to and from the library.

Ruth's behavior wasn't unusual. She locked her door only if she was inside either painting or was in what she called "a funk." And the current situation qualified as a major funk.

So at first Helma didn't worry. She picked up Ruth's newspapers from the front step and set them out of the weather inside a sculpture designed like a small coffin beside the front door. After sorting through Ruth's mail for envelopes that looked important, she added that to the coffin, too.

But by the third afternoon of silence, Helma became uneasy. She rapped sharply on Ruth's door, tried the doorknob and found it still locked.

She didn't condone shouting in nonemergency situations, or talking through closed doors, but now she cleared her throat and said in a conversational tone, as if Ruth might be crouched on the other side of the door, pressing her ear to the paneled wood, "Ruth, this is ridiculous. I'm going home now, and I intend to call the police."

She'd returned to her apartment, eaten a small salad without dressing and a broiled salmon fillet, and even washed her dishes and put them away, rotating the plate she'd just used to the bottom of the stack of six to equalize wear to the set, and wiped her hands on the hand towel she hung separate from her dish towel.

It was time. She wouldn't call out the police force or dial 911, but chief of police Wayne Gallant, whose personal phone number she kept as private as he did.

And that's when her doorbell had jangled.

Helma rehung the hand towel, took a deep breath, and opened the door without first looking through the security viewer.

Ruth stood on the landing that stretched across the third floor of the Bayside Arms. Clothes rumpled, hair wild, her six-foot frame somehow shrunken.

"Were you trying to call me?" she'd asked, her voice brittle and eyes red. "I must have been taking a nap." And she pushed past Helma, a brown bottle-shaped bag cradled tenderly in the crook of her arm.

Now, an hour later, Ruth hiccupped and reached a hand toward Boy Cat Zukas, who'd left his basket by the balcony door and taken a few tentative steps toward the sofa.

"Kitty, kitty," Ruth said, but the black cat hissed and slunk two feet backward, his back arched.

"Even the cat," Ruth lamented. "Even an old scroungy alley cat who's used up ten of his nine lives. Even he knows. I'm doomed."

"Animals are situational learners," Helma explained, turning her wrist to unobtrusively glance at her watch. It was 10:13. "They're accustomed to specific responses in familiar situations."

Ruth grunted. "You're saying I'm not acting in my usual lighthearted effervescent way?"

"Perhaps not in the way an animal is conditioned to expect."

"That's what I just said: even the cat knows."

"You're ascribing intellectual capabilities to an animal. Reasoning. Emotions . . . "

"Call it animal instinct, then," Ruth said. "I don't give a rip." She waved a hand toward Boy Cat Zukas, who had backed up two more steps. "He knows. I know. You know." She paused, brushed her hands through her hair again and asked, "Don't you?"

Helma didn't answer immediately, feeling the intensity of Ruth's gaze, hearing the uncustomary tentativeness, the lingering edge of hope. She believed in honesty, yes, even admitting to painful truths. But Ruth was also her friend, despite their incongruous lives. They'd developed their bewildering friendship back in Scoop River, Michigan, following a bitter preadolescent battle in St. Alphonse School, where Ruth's parents had enrolled her in the vain hope the nuns would instill a modicum of decorum in their troubled daughter.

Ruth and Helma had made their separate ways to the West Coast city of Bellehaven, Washington, and like many transplants who'd only intended to remain "a year or two, just to try it out," they both stayed. Their lives traveled in separate orbits, intersecting briefly by design, since chance meetings, even in a town of only forty thousand, were rare in their daily lives.

"Ruth," Helma said carefully. "You and Paul tried to form an alliance for years, living apart here, then together in Minnesota, and finally next door to each other here."

"An *alliance*," Ruth spat out. She raised her hands behind her head. "But it really *is* over this time, isn't it?"

"I can't speak for either of you," Helma said reasonably, seeing in her mind's eye Paul's calmly sad face as he turned away from her door. "But I believe people reach a point when they want to settle their lives."

Ruth sighed. Her left foot jounced back and forth in a staccato rhythm. The heel of her boot bruised the carpet. "Yeah, there's the rub. He wanted life with a capital L. The white picket-fence thing. A dog and a lawn." Her voice caught. "Children."

"You could . . ."

"I don't want that," Ruth said, and Boy Cat Zukas, who'd returned to his basket, hissed at the tone in her voice. "Never have, never will, and since I haven't been inclined in the past forty-two years, I'm not starting now. Period."

As if Helma had protested, Ruth continued. "I look at kids with jaundiced wisdom, you know what I mean? All those big hopeful eyes, poised to watch their little dreams get pulverized. No thank you. Been there, experienced that. Besides, all that stuff, that capital *L* with a picket fence, disrupts my painting. Putting myself on a schedule dries up the muse. That's why I came back here, remember? Back to sea level."

Ruth abandoned her glass and took a long pull from the whiskey bottle that was still in its brown paper bag.

In the movies, when characters drank whiskey, they grimaced or coughed or wiped their mouths to counter its potency. Helma had never tasted whiskey but she knew that

Ruth's favorite scotch, Laphroaig, was also one of the most expensive. Ruth removed the bottle from her mouth, neither grimacing nor wiping her lips. She might as well have been drinking water.

"Life pulls you along, isn't that what they say?" she asked. "But what life really is, is an accumulation of losses." She clapped her hands together sharply. "And then you die."

"That's very cynical," Helma told her. "Moving forward *is* the only direction we have."

"There are other directions, Pollyanna," Ruth said darkly, and Helma studied her closely.

"Are you saying that for effect, or do you honestly feel that hopeless?"

Ruth waved a hand in dismissal. "Yeah, just for effect. When I do something for attention, I plan to be around to bask in it." She pulled the Laphroaig bottle from the bag and held it to the lamplight, tipping the green bottle. It was half empty. "But you know, Helma, my heart *is* broken into a million bite-sized chunks."

She spoke lightly now, the melodrama replaced by genuine sorrow. Her foot stilled and she turned to gaze out at the night beyond Helma's sliding glass doors, where Washington Bay stretched toward the San Juan Islands. "This is going to be a long haul," she said. Boy Cat Zukas left his wicker basket and sat three feet in front of Ruth, gazing at her, unblinking. "I feel *lower* than sea level."

Helma herself hadn't had an occasion to seek professional help during her lifetime, which she attributed to the ability to extricate herself from unpromising situations before help was necessary.

But she *did* appreciate the value of the disinterested listener. And that might be exactly what Ruth needed. "I could do a search at the library for you," she offered. "There are several highly recommended counselors in Bellehaven."

In one of her lightning switches of mood, Ruth snorted and sat up straight on the sofa. "Spare me. I prefer the fine art of wallowing in my own mire. Besides . . ." She raised the whiskey bottle. ". . . I have all the help I need right here."

Ruth and alcohol, or Ruth and discontent. Either combination meant trouble for Bellehaven. And often, by extension, for her, too. Helma thought furiously. "Keep busy," her mother and Aunt Em advised during times of trouble. And although Helma had once scoffed at the idea of busyness banishing a troubled heart, there had been that one occasion it helped . . .

If Ruth was kept occupied until the rawest edges eroded from her heartbreak, damage to the community and Ruth, and even Helma, might be minimal.

"You could plan a trip," she suggested. She sipped her tea and set it aside. It was cold.

"I don't *plan* trips," Ruth said. "*You* do that. I *go*."

That was true. Planning had never been one of Ruth's priorities.

"Your house," she tried. "You own your house. You could remodel."

"I like it the way it is."

"What about painting?"

Ruth frowned. "Paint my house?"

"No. Your painting. Your art."

Ruth made an erratic living from her art, living high when her paintings sold well and dependent on what she ambiguously referred to as "the insurance" when they didn't. Her paintings—giant oils in mixes of hues that gave Helma a headache if she spent much time in their presence—varied from purely representational to purely chaotic and often controversial. The one sure thing was that once Ruth settled on what she called "the subject," their execution absorbed her body and soul, night and day.

"All I could paint right now is the inside of a hole," Ruth exaggerated, a relief from her quiet sorrow. "What are you trying to do, keep me busy?"

"Yes," Helma admitted. "Painting the inside of holes could be helpful. There are those who believe that exploring a problem helps resolve it more quickly."

"You mean sink so low into the pit there's no way to go but up?"

"In a manner of speaking," Helma said, and was relieved to see a frown of consideration crease Ruth's forehead. "And there are many shades of gray and black paint," she encouraged, "if you truly did want to paint holes, that is."

"Like that joke painting: *Cow Eating Grass at Midnight*?"

"Midnight light *is* different in a full moon than a new moon."

"That would get boring pretty quick, and then where would I be?" Ruth held the whiskey bottle between her knees. "No, I need a bigger subject. Something with lots of facets and angles."

"Bellehaven?" Helma offered eagerly, seeing Ruth's interest pique. "The mountains?" she suggested as Ruth shook her head. "What about painting your life?" she tried.

Ruth bit her lip. "My life," she repeated, absently pushing the cork into her Laphroaig bottle with the palm of her hand. Boy Cat Zukas's ears twitched.

"A lot has happened," Helma encouraged.

"You're saying it's been long." But she was definitely considering the idea, Helma could see it. "The triumphs and the tragedies."

"The ups and downs," Helma agreed.

"The rats and the eagles." Ruth stood, her eyes narrowing but definitely gazing forward.

Helma felt the first prickle of intent gone awry.

"The jerks and the princes," Ruth continued. "A few rodents have definitely jerked their way through my life." She grabbed the whiskey bottle and headed for Helma's door, saying to herself, "I think that just might be a possibility."

And that was how Helma unwittingly set into motion a series of calamitous events.

Chapter 2

Six Months Later

Helma stood in front of the sliding glass doors of her third-floor apartment, snipping the label off a new blouse so it wouldn't scratch her neck. Beyond her balcony, gray water and gray sky joined in a silvery fog, blocking her view of the humped San Juan Islands. The local morning news played on her television.

Spring in Bellehaven, Washington, was a debatable season, in some years existing in name only, as drippy, frigid, and windblown as March or November, or as brightly deceptive as a good day in January. And some years as mildly temperate as a mistake the populace suspected Mother Nature would soon rectify with a vengeance. Closets reflected the season's uncertainty: layers were more than a Northwest fashion statement.

Helma Zukas did not subscribe to the layered look, despite having lived in Bellehaven for over twenty years. During that period she'd studied three books on the peculiarities of West Coast weather and listened carefully to the reasonings and apologies of television meteorologists, until she'd developed an uncannily accurate sense of weather prediction.

She rarely left her apartment in a pile of clothes she had to remove or add to. One of her several thicknesses of coats was always sufficient, as was the sweater she kept at the library, the donning of which was more dependent on the uncertainties of indoor heating systems than the peculiarities of weather.

So, she pulled an unlined coat from her coat closet and draped it over her sofa, sleeves folded backward, knowing it would be adequate.

Boy Cat Zukas had been fed and removed to the balcony. Since she and the cat had never willingly made physical contact, his departure was sometimes complicated. He crouched on her balcony floor as still as a statue, eyeing a sparrow hopping along the railing. Helma tapped on the window to shoo the bird away, not to spoil the cat's fun but because she disliked removing small body parts from her balcony.

Another teen alcohol accident, the news anchor reported, and Helma recalled the chief of police calling the youthful car wrecks "the saddest of the spring rites."

The announcer went on to relate the story of a rogue elk charging a Volkswagen. "And under cover of darkness, the Ground Up organization planted three hundred Douglas firs along the property line of Woody's Car Recyclers. The owner is threatening to sue the extremist organization."

When the news stories switched to sports, Helma donned her coat over a long-sleeved green cotton dress. Her phone rang. According to the clock over her stove, if she spoke less than three minutes, she'd still arrive at the Bellehaven Public Library with ten minutes to spare.

"I've been robbed," Ruth shouted into her ear.

"Have you called the police?" Helma asked reasonably, continuing to button her coat one-handed.

"Of course I've called the police. The 911 lady told me to wait outside until the cavalry arrived. 'No reason to now,' I told her. 'They're long gone.'"

"You were robbed during the night?" Helma asked. "While you were asleep? Thieves were in the house *with* you?"

"Nah, I just got home. They could have turned the knob and waltzed in through the front door, but no, the idiots smashed my kitchen window and hauled themselves in over the sink. I wish I'd seen *that*."

If Ruth even owned a key to her house, Helma suspected it was forever lost. "Locking the door doesn't stop a criminal," she'd claimed. "it just makes him so mad he'll make a bigger mess when he *does* get inside."

"What did they steal?" Helma asked as she removed the lunch she'd packed the night before from her refrigerator.

"Two of my paintings. For my show, you know? 'Ruth Revealed.' The retrospective of my life." The bravado slipped from Ruth's voice. "Can you come over?"

"I'm on my way to work."

"Just for a minute. A little moral support until our beloved blue boys get here, okay? You won't have to come in past my kitchen, all right?"

Ruth lived mainly in her kitchen, a clutter of interrupted tasks that spilled from counters to table to chairs, and finally the floor. The rest of the house had been turned into a studio filled with paintings in every shade of completion. Helma wasn't quite sure where Ruth slept, when she *did* sleep.

"Just for a minute," Ruth pleaded. "Maybe the leader of the pack will pop in."

Helma doubted the chief of police would investigate a simple break-in. Ruth's paintings sometimes sold well, that was true, but it was baffling that anyone would break and enter to *steal* two of them.

"I'm just leaving my apartment," Helma told her. "I'll be there in five minutes."

"I'll clear a space for you to stand."

Ruth's house nestled at the edge of the Slope, Bellehaven's older, more genteel area of town. The small red-trimmed bungalow sat back from the street, nearly on the alley, its narrow front lawn gone, as Ruth said, au naturel. Beside the house, a purple clematis overwhelmed a broken trellis.

Helma parked her Buick along the street, leaving room for a police car to pull in behind Ruth's blue VW. Ruth wasn't outside as the 911 operator had advised, and Helma cautiously approached her house, looking for signs of illegal entry. A soft spring rain had begun to fall, too light for an umbrella. She glanced up at the sky, an unvariegated gray.

A lawn chair with one leg propped by a piece of two-by-four listed on Ruth's small covered porch, an empty wine bottle on the floor beside it. The front door stood open, but Helma walked around to the side door off Ruth's kitchen, avoiding the jumble of colorful objects visible through the open front door.

The kitchen door stood ajar, and Helma cautiously stepped across the threshold. Ruth lived by color and was likely to repaint anything at hand as her moods shifted, which was often, so that now Helma was greeted by not the purple kitchen walls she'd stepped into during her last disastrous visit to Ruth's house but by mud-brown, a color that surely didn't exist on any paint store color chip. Helma blinked. Ruth's refrigerator was painted black. The effect was like walking into a cave, or maybe the inside of the hole she'd once talked of painting.

She tapped against the doorjamb. No answer. Had the thief been hiding in Ruth's house after all? Could he be there now, holding Ruth hostage until the police arrived, a bargaining chip for his freedom?

"Ruth Winthrop," she said in her silver dime voice, a voice that compelled immediate attention, a voice that had once frozen a vandal about to apply an X-acto knife to an especially fine reproduction of the Mona Lisa in an Abrams art book. "The police are on their way."

"I already know *that*." Ruth's voice came from beyond the kitchen. "Come see what I found."

"If it's not evidence, could you bring it here?" she asked as she closed the open door. Mail was piled high on Ruth's counters, an open box of graham crackers and two empty jam jars, dirty plates and ringed glasses, a pair of strappy shoes with three-inch heels. Shards from the broken window shimmered around the sink. She looked up, focusing instead on the brown walls.

"It's evidence in my book."

Helma hesitated. Evidence. "Where are you?"

"In here," Ruth said, her voice cranky. "This house only has four rooms. Come on."

Helma repositioned her purse, holding it close to her body, and crossed the brown kitchen, stepping over a single bar-bell and around a knee-high stack of laundry.

Ruth stood beside what might be her bed: a jumble of clothes on the end, a swirl of blankets and pillows that formed an untidy nest. She wore a denim man's shirt and red leggings, her dark hair in a ponytail tied close behind her left ear. The air drifting in through the open door gave the room a damp and sticky feeling.

"I think this is a warning, don't you? A threat on my life."

Helma knew Ruth didn't mean her bed, so she looked for an anomaly among the disarray, some item that wasn't beddish. A colorful two-inch by three-foot strip of painted canvas lay across her pillow.

"Is that from one of your paintings?" she asked.

"The very thing," Ruth said, nodding glumly at the shred. "Ripped out."

"Do you know from which painting?"

Ruth waved toward the other side of the room. Seven unframed paintings leaned against the wall, all of them bright and big, collections of images that Helma didn't have time to decipher. "Can't you see? Two of them are missing. And this," she pointed to the shred of canvas, "was torn from one of them." She frowned. "I wasn't just robbed. I was desecrated."

Now that Helma had her bearings, she noticed two blank spots in the row of paintings, not next to each other but with three paintings intervening. "What did the paintings depict?" she asked.

"Scenes from my life, what else?"

Helma's original idea to assist Ruth through her crisis by suggesting she paint had taken on a life of its own. Ruth had embraced the idea of exposing her life to the world. And in fact, the title of her upcoming show, Ruth Revealed, hinted at more than just art.

Ruth spread word of her paintings at bars, in post-office and grocery-store lines. She offered dark and dramatic hints that every disappointment in her life would soon be hung on walls for the world to ponder, even that she might be naming names. In a way, the destruction of select paintings wasn't a *complete* surprise.

Before Helma could ask *which* scenes Ruth had portrayed in the stolen paintings, a voice announced at Ruth's open front door, "Police."

"It's about time, you guys," Ruth called. "Come in and solve this."

A single policeman entered, ducking a little, the way people in authority and those who were exceptionally tall did to put people at ease. He was older, tired-looking, as if he'd just come off an all-night shift. A scar dimpled his left cheek. Helma didn't recognize him. "You had a robbery, ma'am?" he asked, looking from Helma to Ruth.

"I did," Ruth told him, pulling herself taller. "Two very valuable paintings. My own." Her voice adopted the tones of a radio announcement, "They were for my show, Ruth Revealed, at Cheri's Gallery next month, opening on Thursday, the seventeenth, with a reception from six to eight. Wine and crudités provided."

He nodded and glanced at the row of colorful paintings, tipping his head to one side then the other, then around Ruth's jumbled house, his face bland. "Any idea why somebody would steal two paintings?"

Ruth shrugged. "They were scenes from the disappointments in my life. Maybe somebody didn't like what I was saying."

"Who else has seen them?" He jotted in a spiral notebook with a mechanical pencil.

"Nobody. I don't show them before I show them. Officially, I mean."

"Did you tell other people about them?"

"Some," Ruth admitted.

More than a few people who knew that Helma and Ruth were friends had cautiously asked Helma if she knew how "open" Ruth intended to be, how much Ruth Revealed would actually reveal, even George Melville, the cataloger at the Bellehaven Public Library.

"The strip of canvas may yield evidence," Helma suggested, putting the investigation back on track.

'Oh yeah, this," Ruth said, reaching for the strip lying across her pillow.

"Don't touch that," the policeman warned, and Ruth jumped back, her hands raised.

"It's a warning. On my pillow like that. If I'd been in bed, they'd have strangled me with it." She touched her neck and added with a touch of dreaminess, "Garroted by my own art."

"I'll call somebody to look at it," he said. "Would you describe the missing paintings?" He raised his eyebrows at the row of remaining paintings, sounding doubtful.

"Certainly," Ruth said. "They depicted two close . . . liaisons I had a while ago."

He held his pencil over his notebook. "So they were faces?"

"Not really."

"Places?" he tried.

Ruth shook her head. "Feelings. Emotions that belonged to that time—and those men. Excitement and disillusionment. I don't remember exactly." She frowned, then brightened. "But I'd recognize them if I saw them, I know that."

"You're not giving us much to go on. What are the names of the men involved?"

"Do I have to?" Ruth asked, crossing her arms.

"It would be helpful."

"They're dead, anyway."

He continued gazing at her, pencil unmoving.

"Okay, okay. Meriwether Scott and Vincent Jensen," Ruth said. "Happy now?"

Tiredness dropped from the policeman's face and he twirled his pencil between his fingers. His brows met above his nose. "You knew both of them?" he asked. "Personally?"

"Yeah, so? I know, they weren't exactly kindred souls, but I have a wide range of personal acquaintances, not just the rich and famous."

"Meriwether Scott was a—" he began.

"Chain-saw artist," Ruth furnished. "Among other things. And Vincent taught at the college. So they were the proverbial night and day, what difference does it make? Just because they're both dead."

"Within a month of each other," he said as if he were talking to himself. He rocked on his heels.

"Well, what's that got to do with my stolen paintings?" Ruth asked. "*I* didn't do it."

Chapter 3

Taking a Fall

The officer closed his notebook and inserted his pencil in the spiral binding. He looked around Ruth's house. "Don't clean up for a few hours, will you?"

"That's not a problem," Ruth told him.

"And don't touch that," he said, pointing to the shred of canvas.

"You got it. Send in the CSI."

After the policeman left, Ruth closed her front door and said to Helma, "He acted funny, didn't he? Don't you think he did? I think he did."

Helma hadn't moved from her position between the doorway and Ruth's sort-of bed, beside the painting Ruth was currently creating. It stood in a pristine island of order. Brushes arranged by size, paint tubes grouped by hue, the canvas centered and upright on the spotless easel.

Otherwise, paint tubes lay every which way on every available surface. A frayed brush was stuck to an empty Snickers wrapper. Clothes dropped here and there, books bookmarking other books and scattered around her bed. Helma blinked overlong, relaxing her eyes. "I believe he was interested in the fact that you had painted two dead men."

"I didn't paint *them*; just the intersecting points in our lives, you know, images and impressions."

"When did you know them?"

Ruth waved her hand vaguely in the direction of Washington Bay. "You want dates, names, and places, right?" She looked up at her ceiling. Helma looked up, too. And saw that one corner had been painted brown, like the kitchen. "Details. Can't tell you exactly. They were both brief encounters."

Helma hadn't heard Ruth mention either Meriwether Scott's or Vincent Jensen's name, but that wasn't unusual. Ruth rarely mentioned and Helma rarely asked about her romantic encounters.

"Last year," Ruth said, and winced. "After Paul and I . . . I was a little bit on the wild, I guess. Meriwether died in early December so I knew him in early fall, and Vincent died right after Christmas, but he and I shared a week in late summer, if you could call that season we had last year, summer."

Helma recalled Vincent Jensen's death because he'd lived on the same side of Bellehaven as she did. A fire had been involved. She couldn't recall the details. "Were they acquainted with each other?"

"I doubt one even knew the other existed. Meriwether lived way the heck out in the county near the Nitcum River. Handy with a chain saw. He carved, too. Tall, shoulders out to here. Vincent taught at the college. Just a nice guy."

"Tall?" Helma asked.

"Not so. But he was funny, for an academic." Ruth picked up a paintbrush and swirled the fibers against her palm, smiling as if the sensation was pleasurable. "Vincent Jensen: say that three times as fast as you can. Why would somebody take those two paintings? Meriwether and Vincent? I don't get it." She frowned. "Stop that."

"What?"

"You're messing up my paint tubes."

Without realizing it, Helma had begun arranging Ruth's oils in alphabetical order: Aborigine, Chestnut, Crimson Blue. She clasped her hands together in front of her. "How did they die?"

"Live by the chain saw, die by the chain saw," Ruth said. "Meriwether was up in a maple tree, cutting off a burl to turn into a table or something. He fell. From on high. With the chain saw." Ruth grimaced, scrunching up her eyes. "Don't think about it."

Helma didn't.

Ruth stopped turning the paintbrush and dropped it into a glass packed with brushes in a multitude of sizes. "I bet his mother named him after the explorer. He probably had brothers named Hillary and Perry. Wait a minute. Meriwether gave me one of his pieces. I'll be right back." And she headed for her bathroom.

Outside, a car door slammed, and Helma glanced at her watch. She was already ten minutes late for work.

"See. I told you he was good with a chain saw." She held out a wooden rabbit about eighteen inches tall, half of its height taken up by long slender ears. The rabbit appeared to be grinning around two buck teeth. On its left ear settled a roll of bathroom tissue.

"That's remarkable," Helma said. "It looks very like a rabbit. How could he do that with a chain saw?"

"Chain saws, like m—people, come in many sizes."

"Are his carvings valuable? Wouldn't someone have stolen the rabbit, too, if they were interested in Meriwether Scott's work?"

Ruth stroked the wooden rabbit's back and shrugged. "Maybe the thieves weren't interested in Meriwether or Vincent at all and they swiped those two paintings because my artistic gifts stirred their hearts."

"What *do* you remember about your paintings?" Helma asked.

"I don't, exactly, and that's the truth. Meriwether's painting had a more woodsy feeling than Vincent's, lots of greens, I remember that. I put a petri dish in Vincent's, I think."

"How did Vincent die?" A lady bug walked across a spoon sitting on Ruth's dresser. With the door closed, the room smelled of paint thinner and oil.

"With his boots on, too. In his home lab, playing Dr. Salk or Dr. Genetic Engineering. Maybe Dr. Frankenstein. Some nasty gas was released and then there was a fire."

"Suicide?" Helma asked in a softer voice. Even saying the word conjured dark sorrow: its sibilant secretiveness and the way the *d* snicked off the word after its last syllable.

Ruth shook her head and said adamantly, "No. That was definitely ruled out. From what I heard, Vincent even left a kettle on the stove in the house. I didn't know him all that well, but if he'd done himself in, all the loose ends would have been tucked in. It would have been tidy, nothing as messy as gas and fire."

Rapping sounded on Ruth's front door, as precise as a measure in 4/4 time, so Helma wasn't surprised to see Ruth open the door to the roundish and very official figure of Carter Houston, detective with the Bellehaven Police Department.

"Why, Carter," Ruth said, beckoning him inside with a sweep of her arm. "We were just talking about you."

Carter Houston was a man who, if he did possess a sense of humor, guarded it closely, a man who Helma had never spotted on the streets of Bellehaven in anything but his official capacity. Always wearing a suit with all his buttons buttoned and his black wingtips polished to a gloss. Ruth claimed he resembled a Fernando Botero drawing, or as

Helma's Aunt Em had once said, "Like one of those blow-up toys that you punch and it pops right back up again."

His dead seriousness made him an irresistible target for Ruth, whose eyes brightened maliciously at the very sight of him. Carter stood one step inside the house, shoulders back and lips tight. A muscle jumped behind his glasses along the lower edge of his left eye.

"Miss Winthrop, Miss Zukas," he said in his carefully modulated voice.

"Detective," Helma acknowledged.

"Oh, Carter," Ruth cooed. "Didn't they tell you one of your compatriots was already here? You missed all the fun."

"I'm aware of the initial investigation," he told her. "I just have a couple of questions for you, if you don't mind."

"Not at all." Ruth peered out the door behind him. "If you'd brought the chief of police we could have made this a foursome."

"I understand the subjects of the stolen paintings were Meriwether Scott and Vincent Jensen." He spoke in a declarative sentence, not as a question.

"Not *of* them," Ruth told him, as she'd told Helma. "I painted impressions of their lives, my life." She joined her hands in front of her face. "The intersection. Etcetera. I already told Cop Number One."

"So they were pictures of . . ." he prompted.

"*Impressions*, Carter. Just impressions, whatever moved me. My deepest, most secret emotions, like these," and she waved toward the paintings leaning against her wall.

He walked along the line of paintings, bending to view them, pausing briefly where the stolen paintings had stood. "Did you do this to all of them?" He pointed to the upper left corner of first one painting and then the next.

Helma, who believed pointing was rarely necessary, nevertheless followed Carter's pudgy forefinger and studied the corner of two of the paintings. "*R.A*" was painted in red on the first painting, a painting that appeared to have an avian theme. And "*J.W.*" on one that made her think of farmyards.

"Well, yeah, I don't want there to be any misunderstandings." Suddenly, Ruth leapt forward and turned an incomprehensible canvas face-in to the wall. "Don't look at this one."

"So the missing paintings had '*M.S.*' in the corner of one and '*V.J.*' in the corner of the other?" Carter asked.

"I guess, but that's a leap. Picture a couple of bad guys stumbling around in here in the middle of the night shining flashlights on my paintings and reading the initials before they grabbed them. And don't forget, they cut a piece out of one of them and left it on my bed. *That* was no accident."

""I'd like to see it," Carter said. "But first, why do you think *two* men did this?"

"It would take two guys to carry both paintings; I mean, otherwise they might ruin them."

For a second Helma thought she saw Carter's face soften. "I understand they did ruin at least one of them," he told Ruth.

"Yeah," she agreed glumly. "The piece they cut out. There's no way I could recreate either painting."

"Could you try?" Carter asked.

"Carter . . . you care," Ruth said.

"It would be interesting to examine them for any similarities," he told her. "There *is* a reason those particular paintings were stolen."

"I could try, but the moment's gone. *Pfft.*"

"Start with the initials in the upper left corners," he suggested. "Maybe that'll help you remember." Before Ruth could answer, he turned to Helma. "And you, Miss Zukas. When did you arrive?"

"Twenty minutes ago," she told him. "I'm going to be a few minutes late at the library."

"C'mon, Carter. Write her an excuse," Ruth interrupted.

"Ruth called me and I drove over on my way to work," she explained.

"Do you recall what the paintings looked like?"

"I never saw them."

He nodded and added a few notes to his spiral notebook. "I'd like to take that strip of painting. Maybe we can pull evidence off it in the lab."

"It's a warning, Carter. They're threatening to slit my throat."

Carter nodded noncommittally and cleared his own throat. "So you'll repaint the two canvases? We can color copy the strip for you. That might help you in your recreation."

"Don't bother. I'll wait until you're finished. I need to smell and touch the original or the artistic juices just won't flow."

Helma was seventeen minutes late when she parked her Buick in her allotted slot in the Bellehaven Public Library's small parking lot, switched off her windshield wipers before she turned off her engine, then entered the workroom through the staff door by the loading dock. The library wouldn't open for an hour and forty-three minutes, but the staff arrived two hours before the public, to prepare for another day of dispensing information to the inquisitive citizens of Bellehaven.

Even with her mind on the crime scene at Ruth's house, Helma sensed disturbance in the overcrowded workroom the moment she stepped inside. The hula lamp on the desk of George Melville, the cataloger, was dark. George was usually the first librarian to arrive so he could start the coffee. "Why brew it at home if I can get it here for free?" he'd said, and often arrived bleary-eyed and slightly disheveled. Harley Woodworth claimed that George kept a shaving kit in the men's restroom, but Helma wouldn't know.

Other desks were empty, too. The usual bustle in the tightly packed room was absent. The most recent plan for a new library had been disastrously squelched, and as often happened when hopes were crushed, the library had begun to feel even more crowded than it actually was.

Helma held her breath and listened, one hand poised at the second button of her coat. The HVAC system hummed as it circulated air; the temperature was comfortable, the electricity on. Then she heard it: the buzz of low voices, men's voices. She tipped her head. The sound came from the staff room.

She slipped off her coat and hung it on the hanger she kept in her cubicle, rebuttoning the top button so it wouldn't slip off, tucked her blue bag in the bottom drawer of her desk and locked it. She paused briefly before she entered the staff room to note the new sign Ms. Moon had pinned on the bulletin board, wreathed in pink paper zinnialike flowers: *When you Assume, you make an Ass of U and Me.*

George Melville, Harley Woodworth, and Roger Barnhard, the children's librarian, stood around the coffeepot, the entire male professional population of the Bellehaven Public Library.

Roger had just poured half-and-half into his cup and was stirring it with his finger.

"I'll tell you one thing," George was saying as he stroked his beard, "it won't be me."

Harley Woodworth, who George referred to as "Hardly Worthit," raised his hand, his usually morose face brightening. "I could—"

Roger cut him off. "I think it'll be Helma."

"That's the most logical choice," George said, "which means that in this zoo it ain't gonna happen." As he raised his coffee cup to his mouth, he saw Helma in the doorway and instead lifted his cup toward her like a toast. "And here she is now."

Helma didn't drink coffee, although she did appreciate its roasty warm fragrance. "Has something happened?" she asked.

The three men glanced at each other, waiting for one or the other to take the lead. George nodded to Harley, who'd already opened his mouth twice while keeping his lips closed, a habit during tense moments.

"You tell her, Harley," George said. "No one can impart bad news with quite your flair."

George was right; Harley was never so eloquent as when contemplating the darker sides of life, particularly medical emergencies, fatal diseases, and potential worst-case scenarios. Now, his eyes widened and his lips formed a smile before he turned them downward into a sad moue.

"It's Ms. Moon," he told Helma. "She was just taken to the hospital."

"Was there an accident?" Helma asked, glancing around the lounge for evidence.

"In an ambulance," Harley continued, casting a longing glance through the walls toward the hospital two blocks away. "Their lights were flashing but they didn't use the sirens."

"Pity," George said. "She would have loved that."

Since the three men actually seemed to be *enjoying* the story, she assumed that whatever had happened to Ms. Moon wasn't life-threatening. "Please," she said, focusing on Roger, the most reliable of the three. "Please tell me the details of the incident immediately."

The diminutive children's librarian complied. "The Moonbeam—I mean, Ms. Moon—was on a kick stool trying to reach some books for the mayor and she fell. I'm no doctor but it looked to me like her leg was broken."

"Oh, it was," Harley said. "The tibia, at least, maybe the fibula, too. Eight inches below her knee." He made motions with his hands like breaking a stick. "I can show you a picture of the leg bones, if you want. I have Netter's *Atlas of Human Anatomy* at my desk."

But Helma was puzzling over more than a broken bone.

The library director on a kick stool? Ms. Moon? Who as far as Helma knew never physically left solid ground, who called a page to pull a book from the shelf and deliver it to her office rather than fetch it herself? George claimed it was because Ms. Moon had never learned the Dewey decimal system in library school.

"She was helping the mayor?" she asked. "Was he here?"

"Nope," George answered while Roger shook his head and Harley asked, "Then you don't want to see the pictures?"

"What material had he requested?" Helma asked, still trying to picture Ms. Moon standing on a kick stool.

"Don't know. She was talking to him on the headset when she fell. He called the ambulance, I think, because it showed up while we were trying to decide whether to pick her up."

"She was in shock," Harley said. "It's dangerous to move somebody in shock. I told them."

The headsets had been Ms. Moon's latest idea. "Picture it," she'd rhapsodized. "All librarians can walk *with* their telephone patrons to the shelf. They'll feel your dedication through the phone lines, enjoy the thrill of research 'as it happens.'" Until that moment, Helma hadn't known Ms. Moon possessed her own headset.

"Where did the fall occur?" she asked.

"In the Local Government section."

A tall tier of shelves overpacked with folders, notebooks, and pamphlets that listed and shifted precariously every time it was touched. At that moment, Helma wasn't sure why she asked the next question. "Did she phone the mayor or did the mayor phone the library?"

"Don't know," George said. "Does it make a difference?"

"Probably not," Helma conceded.

"So we're thinking you're going to be it," Roger said.

"It?" Helma asked.

"Somebody has to be the acting director while she's re-covering."

Harley nodded. "It'll take a long time, a break like that. She'll be out at least six weeks. They might put in steel pins. They do that with bad breaks, especially when both bones are snapped. Maybe a rod."

"It's too early to be appointing an acting director," Helma told them. "Where are Glory and Eve?"

"Our leader requested an accompanying host of librar-ians," George told her. "Females only. It was a good day for you to be late." He frowned. "By the way, you're not usually late; everything okay?"

Helma Zukas believed sharing personal experiences with fellow employees compromised working relationships, but she also didn't believe in rudeness toward those with whom she spent a major portion of her day, so she said, "I needed to assist a friend for a few minutes," feeling that would be adequate enough.

"Uh-oh," George immediately said. "Now what's Ruth up to?"

He'd hear about the theft of the paintings soon enough, probably from Ruth herself, but not from her. Helma smiled as if he were making a joke and asked, "Has anyone phoned the hospital regarding Ms. Moon's status?"

Helma entered the still closed public area of the library and checked the Local Government section. Yes, just like the leavings of a crime scene, there was the kick stool, pushed to the side.

Kick stools were ancient library implements: metal stools with round bases that held wheels and were easy to kick where they were needed. When weight was placed on the stool, the wheels disappeared into the base, supposedly rendering the stool stable enough for sitting or standing. Helma felt that all knowledge should be within the reach of the average-sized American, and kick stools placed in retirement. Many patrons used the stools as seats in the library aisles.

And beside it, in a tumbled stack, was a pile of environmental pamphlets relating to Bellehaven and the surrounding county. Helma lifted the first few and read the titles: *Salmon Enhancement, Invader Weeds, Tree Pests, Wetland Identification.* And beneath those, various legal decisions and committee reports.

"Ms. Moon said not to pick those up."

Helma looked up to see Carolyn, one of the pages, standing at the end of the aisle. Carolyn was one of a new and increasingly common breed of page: older and semiretired, rather than the high school and college-age students the library normally hired. She wore her gray hair in a long braid down her back. The tip was blond.

"After she fell?" Helma asked her.

"That's right. While the medics were attending to her."

"Did she say why?"

Carolyn shook her head. "I think she was worried I'd fall, too. That's a tough place to reshelve material. Even when she was in pain, she only thought of the library, isn't that just like her?"

Helma studied the top shelf. A blank space indicated where the pamphlets had stood. The rest of the shelves were jammed with the loose and sloppy documents.

She was still surveying the scene when Eve, the fiction librarian, entered the public area. "Helma," she called. "Did you hear what happened?"

"I was just looking at the shelves. How is she?"

Eve's eyes misted. Eve's eyes misted when she heard babies cry or saw elderly couples holding hands, or when she helped slender young women find books on dieting. "She's in surgery. Glory's staying with her. I think they're putting pins in her leg."

"Did you see her fall?"

Eve shook her head. "Nobody did. Luckily, Glory came out to survey our atlas collection and found her on the floor." The mistiness turned into real tears. "Poor Ms. Moon. She's so worried about the library. She asked us to tell the mayor it wasn't his fault she couldn't reach his book on the crowded shelves. It wasn't his fault at all."

Chapter 4

Researching Death

At one minute to ten, despite the furor over Ms. Moon's calamity, Helma took her position behind the public reference desk.

Dutch, the retired military man who now commanded the opening of the library as well as his former rule of the circulation desk, stood five feet to the left of the plate-glass doors, out of sight of eager patrons gathered outside. He held up his wrist, gazing at his watch, his lips moving as he counted down. At five seconds to ten he sharply nodded his thumb-shaped head and marched to the doors. The night employees repeated the same procedure in reverse at 9:00 P.M. Mostly, Helma suspected, because Dutch was prone to suddenly appear in the library at 8:58 or be glimpsed standing in the shadows on the front sidewalk monitoring his upheld watch.

The usual patrons entered the library, those who raced for the computers or the morning's *Bellehaven Daily News*, or the fewer and fewer who had a burning question they didn't trust the Internet to answer.

Ten minutes later, during a lull after Helma had verified the complete names of the Curies, helped a computer user find a dating Web site, and gently explained why the library didn't own an actual map of Marlboro Country, she looked up to see Harley standing beside the desk.

"Has anybody asked about Ms. Moon?"

"Not yet," she told him.

Harley had abandoned his eyeglass leashes in favor of raising them to somehow rest on his forehead like an extra pair of eyes, which he did now. "Did you hear?" he asked. "Pins. They're putting pins in her leg." He looked up at the clock over the circulation desk. "Right now. Pins to hold the bones together. Sometimes they just use screws. They'll have to cut her leg open to get to the bones." His hands made sawing motions.

"I'm sure the doctors are doing what's necessary for her recovery."

"It's a bad one," he said, nodding gravely. "And George is all wrong. Nobody'd do that *on purpose*."

"Insert pins?" Helma asked.

Harley's jaws separated in his closed mouth, elongating his already long face. "No," he said in a low voice, glancing behind him. "No. *Fall*. George said Ms. Moon fell on purpose."

"I'm sure it was an accident," Helma told him firmly.

"That's exactly what I told him. I saw her on the floor and she was definitely in pain. Agony. People don't inflict pain on themselves intentionally." He stopped and his forehead furrowed. "I mean, not usually. You can pay . . ." His face turned red and he nudged his glasses from his forehead to his eyes. They dropped like a curtain. "No. Thanks, Helma. I guess I'll go . . ." and his voice trailed off as he walked away.

Helma reached for the *Bellehaven City Directory* for a young businesswoman, smiling at her but distracted by Harley's words. George Melville was cynical and sarcastic about everything from the degradation of the Anglo-American cataloging rules to vegetarians, while Harley frequently couldn't differentiate teasing from simple declarative sentences. George had certainly been teasing Harley with one of his questionable jokes.

But she paused, the directory frozen between herself and the eager patron's waiting hands. Hadn't she herself felt a niggling sense of suspicion on hearing of Ms. Moon's accident? Ms. Moon standing on a kick stool while searching for information for the mayor? While talking *to* the mayor? On a headset?

The very mayor who'd recently been quoted in the *Bellehaven Daily News* as proclaiming the Bellehaven Public Library didn't need a new building after all, that with the changing reading habits of the public, fewer citizens would be frequenting the library, so it was smart government to take a wait-and-see approach.

When the building plans for a new library had collapsed the year before, Ms. Moon had taken the blow hard. For days she'd sat at her desk in her office, eating chocolate mint Frangos and playing Yanni music.

Not that exploding buildings or failed bond issues had deterred her so far. "But I've already designed a new logo," she'd cried on hearing the mayor's statement.

"Is there a problem?"

Helma started and looked up into the quizzical face of the young woman. "No, I'm sorry," she said, relinquishing the directory. "I was considering other possibilities."

"You're so thorough, but this should do it," the woman said, and carried the directory to the nearest table.

At the end of her reference shift, Helma retidied the desk for a left-hander after glancing at the schedule and seeing that Harley's shift followed hers.

He appeared, his arms laden with medical texts. "I found a couple good ones in closed stacks, too," he announced as he dropped them on the desk with a thump, then leveled them up so they wouldn't topple to the floor.

"What are you planning to do with these?" Helma asked.

"I'm putting together a notebook of materials for Ms. Moon." He touched each book with a long forefinger. "Surgical procedures, recovery and rehabilitation, diet, information on dressings. And this one." He stroked the spine of a green tome, titled, *Complications in Wound Recovery*. "It has a lot of dangerous symptoms and warning signs. Pictures, too." He smiled. "In color."

"She requested this information?"

Harley shook his head. "It's a get-well gift. I'll photocopy the best articles and put them in here." He held up a pink three-ring binder. "Isn't this cheery? So, what do you think?"

"I think she'll be surprised," Helma told him.

"Good. Oh look, here's your policeman."

Before Helma could claim he wasn't *her* policeman, Chief of Police Wayne Gallant joined them at the reference desk. He wore a dark suit, with the tie loosened as if he'd already put in a long day, instead of it still being morning.

"Helma, Harley," he said, nodding to each of them, his manner all business; police business. "Can one of you show me where Ms. Moon fell?"

"Sure," Harley said, then looked at Helma and said, "I'm on duty here, but after Helma shows you, I can tell you what I saw. I was a witness. Almost."

"Excellent," and he waved a hand for Helma to lead the way.

"I wasn't here," Helma warned him as she led him toward the Local Government shelves. "So I can only show you what I was shown. Second-hand knowledge, so to speak."

"That'll do for now." She smelled his aftershave as he followed her and avoided breathing too deeply, allowing the spiced fragrance to linger.

"You're investigating Ms. Moon's fall?" she asked. "I understood it was an accident."

"The mayor asked me to drop by and take a look as a personal favor, that's all." He spoke easily, but Helma noted how his eyes shifted away from her.

"Right here. Harley said she was on the kick stool and fell while she was reaching for this material." She nodded toward the stack of environmental information still on the floor.

Just like Helma had, he lifted the first few publications and read the titles, then pulled out his notebook, identical to Carter's and the policeman's at Ruth's house, and jotted in it.

"She reportedly was speaking to the mayor when she fell," Helma said.

He nodded as he wrote, then looked up at her. "Had she said what project she was working on for him?"

"No, she hadn't," Helma told him, thinking Wayne should already know the topic since the mayor had asked him to "drop in and take a look."

He nodded, then examined the kick stool and the floor.

"Do you know her condition?" Helma asked, watching him. When he leaned over, a strand of graying hair fell forward and covered his widow's peak.

"Out of surgery. Sounds like it went well. No complications." He gently pushed on the shelves to test their sturdiness. "But she'll have a long recovery. Might be a little disruption for you over here. Somebody else will have to take charge."

Helma recalled George, Roger, and Harley in the midst of their speculation in the staff room. Why would they think *she* qualified to be acting director?

"Ruth had a theft at her house last night," she said, changing the subject.

"I heard about that. There are some interesting coincidences there."

"Because the subjects of the stolen paintings are dead?"

He grinned at her and she felt the full focus of his bright blue eyes. "That's one aspect that's definitely interesting. Are you aware of another?"

"I'm sure if you or Carter were to share your information, I might be able to find other facets."

He tipped back his head and laughed aloud, causing several people to glance their way. An elderly woman smiled, then closed her eyes and bent her head. He relaxed and his police demeanor slipped away. "I'm sure you could. In the meantime, why don't we go out to dinner tomorrow night?"

"When you say, 'in the meantime,' are you implying that you *do* intend to share?" Helma asked, and was rewarded by another laugh.

"You are persistent," he said.

"Thank you," she replied.

Helma returned to her cubicle in the workroom, sitting uncharacteristically idle at her desk for a few moments, thinking of Wayne Gallant's appearance in the library. She knew he and the mayor played racquetball together, that they might even be friends. But why had the mayor asked Wayne to investigate Ms. Moon's fall as a *personal* favor to him?

And Ms. Moon had asked the page not to reshelve the materials that toppled from the high shelf. Was there something significant in the materials that tumbled to the floor with Ms. Moon? She had only looked at the first few titles, and later her attention had been given to the chief, naturally. She'd bring up the subject at dinner the next night. They often shared insights into Bellehaven's local crime, although Helma believed she was far more generous with information than he was with her.

Helma stood, intending to return to the Local Government shelves, when Ruth appeared at her cubicle entrance.

"Do me a favor, okay?" Ruth asked. Her wiry dark hair with its Bride of Frankenstein streak was roughly and temporarily tamed into a tail. Her makeup was restrained—at least for Ruth.

"If I'm able," Helma said, and beckoned to the chair that barely fit in the small confines of her allotted space. "Sit down."

"Nah, I can watch my back better from up here." Few of Ruth's shoes had heels less than two inches. From her vantage point draped over the wall of Helma's cubicle, she could survey the entire workroom. "Hey, George," she called across the room.

"Ah, Beautiful Ruth," he replied as if it were a title. "You're not telling any tales about me in those paintings of yours, are you?"

"Only if you broke my heart, George."

"You gotta give me a chance first," George replied.

"I have a research question," she said, turning back to Helma. "Don't you think it's a little funny that Detective Carter Houston showed up so pronto after my little theft?"

"No. The responding officer probably reported the break-in to him. And both the subjects of your paintings are dead."

"Yeah, so?" Ruth bit her lower lip, concentrating. "Lots of people I know are dead. I think it's because Meriwether and Vincent were murdered and our cops couldn't prove it, so both their deaths are, whaddaya-call-its. Ice chests?"

"Cold cases?" Helma supplied.

"Definitely. So do your librarian stuff. Look them up." Ruth didn't own a computer, nor would she use one. It wasn't that she was incapable, but like many subjects in life that didn't interest her, she simply dismissed all things computerish with an airy, "I can't be bothered."

"It's too soon for the case to be cold," Helma told her. "The police are still investigating. The only information online will probably be the newspaper articles."

"Then let's read the obits. Who can remember the details that long ago?"

"Both of them only died four months ago."

Ruth raised her eyebrows. "And your point is? C'mon." She made typing motions with her fingers. "Be a good public servant."

"I assure you I am."

Three hits came up for Meriwether Scott in the Bellehaven News database: one an article on his carvings two years earlier, accompanied by a photograph of a smiling handsome man standing between two credible life-sized wooden bears. As Ruth had claimed, he had "shoulders out to here." The other two pertained to his death: one detailed the fall from the tree, citing the vague "multiple injuries," and the other his obituary.

Ruth read over Helma's shoulder. "Minnesota," she burst out. "He never told me he was from Minnesota. You'd think I'd learn. He should have hightailed it back to the old country, just like Paul did." Her voice had darkened and now she slumped against the cubicle wall, bowing it inward.

There was no point in reminding her *why* Paul had left Bellehaven and returned to Minnesota, so instead Helma did a quick search for Vincent Jensen. "Look," she told Ruth. "He was dean of sciences."

"I told you he was something at the college," Ruth said, still glum. "I'm not looking at that screen until you tell me whether he was another Minnesota man."

Helma skimmed through the article. Most everyone in Bellehaven came from elsewhere, bringing to the city so many brands of beliefs and passions that its workings occasionally twisted back onto itself. "No," she told Ruth. "He was from Seattle."

"Vincent from Seattle," Ruth murmured. "That's a relief. Where does it say how he died?"

"Second paragraph. There isn't much detail. He was

overcome by a deadly gas in his home lab. Police suspect it sparked a fire."

"You'd think a scientist would be more careful, wouldn't you?" Ruth said. "He didn't seem that careless to me. ' . . . never regained consciousness,'" she read.

"Ruth, he was survived by a *wife*."

"Don't look at me like that. He was separated when I knew him. I don't do married men and I don't do lunch."

"How long did you date him?"

"I don't *date*, Helma Zukas. We got together a few times at Joker's, a few more times here and there. He was funny, as in ha-ha funny. Nice guy, but we didn't have much in common." She shrugged.

"Then why did you paint him?" Helma asked as she exited the obituaries. "I thought you were painting significant encounters in your life."

"He dumped me," Ruth said flatly. "Saw the light and went back to his wife. Hell hath no fury, you know, so that's why he got a healthy dose of my paintbrush. I have more imagination than to just sit in a corner and quietly despise some guy who leaves me in the dust."

"Did Meriwether dump you, too?" Helma asked, beginning to see the pattern of Ruth Revealed.

"Not exactly, but it didn't end well. He got cozy with some chickie who made leaf impressions on cement and turned them into earrings or something."

"Cement is the mix, concrete is the product," Helma corrected. "The impressions would have been made on concrete."

"Okay, so concrete. But that did effectively end the association." She tossed her head. "If I'm not number one I'm not interested."

"So the only connection the two men had with each other was that their associations with you ended unhappily."

Ruth shrugged. "I guess. And I painted impressions of

them, but I don't see why that would make my paintings so desirable."

"Me, neither," Helma agreed, then seeing Ruth's expression, she added, "We're discussing the act of stealing, Ruth, not purchasing."

"Yeah yeah. I *needed* those paintings. For my show. Now I have to come up with two new ones."

"Have you started reconstructing them, as Carter Houston suggested?"

"That's not the way art works," Ruth said, adding a dramatic sigh. "I could never exactly recreate them. That moment's gone forever."

"But seeing exactly what you'd painted *is* probably the only clue to why they were stolen."

Ruth glanced toward the workroom door and rolled her eyes. "Look who's here," she murmured. "Oh lucky lucky us."

Helma heard the unmistakable twittering voice of Gloria "Call me Glory" Shandy, Bellehaven Public Library's newest librarian.

"Oh, Ruth," she cried. "Are you here about May Apple, I mean, Ms. Moon? I just came from her bedside, and the news is good."

Glory danced into Helma's view, her red hair tousled as if she'd been running, her eyes wide and eager. She was as small as a twelve-year-old, a fact that was emphasized by Glory's choice in clothes and jewelry. A dispenser of fulsome praise, ever eager, her presence left Helma exhausted and set Ruth to chewing the inside of her mouth as her eyes darkened dangerously.

"Her bedside?" Ruth asked. "Were you playing doctor?"

"Oh," Glory turned to Helma. "You didn't tell her?"

"Not yet."

"I'm surprised." Glory cast a disappointed look at Helma and lowered her voice. "She fell, here in the library, helping the mayor. And now they've put steel pins in her leg." She shuddered and rubbed her arms. "Isn't that *awful*? She'll be in a wheelchair just forever. But she's out of recovery now and the first thing she wanted was for me to assure everyone she's going to be all right. Isn't that fantastic news?"

"I'm so relieved," Ruth said, rocking the wall of Helma's cubicle. "So who's going to be running this institution while she recovers?"

For a moment Glory looked blank, then puzzled. "Why, Ms. Moon, of course."

"How?" Ruth asked." Ruling from her hospital bed?"

"No," Glory told them. "She's coming in herself. Tomorrow. She wants to be here, isn't that brave?"

Even Helma was surprised. "Tomorrow?" she repeated. "So soon."

Glory bobbed her head up and down, up and down. "I'm going to help. It's all set."

After Ruth left, Helma completed an order for the new edition of *Best Places in the Northwest*, then walked past Ms. Moon's office on her way to the staff lounge, pausing when she heard the low purr of a voice. Glory Shandy sat behind Ms. Moon's desk, speaking quietly into the telephone while she absently stroked one of Ms. Moon's baseball-sized crystals.

Chapter 5

Unusual Habits

"Hello, dear. I've heard something very disturbing."

Helma held the phone to her ear while she unwrapped a new roll of paper towels she'd just retrieved from her dishwasher.

The electric dishwasher in her apartment hadn't been used since she moved in fresh out of library school twenty years earlier. She'd never liked the suspiciously slick way dishes pulled from a dishwasher felt, and she supposed by now the moving parts and gaskets of the dishwasher were frozen beyond repair. Instead, she stored excess paper towels and cat food on the lower gridded shelf, along with a few gifts that didn't suit her tastes but were given to her by people whose feelings she didn't want to hurt, always at hand to be pulled out when they visited.

"What did you hear, Mother?" Her mother, Lillian, and her Aunt Em were both Michigan transplants who shared an apartment in the Silver Gables, senior apartments with a lively reputation. One Saturday night, a month earlier, the police had been called to the complex after complaints that "hound dog music" was getting out of hand. Helma's own mother had been responsible for "turning the platters" at the Rock On party and deftly worked the "bust" into any conversation she could.

"Well," Lillian began after taking a deep breath. "You know how your Aunt Em's always looking for somebody new so she can repeat those old stories you've heard a hundred times, always changing the details to make herself look better?"

Aunt Em had recently turned eighty-eight. Her once sharp mind was beginning to veer off, most often into the past, sometimes slipping into Lithuanian, and causing Lillian to say, her eyes fearful but her voice exasperated, "Now just stop that, Em. Right now."

"Aunt Em told you something she'd heard?" Helma prodded as she folded the plastic wrapper and set it in her trash basket.

"You know the café downstairs? She'll hog a table for hours nursing one cup of coffee. She looks a hundred years old, so people are always checking to see if she's still breathing. That's how she got to talking to the meter maid's mother. And *she* said . . ." Lillian paused dramatically. ". . . that paintings were stolen from an artist on the Slope. Now, I know there are a lot of artists in this town, but it *did* pique my curiosity, naturally."

"Naturally," Helma repeated.

"Maybe I get it from you, the sleuthing bug." Lillian laughed. "But anyway, I made a few teensy phone calls. And I was right. It was your friend Ruth. Her paintings were stolen. She was robbed. Did you know about it, dear?"

"I did," Helma said warily. "It only happened this morning."

"Why would anyone *steal* Ruth's paintings?" she asked. "I can't understand why anyone even *buys* them, let alone breaks into her house and *takes* them on purpose. Do you know the details?"

Helma's mother couldn't hide her disapproving, yet abiding fascination, with Ruth's life. Once when Helma was in ninth grade she'd asked, "Can't you find any *nice* girls to be friends with, Helma? Girls more like you?"

"I only know that two paintings were taken, Mother. The police are investigating."

"Oh. Which policemen would that be?" she asked, trying but not succeeding at sounding casual.

"I didn't recognize him."

"I suppose the chief of police is way too busy for a minor break-in?" she asked.

Helma thought of Wayne Gallant examining the site of Ms. Moon's fall as a favor to the mayor. She wouldn't tell her mother *that*, but knew exactly how to redirect her mother's attention from her daughter's love life. "You may not have heard yet, Mother, but Ms. Moon fell in the library this morning and broke her leg."

Lillian gasped, and Helma related the basic details of Ms. Moon's mishap to her mother, absent all conjecture and suspicion, naturally.

"I know who did it."

"Ruth, what are you doing here? It's six o'clock in the morning."

"I was out driving around, thinking. Is that a new robe? And no, I wasn't out all night. I just woke up early."

Ruth wore different clothes than the day before. That was a good sign. Her blue Volkswagen was parked in front of the Bayside Arms Dumpster.

"Come inside. You know who did what?" The pink of a sunrise tinted the rising dawn behind Ruth, but Helma caught sight of a misty fog on the hills behind Bellehaven. She judged the mist would lift by late morning because the air already had a spring warmth to it.

"What do you think? I know who broke in and ripped off

my paintings. They were stolen, remember? Dead guys and all that? I can't believe you could dismiss a felony like it was an overdue book."

"Ruth, you're distraught," Helma said. She took a glass from her cupboard. "Have a glass of orange juice."

"Do you have coffee?"

"Research has shown that fruit juice can be as stimulating as coffee."

"Except it tastes funny. Besides, I have a legit reason to be, as you say, 'distraught.' Art theft is a crime. Look at Munch's *The Scream*. It disappears every time you turn around."

"It was stolen for ransom money," Helma pointed out.

"My thief doesn't want money. That strip of slashed art left on my bed wasn't just a threat to my life. It was worse: the rat intends to stop my show, *Ruth Revealed*."

"And your suspect is?"

"Roxy Lightheart," Ruth emoted, as if announcing a vaudeville act. "What are those three things the cops say a criminal needs?"

"Means, motive, and opportunity," Helma supplied. "Who is Roxy Lightheart?"

"A poseur," Ruth said. "That name is fake, too. She can't get by on her own talent so she has to throw in a ridiculous name to catch a little attention. Add a little zing, a hint of cool Indian blood. Her name's really Rose Anne White Bread or something like that. She paints, she sculpts, she makes cutesy panels. A one-woman art factory. I should have known she'd try a sneaky trick like this, the jealous—"

"Means, motive, and opportunity?" Helma broke in to remind her. She poured the orange juice and handed it to Ruth, who finished it in two gulps.

"Okay: motive," Ruth said, wiping a hand across her lips. "My new show is replacing hers on the Cheri's Gallery calendar. She was so pissed about that, she called me at midnight to spit incoherently into the phone for twenty minutes.

She wanted to dance on my bones or pound sand in my ears, something juvenile." Ruth shrugged. "She knows where I live and my door was unlocked. That's opportunity. What else do you need to know? It was her, I'd swear to it."

"Would she risk arrest to steal two paintings and leave you a threat just because your show replaced hers?"

"Obviously." Ruth poured herself more orange juice. "Want some?" she asked, holding up the juice carton.

"I don't drink standing up," Helma told her. "But why those two paintings? They were *chosen* and both were of dead men. Why would Roxy Lightheart want *those* two?"

"Coincidental?" Ruth offered. "She grabbed a couple to stall out my show."

"If that's true, it would have made more sense to destroy more paintings, even all of them," Helma pointed out. "You can easily repaint two more to replace the stolen works."

"Says you."

"I have to get ready for work, Ruth," Helma said, glancing at the clock over her stove. It was synchronized to the library's clock, which ran two minutes fast. "But if you have suspicions, call the police. Call Carter Houston."

"I've already talked to the charming Mr. Houston five times since the crime. And what's he done: nothing,"

"You told him about Roxy Lightheart?"

Ruth shook her head and pursed her lips. "Not yet. Maybe I'll drive over and wait on his doorstep. She can't get away with this."

Ruth left, frowning, barely telling Helma goodbye, her boots thumping down the stairs.

Helma heard rhythmic footfalls along the deck that stretched across the floors of the apartment building like decks on an old-fashioned motel. It was 7:15 A.M..

She pushed aside the blinds in her kitchen in time to see TNT, the retired boxer who lived in 3E, the apartment next to hers, jog past the window, his knees high, arms up as if prepared to defend himself from a punch by an invisible opponent. He wore gray sweats, as usual, a towel wrapped around his neck, but his sweat-beaded face was grim, his eyes half closed.

TNT jogged every morning, and often again in the afternoon or evening, and in between sparred at the gym or worked out on incomprehensible steel mechanisms that filled his living room.

But never along the decks. Something was wrong.

She opened her door and stepped onto the deck just as TNT bounced his way back toward her. A docking ferry sounded in the bay, and sea gulls screeched in answer.

For a moment she doubted he recognized her, so inward was his vision. She held up her hand and he stopped, continuing to rhythmically shuffle his feet. TNT's face was grizzled, his nose bore the signs of having been broken at least once, but as Ruth had noted with raised eyebrows, he was a "superior specimen of graceful aging." His body was vigorous and trim, his gray hair thick and full, as if exercising had invigorated it, too.

TNT nodded, then nodded again. "Helma," he said, and nodded yet again.

"Good morning," she said. "Is everything all right?"

He seesawed the towel around his neck. "Why? Oh, you mean because I'm out here shaking the building awake?"

"Yes," she admitted. His eyes were red, as if he hadn't slept all night. "You usually begin your jog in the parking lot."

"I didn't want to miss my phone . . . in case it rang." He shook his head. "That sounds stupid, doesn't it? An old man like me, waiting by the phone like some teenager."

Helma didn't say anything, waiting for him to enlighten her or not, as he wished, although she *was* curious; she'd never seen TNT like this, so . . . well . . . unsettled.

He gave a short self-deprecating laugh. "Ignore me. I'm an old fool, and the devils were raising hell last night."

"My Aunt Em has a Lithuanian saying that whenever she lies down the devils climb into her head."

"Right she is. My devils bored their way in and danced a jig. Don't even think about me, girlie girl. You've got a real life to live; my problems aren't worth a darnik in hell. Sorry I disturbed you. You have a fine day; it looks like a good one out there," and he waved a hand toward the bay before he gave her one last nod and jogged on down the flights of stairs to the parking lot.

Helma watched him for a few moments, filing away the word "darnik" to look up later. It was likely a boxing term or one of TNT's Irishisms.

Chapter 6

The Return

"So what do you think? Are we supposed to all raise our cups and doughnuts and sing, 'For She's a Jolly Good Trouper'?"

Helma gazed around the workroom. Blue and pink helium-filled balloons were tied to bookshelves and furniture, bobbing and swaying with the air currents in a most irritating fashion. A banner stretched across the wall above Ms. Moon's door. It was decorated with daisies and yellow globes of sunshine, and read, WELCOME BACK, MS. MOON!!

"Who did this?" Helma asked George. A plate of chocolate chip cookies and two bowls of nuts—one of salty-looking cashews, one of dry roasted peanuts—sat on top of an unopened box of new books.

"Glory and cohorts," he said. He ticked off his fingers. "The Moonbeam fell yesterday, had surgery yesterday, and from what I heard, was released from her bed in our local hospital only this very morning." He motioned toward the banner. "'Welcome back,' when she wasn't even gone a full day?"

"She can't be well enough to work," Helma said. "They're preparing this for tomorrow, or the next day."

"Nope. I saw the Glory herself. She's scampered off to escort our leader into our presence. She probably has a trumpet tucked under her arm."

For the first several months after Glory Shandy had been hired, the normally impervious George Melville had gone dewy-eyed in Glory's presence. Flushing, occasionally even stammering, anxious to offer a chair or hold her coat. But something had happened two months earlier and now George treated Glory as he treated everyone, with raised eyebrow, stroked beard, and an overlay of mockery.

"Hello?" a woman's voice called from the rear of the workroom. Helma and George exchanged glances. George didn't move but Helma threaded between the cubicles and mending area and books in various stages of processing to the back door.

She recognized Maggie Bekman, crack reporter from the *Bellehaven Daily News*, standing inside the workroom. "So where is she?" She glanced at a notebook similar to the notebooks the police carried. "It's 9:45. And I'm here."

"This door is the staff entrance," Helma informed her. "The library isn't open to the public until ten o'clock."

Maggie ran her free hand through her blond hair. It was the same wiry texture as Ruth's, only more controlled. "If you don't want the public in here, then try locking the door. That usually works."

Helma examined the door. The lever above the handle that was always kept pushed to the right, which automatically locked the door behind anyone entering or leaving, was now pushed to the left. Maggie was correct. The door *had* been unlocked. She stepped forward and repositioned the lever to the right.

"Hey," Maggie objected. "Wait a minute." She flipped the lever back to the left. "My photographer will be here any second. We would have come together but he went to that accident over on Fourth. I told him it wasn't worth covering—nobody dead or maimed—but he was looking for a drama shot. Didn't get it, just like I told him."

"This must be a mistake," Helma said. "There's no accident here. We're simply preparing to open the library."

"News, news. It's all about the news." Maggie flipped back a page in her notebook and read aloud, "Nine forty-five. Library. Interview May Apple Moon."

"Who called you? When?"

Maggie pulled her notebook to her breast as if Helma were trying to peek at test answers. "Newspaper sources are confidential. Is she here yet?"

"No, but—"

With a clatter, the staff entrance door banged open and a man with a black camera case over his shoulder tumbled inside, stumbling and reaching out to brace himself against the wall. Maggie deftly caught the camera bag and rolled her eyes. "Geez, Josh. Do you always have to make an entrance?"

"Sorry," he said, taking the camera bag from Maggie and gently shaking it. "I thought the door would be locked, didn't expect it to open like that." He glanced at Helma as if she'd been derelict and any camera damage was her fault. "Where do you want to set up?"

"Wherever the light's good," Maggie told him.

The photographer swiftly glanced around the workroom. "This place is a mess. It won't work."

George Melville stepped up beside Helma, his beard twisted in a way that told Helma he was grinning. "Well, folks. I have a suspicion you're supposed to be out front. That's where the festivities are taking place."

"So how do we get out front and out of here?" Josh the cameraman asked.

George made a "Wagons ho" motion and led Maggie and Josh toward the library's public area. Helma stopped by her cubicle to take a fortifying plain M&M from the ceramic container on her desk. It was an unappealing orange color but she bit it cleanly in two, chewed and swallowed it before she left her cubicle for the public area. It was 9:56.

"Oh, this is so good," Maggie was telling her photographer. "Get as much as you can."

An ambulance had backed up to the front doors of the library, its lights gyrating. Emerging from the open back doors, assisted by three EMTs in sharply pressed whites, came Ms. Moon in a wheelchair, with Glory Shandy hovering behind her. The glass double front doors of the library were blocked open to receive her.

Clicking filled the air as the cameraman bobbed and squatted, snapping shots from every angle. The reporter's pen raced across her notebook.

Helma stood back and watched as Ms. Moon in her wheelchair was maneuvered onto the sidewalk and up the sloped ramp beside the library steps. Her normally tousled blond hair hung tragically limp, a brave but pained expression on her face as waiting patrons parted to allow her and her entourage to pass. Ms. Moon nodded toward each and every person, even raising her hands humbly to her heart.

Into Helma's mind flashed a scene from Shirley Temple's *The Little Princess*, the first video her mother had ever owned, and that Lillian had played over and over again, tears spilling each time Shirley discovered her father languishing in a veterans' hospital. In the film, a desperate little Shirley meets Queen Victoria being wheeled through the hospital halls, dispensing benediction to the staff and fallen warriors alike.

Ms. Moon's right leg was raised, supported straight out

in front of her and encased in a blue cast. Pain and exhaustion filled her face, but something more, too, Helma saw. Almost . . .

"She's loving every second of this," George said from beside her. "Basking in it. There hasn't been an entrance like this since Cleopatra did her thing in Rome."

Harley Woodworth stood beside the circulation counter as Glory pushed Ms. Moon inside. Clutched in his arms was the pink three-ring binder bulging with copied articles on wound recovery. He gazed with intense speculation at Ms. Moon's leg and cast.

"It was over here," came Ms. Moon's melodious voice as she pointed toward the Local Government area of the stacks. Maggie Bekman walked beside her, nodding and flipping pages. "I was standing on a stool, reaching for material and talking to the mayor at the same time." She paused and squeezed her eyes closed, then continued, her voice wavering. "We in the library pride ourselves on service to the public, whether it be a homeless derelict or a city official. Our patrons are our body and blood."

"Uh-oh," George whispered. "Here it comes."

A tremor passed through Ms. Moon's hand as she pointed to the disturbed upper shelf, the kick stool nearby, the environmental documents still on the floor. Surely they hadn't been so disorderly the day before, Helma thought.

"When we're forced to work in such overcrowded conditions, accidents are bound to happen," Ms. Moon said. "I certainly don't blame the mayor. He needed information and I was proud to provide it. His reluctance to support a new library has nothing to do with this unfortunate mishap. Absolutely nothing at all."

The camera snapped furiously, and Maggie's pencil moved so fast it made scratchy whispery sounds as she bobbed her head to Ms. Moon's words.

"No," Ms. Moon said, her voice firm yet curiously even

weaker, more unsteady, as she peered at Maggie and made
an appealing face for the camera. "It's not the mayor's fault
I fell reaching for material for him on our overcrowded and
unbalanced shelves. It's entirely my own fault."

After the reporter and the cameraman left, Ms. Moon, who
normally spent as little time in the public area as possible,
asked Glory to wheel her to a spot beside the reference desk.

"Helma," Ms. Moon said, "will it distract you if I sit
here?"

"Only if it keeps me from my work," Helma told her honestly.

Ms. Moon's eyes darkened briefly.

Each time a patron stepped up to the reference desk, Ms.
Moon looked up, smiled wanly, and said, "Please, pay no
attention to my injuries. They happened while I was serving
the public, but they in no way intrude on my abilities."

Harley approached Ms. Moon, head bobbing and holding
out the pink three-ring binder in both hands, like a price-
less gift. His stance reminded Helma of the three magi her
mother had constructed in a craft class from dryer lint and
white glue. Within seconds the two of them were huddled
together, whispering and oohing over the "recovery"
binder.

And in the periphery, in all aspects except for sound,
buzzed Glory, darting in to bring Ms. Moon a cup of water,
offering her a mint, asking if she was cold, or tired, or needed
to be wheeled away "for relief."

Between patrons, Helma searched for the word TNT had
used: "darnik". It wasn't in the usual dictionaries, or online,
either. She even checked the *Oxford English Dictionary*
without luck. Perhaps she'd misunderstood TNT's pronun-
ciation. She'd ask him later.

When Harley left Ms. Moon to find a medical dictionary,
the director shifted in her wheelchair and winced. "You're

not wearing your headset, Helma. You could serve more patrons at once if you did."

"I prefer to give each patron my full attention," Helma said.

Surprisingly, Ms. Moon let her newest favorite topic drop. "I heard the chief of police was here yesterday to look at the spot where I fell."

"Yes," Helma said. "He was."

"And what did you tell him?" Ms. Moon asked in a pleasant voice.

"I showed him the location, but informed him I hadn't been present. I was a few minutes late for work yesterday."

"The chief of police," Ms. Moon mused. "I wonder why the chief of police himself came to investigate."

"Perhaps all injury accidents on city property are investigated," Helma suggested.

"But the chief of police," Ms. Moon continued. She turned her head and gazed at Helma. "The next time you're with him, I'd appreciate it if you'd ask him."

"I don't become involved in police business," Helma told her. She gave a man patting his pockets a pencil and asked Ms. Moon, "What were you researching for the mayor when you fell?"

"Environmental issues," Ms. Moon said vaguely. She raised her hand wearily from the armrest of her wheelchair and waved it toward the Local Government shelves.

"I can finish finding the information for him," Helma suggested. "I know your search was interrupted by the fall."

The expression on Ms. Moon's face changed from vague to confused to, yes, panicked. "No need," she said hastily. "It's not necessary now."

"What was the topic?" Helma asked.

Ms. Moon bit her lip, then nodded to herself. "Trees. Yes, trees."

"Growth issues? Pollution effects? Logging?"

"Just . . . trees. Living and growing and dying and being born again from seeds and acorns and nuts, the way they do." She closed her eyes for a long moment. "I can't remember right now. A serious fall can make you forget. Harley says trauma has many inexplicable side effects."

Helma touched the telephone on the desk. "I'll call the mayor for you."

"No!"

Glory suddenly appeared at Ms. Moon's elbow, a crease between her brows. "Are you okay, Ms. Moon?" She cast a look at Helma and spoke as if Ms. Moon had left the room. "She's exhausted. I'll take her back to her office."

"Thank you," Ms. Moon murmured weakly to Glory. "Yes, I'm exhausted."

Helma watched Glory wheel the director through the public area and pause by the door to the workroom until a man reading a magazine jumped up and opened the door for them.

Chapter 7

A Bird in Glass

Helma returned to the site of Ms. Moon's accident and began sorting through the stack of studies, publications, and brochures that had fallen to the floor. Slender, soft-covered materials like these were often misfiled, lost between hardcover books and impossible to retrieve. If they ever actually moved into a new library, she already had in mind just the filing system that would make such disorder a task of the past.

As Ms. Moon had said, the publications *did* all pertain to trees, some published by the state of Washington, others by organizations or local groups with a specific focus. Tucked between *Name That Tree* and *Salvage Burning Specifications* was a crudely printed pamphlet titled *Tree Killers*, advocating guerrilla tactics to halt logging: lying in front of bulldozers, spiking trees, funneling sand into the gas tanks of heavy equipment. It wasn't marked with the library's stamp and had probably itself been slipped into the collection by guerrilla tactics.

She removed the *Tree Killers* publication, as well

as another unmarked but more professional pamphlet from Ground Up!, the private tree-restoration group that surreptitiously planted trees in open areas around Bellehaven, often under cover of darkness, leaving only a new flock of seedlings with trunks wrapped in the group's signature pink tree tubes. Their name was usually followed by an exclamation point, which Helma considered an awkward form of written presentation.

Then, a stapled set of pages advocating artificial Christmas trees with instructions on adding "real" pine scent and natural decorations. To these she attached a note to the Collection Development committee and finished sorting the stack in Dewey decimal order, ready to be reshelved. She wondered which one Ms. Moon had been searching for.

"Howdy, Helma. You studying up on trees?"

It was Boyd Bishop, the tall and lean western writer who'd become a friend of hers during the past year. He'd moved to Bellehaven after his wife's death, and she alone in all of Bellehaven knew of his secret life. The pointed toe of his leather boot touched the stack of fallen materials.

"Hello, Boyd." His clothing was at odds with normal Northwest style, in jeans and boots and shirts that snapped instead of buttoned. But somehow on him it didn't matter. All that he lacked was a cowboy hat.

"I heard your friend Ruth had a little to-do at her house the other night."

"How did you know?"

He grinned. "She told the tale at Joker's. Nearly got strangled, I heard." Ruth's version of her theft had no doubt reached cinematic heights. "Stolen paintings of murdered men. Chain saw murders, explosions. Quite the yarn."

Exactly, Helma thought, but to Boyd she said, "Is there something I can help you find?"

He leaned against the bookshelves. "I came to ask you to go to—"

"Oh. Are you putting those away?"

Glory Shandy stood at the end of the aisle, frowning. She spoke to Helma but her eyes drilled into Boyd Bishop, the fingernail of her index finger between her two front teeth.

"They're taking up valuable floor space," Helma told her. "Is there a reason *not* to reshelve them?"

Glory shook her head. "No," she said, but sounded doubtful. Her eyes were still on Boyd. "I'm Glory," she said, holding out her small hand.

"Boyd," he told her, touching his forehead as if tipping a hat. "Pleased to meet you."

"I'm a librarian, too," she said, "but I haven't had as much experience as Helma. She's had a *lot* more experience than me. Isn't the library lucky to have had her for so many years?"

"I'd say so," Boyd said, and turned back to Helma. "I'll be talking to you soon, Helma," and he nodded to include both women.

Helma and Glory watched his loose-strided exit. "Ooh," Glory said, pressing her hands over her heart. "He looks like a cowboy, doesn't he?" Helma didn't answer, and she continued. "I *love* cowboys." She turned back to Helma. "Do you know him? He sounded like he knew you."

"He's a library user, Glory. He's here often."

"Oh goody." A thought visibly passed through Glory's head. "Does Wayne know about him?"

"I'm sure the chief of police knows most people in Belle-haven," Helma told her.

"I meant—" She stopped, and then added, as if it had relevance, "We're taking Ms. Moon home now, anyway. Harley's going to drive the bookmobile so we can fit in her wheelchair. She'll be back tomorrow."

"Be sure the brakes of her wheelchair are securely fixed," Helma advised, suddenly imagining Ms. Moon's wheelchair in the narrow bookmobile aisle as Harley wheeled around a corner.

After Glory left, Helma pulled the kick stool to the book-shelves and tentatively stood on it, testing it with her weight, moving back and forth a little. It remained completely solid, its wheels tucked up into its circular stand. It obviously hadn't slipped out from beneath Ms. Moon's weight, which *was* less than last year's but still *more* than her own.

As she reshelved the loose and sloppy documents, she found a classic children's picture book titled *In the Night Kitchen*. She opened it to the page of an anatomically cor-rect baby boy to be sure it wasn't one of the copies that some-one had pasted diapers over—it wasn't—and set it aside to send to the Children's Room. It was evidence of a curious moral code: people who didn't destroy or steal the books they found offensive, but hid or censored portions of them, in their minds not really compounding one crime with an-other.

Glory and Harley returned from delivering Ms. Moon. Harley stood in the staff room, a glass of water on the coun-ter, flexing his shoulders as he tipped aspirins from a plastic bottle into his palm. George Melville poured himself a cup of coffee.

"If you're going to play he-man," George advised Harley, "you'd better wear a weightlifter's belt."

"I've already moved up my chiropractor's appointment," Harley said and palmed the aspirins into his mouth.

Dutch marched into the staff lounge and they all fell silent. "I'm transferring a call I believe is for you," he said, nodding to Helma, and as he turned smartly on his heels to return to the circulation desk, he added, "She's very upset."

"Sounds like trouble," George called after Helma as she returned to her cubicle. "I bet our leader's lonely already."

Helma braced herself for a conversation with Ms. Moon, taking three fortifying breaths before she picked up the telephone receiver. Inhale for four, hold for four, exhale for eight.

"Wilhelmina. Is that you?"

"Aunt Em. Are you all right?"

Her aunt's voice shook, her accent so strong Helma wasn't surprised when she slipped into Lithuanian, speaking too fast for her to understand anything except that Aunt Em was grievously upset.

"Is Mother all right?" she asked, keeping her voice low and calm, but still she caught sight of one of the pages pausing by the entrance to her cubicle.

"Lillian? No, she's good. I'm not at home. I'm coming. Right now. To talk with you. It's an emergency."

"Why?" Helma tried again. "What's happened?"

"It's about Hannibal Lecter," Aunt Em said. "You wait there." And she hung up.

Helma stood, confused. Hannibal Lecter? The only Hannibal Lecter she was aware of was a fictional killer who supplemented his diet with his victims' flesh.

She waited in the library foyer, with a view of the street. Aunt Em had said she wasn't in the apartment she shared with her mother. Where was she?

"Everything okay, Helma?" George asked, joining her in the foyer. "You're pacing."

"I don't pace," Helma assured him, stopping beside the Naugahyde chairs. "Are you aware of anyone besides the Thomas Harris character who's named Hannibal Lecter?"

"You mean, in real life?"

"Yes."

He shook his head no. "And if they were, they've probably already hightailed to the nearest courtroom to petition for a name change."

A yellow taxi pulled up in front of the library, and Helma spotted Aunt Em's thick white hair through the window. She ran outside and opened the taxi door. Her aunt held a folded newspaper in shaking hands. "This is not right, Wilhelmina," she said, jabbing at an article with an arthritic forefinger.

"Let me help you out of the cab, Aunt Em, and we'll talk about it."

She took her aunt's arm and ushered her into the library foyer. Aunt Em leaned against her, holding up the newspaper. "Read it."

"I will, but first sit down here." Helma guided her to one of the sofas and sat beside her. She took one of Aunt Em's hands, which had grown thin and more veined as she'd shrunken in the past two years. Helma wanted to push back the air of insubstantiality that was growing around her.

During times of excitement, it worked best to speak slowly to Aunt Em, and in simple sentences. "Now tell me."

"This," she said, waving the newspaper. "Zita sent it to me. In this, it says Hannibal Lecter is Lithuanian." She pronounced it Lit-wane-yun. "*Lithuanian!* How can that be?"

"Hannibal Lecter is not real."

"Yes, he is. It says here: Lithuanian, from Vilnius." She placed her hand on her heart. "*I* am from Vilnius. I know nobody who eats people."

"The author invented him, Aunt Em. For his books. He just said he was from Lithuania."

"But why? It's not right. Is *he* Lithuanian?"

"I don't know."

"You are *bibliotekininké*. Can you find out?"

Aunt Em rocked on the sofa. Her face was flushed and Helma felt her pulse flutter beneath her fingers.

"I know what we should do," she said, and waited for Aunt Em to give her her full attention before she continued. "I'll find the author's address and you can write to him. You can ask him."

Aunt Em's old eyes narrowed. "He would answer an old lady?"

"I'm sure he would."

She considered, letting the newspaper fall to her lap. "You will help me?"

"I will," Helma promised. "We'll do it together."

"On computer," she said, nodding. "So he won't mistake what we're saying."

"On computer," Helma agreed. "Now let me take you home, and I'll find the address for you today."

She looked up at George, who'd managed to stick nearby until he discovered what was going on. George nodded and said, "Don't worry about it. I'll cover for you."

"Thank you," she told him, and helped Aunt Em to her feet.

Once in her car and driving back toward the Silver Gables, her aunt said, "Am I too old to think right anymore?"

Helma felt Aunt Em's eyes on her, waiting. The question was too important to answer in any manner but the truth. Helma moistened her lips and said, "You *are* old."

Aunt Em grunted—and waited.

"You get mixed up sometimes."

Aunt Em nodded.

"But you are a good thinker, Aunt Em, a smart cookie."

Her aunt laughed.

As they pulled into the circular parking lot in front of the Silver Gables, Aunt Em pointed to one of the handsome young gardeners. "See him? He's fixing the ground. They came in the night last night."

"Who did?" Helma asked, wondering if Aunt Em was drifting again.

"The tree planters. We woke up this morning and there were ten new trees in the middle of the gardens, with those pink . . . " She made circular motions with her hands.

"Tree tubes?" Helma provided, remembering *Ground Up!*, the brochure she'd found in the Local Government stacks. "They planted trees during the night?"

Aunt Em nodded, and her voice dropped to a whisper.

"Last night. None of us wanted *trees* in the middle of our garden so the men—Charlotte's husband and Frederick from fourth floor—pulled them out and hid them in the garbage. Those pink . . . tubes, too." She raised a finger to her lips. *"Shhh."*

When Helma unlocked the apartment door for Aunt Em, her mother stood there, hands on hips. "I've been worried sick, just *sick*. Where *have* you been?"

Aunt Em raised her nose and pointed to Helma. "To the library."

"You didn't tell me," Lillian accused her.

"I had to do important research."

A loud thump sounded against the window, and Helma's mother glanced at the smudged glass and tsk-tsked. "There goes another bird. I shouldn't have washed those windows. I was just so nervous, I had to do *something*."

Chapter 8

Two Unusual Encounters

A spring sun burned off the morning mist, and after wiping the seat with an extra paper napkin, Helma sat on a bench behind the Bellehaven city hall to eat her lunch, a half block from and out of sight of the library. If library patrons spotted her near the library, they were reminded of questions they'd forgotten to ask, or hurried past with guilty bobs of the head and excuses for unpaid library fines and lost books.

She spread another napkin across her lap and re-wrapped the second half of her roast beef sandwich, setting it aside while she ate the first half. With a plastic knife, she cut the crusts from the bread and lined them up at the edge of the napkin. Purple, almost black, tulips bloomed in pleasantly straight rows at the base of the city hall building. The new gardener hired the previous fall had an admirable geometric sense.

Sunlight filtered through the fresh green of the maple trees, warming her enough that she unbuttoned the top two buttons of her sweater.

"You're from the library, aren't you?"

Helma braced herself for library talk and shaded her eyes to look up into the face of Mayor Ron Morris, whom she'd heard referred to as "Mayor Morose," which honestly he did look like at the moment. He was a small man with a paunch and large brown eyes that sloped downward at the outer corners, giving him a perpetually sorrowful air.

"I am," she admitted. "Miss Helma Zukas."

He nodded in the way of people who hadn't really heard. "Were you there when *she* fell?"

There was no reason to ask who *she* was. The mayor and Ms. Moon had never exactly been friends. "No. I arrived a few minutes later."

Again the nod. "I was talking to her on the telephone the moment she went down."

It was wisest to remain silent if one was curious about the details of a story, so Helma did.

"I called the ambulance after I figured out she dropped the phone," the mayor continued. He looked at Helma, and she felt his watchfulness. "I heard she's at work today."

Helma nodded. An ant scurried across the bench toward her sandwich and she flicked it away with her thumb and forefinger. "She went home an hour ago," she volunteered. "To rest." She waited two beats, then said, "She was concerned about the research she was conducting for you. Could I help?"

"I doubt it. She called and said she had information on something I'd said at a city council meeting."

"But you don't recall the topic?"

He shook his head.

"Was it about forestry?"

He frowned, and if it were possible, the corner of his eyes drooped more. "I honestly can't say. Every subject comes up at those meetings: parks, loose dogs, land management, water use. You name it, somebody's got an axe to grind."

"But you didn't phone her?" Helma asked.

"No," he said as if the possibility would never occur to him. "She claimed she had information I wouldn't find on a computer."

"Then it must have been a local or private issue," Helma mused, "a subject not connected to Bellehaven government. Most of the city's business is available online."

"We've made great strides during my tenure as mayor," he said, straightening into an oratory stance, reminding Helma that the next election was only eighteen months away. "No more unfiled notes or messy stacks of reports. All you have to do is fire up your computer and connect to the city's Web site." He snapped his fingers to illustrate just how fast *he* believed it was to burrow through pages and pages of Web site information to find a single statistic.

"Not every citizen has access to a computer," Helma reminded him.

"Well, that's where the library comes in handy, isn't it? Access for all. Just pop on in and click a few keys."

"*If* they're only looking for government information," Helma pointed out. "But libraries house far more than government information."

He waved toward a sparrow hawk that suddenly swooped in over their heads and lit on the cap of a streetlight. "Look at that. They've adapted to city life. Wish they'd land on a few more of these pigeons." Then he turned back to Helma. "I know, I know. It's an old argument: how to prepare for the future. We'll just have to wait and see."

"I know which materials Ms. Moon was looking through, if you'd like to come to the library and peruse them," Helma offered. Only six minutes remained of her lunch hour.

The mayor shook his head. "No, it was *her* idea. She can remind me of it later if she wants to." He shifted on his feet. "I wish she'd stop saying her fall wasn't *my* fault, though. What's the point of that? I wasn't even there."

"You could talk to her," Helma suggested. "Express your concerns."

"That would just draw attention to it. You know how little things can get blown out of proportion. But if *you* asked her . . . "

Helma tucked her wrapped sandwich and pared crusts back in the lunch bag and stood. She and the mayor stood eye-to-eye, the same height. "One should always speak for oneself," she told the mayor. "It avoids misunderstandings."

"And could get me neck-deep in alligators," he said.

"All the quicker to extricate yourself," Helma said. "Excuse me now. My lunch hour has ended."

"Thanks," the mayor said vaguely, his attention, Helma suspected, on Ms. Moon's suspiciously helpful protestations that the mayor, and therefore the city, had nothing to do with her fall and injury in an overcrowded and possibly dangerous public building.

Helma followed the graveled path from the bench around the side of city hall, beneath an ornamental cherry tree. A breeze had risen and stirred the fragrance of the blossoms. She inhaled the perfumed air. The tree stood in the shade, a late bloomer. In a week the pink blossoms would be gone, and in fact were already drifting to the grass.

Twenty feet beyond the tree, Helma glimpsed a furtive yellow movement in her peripheral vision. She stopped and turned toward a line of droopy cedars planted along the east sidewalk. The trees had been planted years ago, and in the moist maritime climate had grown beyond expectations. They now had to be pruned once, even twice, a year, or they crowded the sidewalks. "People are *sleeping* under them!" had been a recent outcry.

A woman stood near the trees wearing a stylish if unfortunately colored yellow coat. Her tinted hair was swept back in an old-fashioned chignon. She stared at Helma. Intently.

Helma waited for the woman to beckon but she continued

gazing in her direction, unmoving. Helma stepped off the path and began walking across the lawn toward her.

The woman raised her hand toward her mouth and shifted her stance as if about to duck behind the branches, but then dropped her hand and waited.

She was middle-aged, well-tended. Helma noted the carefully plucked and drawn eyebrows, the tan pumps, the flattering lipstick. It was only the yellow coat . . .

"Excuse me," Helma said when she was close enough so there was no need to raise her voice. "May I help you?"

The woman moistened her lips. Her neck moved as she swallowed. "I've heard rumors," she said without preamble. Her voice was modulated, educated. "About your friend, the artist."

"Yes?" Helma said, not about to provide Ruth's name.

"About her paintings, that there was a robbery." She folded her hands in front of her, clasping them together, her knuckles turning white. "Do you know which paintings were stolen?"

"I'm Miss Helma Zukas," Helma said.

"I know, from the library."

"And you are?" Helma asked. She knew or recognized many people from her years serving the citizens of Bellehaven, but this woman was unfamiliar.

"It's not important." It was a coolish day but perspiration dotted the woman's forehead like dew. "I thought . . . " She frowned. Her eyes filled and she swallowed again, struggling.

"Please," Helma told her, and pointed to the bench where she'd eaten her lunch. "Let's sit down."

"No." She violently shook her head. "No. This was stupid. I'm sorry." She spun around, away from Helma, catching her heel in the grass and stumbling.

Helma reached out a hand and the woman jerked away from her. "Just forget it. I'm sorry."

"Please," Helma said again.

But the woman hurried away, her heels staccato on the sidewalk. For a moment Helma contemplated following her. Instead, she stood on the city hall lawn watching the woman stride down the street, her yellow coat pulled tightly to her body, until she turned the corner by the hospital and disappeared.

Helma committed to memory every aspect of the woman she could, including her voice and the tilt of her shoulders. She'd known about the theft of Ruth's paintings, had wanted to know *which* paintings. Helma was sure she would see the woman again, and next time she would recognize her. But mostly she wondered how far and wide the news of Ruth's show, Ruth Revealed, ranged across the region.

Before she left the library, Helma searched the Internet for Roxy Lightheart, the artist Ruth suspected of stealing her paintings, whom she'd called a "one-woman art factory."

Her name popped up as an exhibitor on a long list of craft shows and bazaars, but Helma had no luck finding a photo of Roxy or any of her artwork.

Chapter 9

A Threatened Home

Helma blinked. She braked her car at the entrance to the Bayside Arms and stared at the white sign gently swinging from a white post beside the drive.

FABER REALTY, the sign read. FOR SALE.

The Bayside Arms, her apartment building, was *for sale*?

Faber Realty was sometimes called the "big muscle" realty company in Bellehaven. Their signs popped up on building walls, billboards, the sides of buses, and on top of taxis, even gracing grocery carts at Hugie's.

Residents of the Bayside Arms had feared for years that the apartments might be turned into condos, but *for sale*? Apartment 3F had been Helma's first home for her first job after library school. At the time, the Bayside Arms had been a new, highly desirable address. Since then it had been overshadowed and outpaced by sleek condos and multilevel homes with sweeping views of Washington Bay.

Helma parked her car and knocked on the manager's door. Moggy sat on the back of Walter David's sofa, watching her. Helma looked away from the Persian cat's flat eyes. After knocking twice more without a response, she climbed the outside stairs of the building, considering the implications of the For Sale sign.

TNT's door stood open. She glimpsed the retired boxer's black and metal exercise apparatus, which took up most of the living room, resembling an updated torture machine. TNT's only furniture consisted of a lounge chair and a television positioned so it could be viewed from the chair or the machine.

The clanking sound of pulleys and metal ceased and TNT called, "Boy Cat Zukas is here."

Helma rarely worried about the wandering cat. She had no idea how old he was, and even though he wasn't actually showing signs of age, he'd begun to stay closer to home, as well as sleep more. And maybe not quite hissing at her as much. She'd never touched the cat but they'd formed a mutually wary and respectful affiliation.

She stepped into TNT's doorway as he climbed off the machine, mopping his forehead, and pointed to Boy Cat Zukas curled on a towel in the corner. TNT's walls were bare except for an old framed poster with the words TNT—DYNAMITE MAN! arced over a picture of a young TNT in a fighting stance challenging the viewer.

"If you let him on your balcony," Helma told him, "he'll jump across to mine." Boy Cat Zukas hadn't even glanced her way.

TNT uncapped a water bottle from a case on the floor. "Nah, if you don't care, I'll let him stay. He's good company. I just didn't want you to worry."

"I won't," Helma assured him.

"Did you see the For Sale sign?"

"I did."

"I talked to Walter for a minute. He thinks it'll be sold for condos."

"The building was nearly turned into condos a few years ago," Helma said.

TNT shook his head. "Not turned *into*, torn *down*." He waved toward his sliding balcony that overlooked Board-walk Park and the wide blue bay beyond. The islands piled up behind one another to the west, each a mistier shade of blue. "With this view, in this location, condos would be worth more than apartments. We're talking major bucks."

It had happened elsewhere in Bellehaven, in fact, just down the street.

"I guess I'd better start looking for a new apartment," TNT said, shaking his head. He stood beside the poster of his young self, the resemblance like father and son.

"My aunt always recommends not borrowing trouble," Helma told him. "It makes sense to wait and hear the new owner's intent. It could take months to sell."

He nodded. "I don't mean to be nosy," he began, which in Helma's experience usually meant someone was about to say something intrusive, "but your phone's been ringing off the hook. I could hear it through the walls. Your answering machine must not be working."

"I don't have an answering machine," Helma told him.

"That explains it then. Can I get you a Coke? Water?" He waved toward the case of water.

"No thanks. I'll go home now."

He nodded. "Catch that phone call."

She was stopped in the door by TNT asking, "How's your mother?"

Her mother? Helma turned. "My mother? She's fine."

TNT nodded. "That's good, really good."

Inside 3F, before she locked her door and with her hand still on the doorknob, Helma made a quick appraisal of her apart-ment, as was her habit. Dish towels still hung squarely, cush-ions in place on her sofa, westward-facing window shades pulled down against the sun, magazines and books on her coffee table still aligned.

She tried phoning Ruth but there was no answer, only Ruth's new answering machine, which suggested in a haughty British accent that the caller "leave a brief, appropriate message." It was a more agreeable message than Ruth's last machine, which had only said, "Talk," in Ruth's bored voice, but still, Helma didn't give out her personal phone number, order her phone number printed on checks, or speak into mechanical devices, so she hung up.

If Ruth had let the phone "ring off the hook," she'd call back later. Ruth didn't give up. She'd phone her in the morning and describe the woman in the yellow coat. The woman didn't fit Ruth's description of Roxy Lightheart, but she might have information about her stolen paintings.

But now she had to prepare for dinner with Wayne Gallant. She and the chief had been friends for a long time. Actually, for years. And actually, more than friends. Ruth called Wayne "gun shy," because of his divorce, which although he rarely mentioned it, Helma knew had been long and painful. Their association had originally centered on unfortunate events in Bellehaven, and through the years it had fluctuated between close and closer. They had only recently recovered from a misjudgment on the chief's part regarding another library employee.

From the blue portion of her closet, Helma chose a pale blue dress with a heatherish weave. It buttoned up the front from hem to neck. She buttoned it all the way to her neck, then pinned her grandmother's cameo at her throat. Studying herself in the mirror, she thought of Ruth, whose clothes were a jumble of color and cut. Too low, too short, too long, or simply wildly mismatched. Helma's shoes and belt were the same shade of soft matte black. She frowned, removed the cameo and unbuttoned the top button of her dress, turning in front of the mirror.

No. Rebutton and repin. But as her doorbell rang, she checked the stubborn curl on the left side of her head and leaned down to unbutton the bottom two buttons above the hemline of her dress. There.

Wayne Gallant wore a sport jacket and turtleneck sweater. She couldn't help noting how the fabric stretched across his shoulders and chest and then hung loose over his midriff. He'd joined a local gym and his stomach had shrunk to a definite taper.

"That's a nice dress," he said, grinning at her. "Like spring. Which it is."

"It is," she answered. "Spring, I mean."

When they were in his car, he nodded toward the For Sale sign. "That's new."

"It went up today. I haven't talked to the manager so I don't know the details."

"Progress," he commented. He took his eyes from the street for a moment longer than was safe, gazing at Helma. "You may need a new place to live."

"Perhaps," was all she said.

They ate dinner at Alpaca's, a new seafood restaurant by the bay.

"What's an alpaca got to do with salmon?" Wayne asked after they were seated, pointing to his menu, which had two alpacas nuzzling each other inside a heart on the cover. A passing waitress overheard him and paused beside their table. "They just liked the name. Isn't it cute?"

Since Helma broiled, braised, and baked excellent salmon herself, she ordered sautéed shrimp, while Wayne requested stuffed trout. He ordered wine for both of them: white for Helma, red for himself.

"I heard Ms. Moon went directly from her hospital bed to the library," he said after they'd ordered. "How is she?"

"She stayed part of the morning and then members of the staff took her home."

He nodded. "Bad break."

Since he'd brought it up, Helma told him, "I talked to the mayor today. He mentioned he was concerned about Ms. Moon's fall."

He swirled the wine in his glass. It rose dangerously close to the rim. "'Concerned' is one word for it."

"And another word might be?" she asked.

He leaned back in his chair and studied her. "I wish you'd been there when she fell. I'd like your perspective on the whole thing."

Helma felt her cheeks warming and picked up the glass of white wine, lowering her eyes. "You don't think anyone else was involved, do you? That she was pushed?"

"There's no indication of that," he said.

"The mayor's afraid she's going to sue the city," she guessed, "because the library's overcrowded and should have been replaced years ago."

"A certain amount of publicity might help her cause."

Helma set down her wineglass, accidentally banging it against her bread plate. George had suggested the same thing, but then George viewed every small child as a potential book abuser. "You're not implying Ms. Moon would fall and break her leg *on purpose* in order to push her case for a new library, are you?"

When he didn't answer, she shook her head and said, "Ms. Moon would never . . . She isn't . . ." Imprecise language was a sign of an imprecise mind but she couldn't help it.

Helma closed her lips, recalling Ms. Moon's previous dubious dealings: trading her to another institution without her knowledge, tricking her into group counseling, using murders to publicize the library, entering into "suspect" negotiations to procure a site for a new library. Ms. Moon was a woman who was open to the advantage of any occasion, good or bad. The disappointment of being thwarted never fazed her.

"Did the mayor come to the library?" Wayne asked.

"No. I was eating lunch near the city hall and he stopped to speak to me."

Remembering her lunch reminded her of the woman in the yellow coat and Ruth's crime scene. "Do you have any information on Ruth's missing paintings?" she asked him.

"Carter's taken the lead, and I haven't talked to him since a briefing this morning. The connection to the two dead men is a problem. Both deaths were suspicious when they occurred. And there's no known connection between Meriwether Scott and Vincent Jensen." He smiled. "Except Ruth, of course."

"How did Vincent Jensen die? The newspaper article was vague."

"He was working in his home lab and was overcome by gas, we suspect."

"I thought there was a fire."

"There was. Not a large one, but a reaction to the gas in the air. He may have turned on a light or somehow sparked it. He could have dropped metal on metal. It doesn't take much."

"Wouldn't he have had a fan? What kind of gas?"

He hesitated, buttered a roll that had too many seeds in it, then said, "There was an empty hydrogen sulfide container in his lab. But hydrogen sulfide isn't detectable in the body."

"So you couldn't *prove* hydrogen sulfide killed him, or that it was murder."

"That's correct. A neighbor walking her dog in the alley heard the explosion and called the fire department. A truck arrived within seconds."

"And Meriwether Scott's death?" Helma asked. "Was his fall suspicious?"

"It didn't feel right to me," Wayne said, then ducked his head. "That doesn't sound very professional, but that's the way it was."

"The mind pays attention," Helma said.

"There's also the possibility that the paintings depicted two dead men is a coincidence."

"But the two paintings weren't even near each other," Helma said. "Ruth had lined her finished work against the wall and there were three other, untouched, paintings between the two that were stolen, so those two were definitely chosen. And don't forget that a strip of canvas ripped from one of them was left on her pillow, which seems very sinister to me."

"It does, I agree." Their dinners were served and he picked up a slice of lemon perched on top of his fish and set it on the rim of his plate. "Carter's a pretty thorough detective. I'll wait and see what he turns up."

"Before you become involved?" Helma finished for him.

He laughed and pointed toward her sautéed shrimp beside a bed of rice, not on it, just as she'd requested. "That looks delicious," he said, changing the subject.

Since they both worked the next day, Wayne brought Helma home by 9:30. As he walked with her up the outside staircase of the Bayside Arms, even though she knew their footsteps were barely audible, she spotted the blinds on Mrs. Allen's second-floor apartment move.

The night was soft with the slightest breeze from the south, bringing a fragrance of the sea at low tide. "Would you like to come in?" Helma asked as she unlocked her door. "I can make coffee." She could, too. She'd bought a four-cup electric coffee maker after carefully studying *Consumer Reports*, and then exactly memorized the directions that came with it.

Wayne Gallant shook his head. "I'd like to, but I think I'll go back to the station and look over a couple of things."

"You have an idea about Ms. Moon's fall? Or Ruth's stolen paintings? Or the deaths of two men?"

He laughed. "You got me thinking. I just want to review the details. Sometimes that's enough to get my mind going."

Helma nodded. That was exactly how *she* dealt with puzzling situations, to step out of the way and let her mind wrestle with the details. More often than not, hours later she discovered herself on the way to a solution.

They faced each other on the doormat. Helma swallowed as Wayne touched her hair. He leaned toward her, bending slightly, and she leaned toward him. She felt his arms go around her and smelled his aftershave and the night on his jacket, felt his heart beating. And maybe her own.

They stood like that until she was startled by a hissing sound and looked up to see Boy Cat Zukas sitting on the roof above them. He stared down, unblinking, his black pupils eerily filling his eye sockets in the darkness, reminding her of why she'd always avoided cats.

"A voyeur cat," Wayne commented.

"More likely he's hungry," Helma told him. "He didn't show up at his usual dinnertime tonight," although she suspected TNT had offered him food of some kind. As if he actually remembered his alley-cat days, Boy Cat Zukas never took food for granted and gorged himself whenever he had the opportunity.

"I'll talk to you soon," Wayne said. And then in a surprise motion he lifted her hand and kissed her palm. "Thanks for tonight."

Even more surprisingly, Helma found herself unable to answer and stood on the doormat watching Wayne Gallant stroll to his car before she awkwardly turned her doorknob with her other, unkissed hand, barely hearing the thump of Boy Cat Zukas as he jumped down and slipped into the apartment ahead of her.

Chapter 10

A Stealthy Escape

Helma was flossing her teeth with a new "profession-ally engineered" green ribbon floss with an overt spear-mint taste the dental hygienist had given her at her last cleaning, and thinking it was hard to improve on plain white flossing string, when her phone rang.

She paused, floss held between first and second molar. The digital clock on her bathroom counter read 10:02, so she waited.

After seven rings she left off flossing and answered the telephone, bracing herself. Very little good news arrived after ten o'clock in the evening.

"Hello?" she said warily.

The whispered answer was unintelligible.

"Ruth, is that you?" Helma asked.

"*Shh*. Just come pick me up."

"Why? And where are you?"

"I'm not in a bar. I'm cold sober and I'm not in trou-ble. At least not yet."

"Call a cab."

"Too obvious. If you just drive over to the corner of

Merritt and Orca, I'll jump in. That's all you have to do."
Ruth's voice echoed, as if she was calling from a small en-
closed space.

"Where's your car?"

"Helm."

"Helma," she corrected. She was still dressed. She only
needed to put on shoes and retrieve her coat from her coat
closet.

"It's about my stolen paintings," Ruth said in a cajoling
tone. "I have news."

"Is it important?"

"Are you coming or not?"

If she didn't pick up Ruth, who knew what Ruth would
do. "All right," she told her. "On which corner of Merritt
and Orca?"

"You know I can't tell north from south. Just stop in the
parking lot of the Malibu Tanning Salon and I'll appear,
okay? Whoops. Gotta go. See you in a minute. Hurry. And
don't honk, okay?" And the line went dead.

In five minutes Helma was pulling out of the Bayside
Arms parking lot. Merritt and Orca was on the north side of
town, in a mix of older houses and a new box-store development. It was the direction of Bellehaven's inexorable expan-
sion, and usually deserted after business hours.

It was a quiet night; Helma eased her Buick past dark
stores, empty parking lots, and houses where lights were
being flicked off. An empty grocery cart tilted off a sidewalk corner. During the day the street past the commercial
development was filled with cars, creating Bellehaven's first-
ever traffic jams. On this street it was rare to see loose dogs
or oversized trees. It was indistinguishable from any developing area in the United States.

She turned onto Merritt and drove away from the developed area toward the older homes, many of which had
been turned into small shops and offices, last-ditch efforts

before they too were gobbled up and turned into commercial buildings.

Her Buick suddenly jerked and she leaned forward, removing her foot from the gas pedal and listening to the engine. Helma knew nothing about automobile mechanics but after this much time knew how her car *should* sound. It had been her high school graduation present, and except for a replaced passenger window and a small repaired scratch on the driver's-side door, it was in the same pristine condition as when it was brand new and her father had tied a roll of green garden hose into a messy bow and perched it on the hood.

When the engine noise wasn't repeated, she sat back and discovered she'd driven past the Malibu Tanning Salon. She peered in front and behind her. No other cars traveled the street, so she stopped and made the policeman's turn her father had taught her: back up, go forward.

The tanning salon was closed and dark, but Helma parked in a space in front of the door and waited, seeing no sign of Ruth. The building had once been a small bungalow home and the parking lot its front lawn. She was sure this was where Ruth had said to meet her.

A minute later, at the edge of her headlights, Ruth darted into view, crouched and running toward her car. She wore black. Before Helma could unlock the passenger door, Ruth jerked on it, her mouth moving in furious unheard words.

"Okay," she said when Helma had unlocked the door and she'd lunged inside but left the door open, sprawling onto the seat. "Drive away like you haven't done anything wrong."

"I haven't," Helma told her. "Close the door."

"Not yet. I don't want to attract attention."

"Ruth, I'm not leaving until you're all the way inside my car and the door is completely closed."

With exaggerated care, Ruth gripped the door handle and closed the door. It barely made a sound. "There. Are you happy now? Let's go."

"Go where? And why are you dressed in black? You said you had information about your missing paintings."

"Not information, news. Wait. Don't go that way!" Ruth slapped her hand on the Buick's dashboard.

Helma stopped. "Ruth. I see police lights down there. Do they have anything to do with you?"

Ruth leaned back and slouched as far as the seat belt would allow. "Roxy Lightheart is such a whiner. Just because she hears a little noise she calls the police. Whine, whine. What a wuss. *I* wouldn't do that. I'd at least look first."

"You went to Roxy Lightheart's house to look for your stolen paintings and she saw you and called the police," Helma summarized for Ruth. "Where'd she see you, in her yard?"

"Not exactly." Ruth said crankily.

"Oh, Ruth, you weren't *inside* her house, were you?"

"How else was I going to look for my paintings? I didn't know she was home. She was in her bathtub, and she called the police from her *bathroom*. A phone in her bathroom, how paranoid is that?"

"Did she see you?"

"Nope. Luckily I heard her screeching and splashing around. She's lucky she didn't drown herself."

"Breaking and entering is a crime. You could be in terrible trouble."

"I already said she didn't see me. I'm in the clear."

Helma turned her car off Merritt and toward the center of Bellehaven. "Then what news do you have?"

Ruth shrugged. "Not much. I didn't see my paintings anywhere, not even in her trash. I did see the stuff she's working on." She sniffed and waved her hands into incomprehensible shapes. "Stuff you'd see at a church bazaar. Absolutely not competitive. How'd she ever get a show scheduled at Cheri's Gallery in the first place?"

"There must be some commercial value in it or the gallery wouldn't exhibit her work."

Ruth grunted.

Helma drove to Ruth's small house and stopped at the curb in front of it, setting her emergency break.

"Thanks for saving me from embarrassing myself," Ruth said as she opened the car door and stepped out. "*Brr,* it's chilly out here." She reached back into the car, feeling along the bench seat, then on the floor, and finally beneath the seat.

"Oh crap," she said.

"What is it?" Helma asked her.

"My gloves," Ruth said, her eyes troubled in the car's overhead light. "I left my gloves behind."

Chapter 11

And if the Glove Fits

"You left your gloves at Roxy Lightheart's house?" Helma asked.

Ruth grimaced and climbed back into the car. "Looks that way. You might as well take me down to the police station and let them slap on the cuffs. I'm sunk."

"Think, Ruth," Helma advised. "*Where* did you leave them? *In* her house? Outside?"

She shook her head. "I'm trying to remember. Must have been inside. Why would I have taken them off *outside*? I wore them so I wouldn't leave fingerprints."

"Then maybe you didn't take them off until you left her house, perhaps near the tanning salon."

Ruth hadn't closed the car door, and in the overhead light, the sad light that had edged her eyes since Paul left Bellehaven was deeper, darker. "No. I swear I didn't have them when I ran for my life. But I can't remember taking them off, either."

"What kind of housekeeper is Roxy?"

"That is so pertinent, Helma. Leave it to you to ask a question like that."

"No," Helma explained. "If she's a relaxed housekeeper, she may overlook a pair of gloves left on a table or counter. Black gloves might not be too out of place."

When Ruth didn't answer, Helma asked, "Roxy was an orderly housekeeper?"

And when Ruth still didn't answer, she said, "Your gloves *were* black, weren't they?"

"I couldn't find my black ones, so I wore my red ones. In the dark, red and black are indistinguishable. It has something to do with wavelengths and reflected light. I thought . . . I mean who could tell? They were better than lily white bare hands."

"Not the red gloves with the dragons stitched on the back?"

Ruth nodded miserably. "The very ones."

Gloves Ruth had worn all winter long, inside and out, showing them off as a "score from an estate sale." Elegant, tight fitting, from a bygone era. Overlong and obvious. Probably not another pair like them in all of Washington State, maybe the country.

"I'm in trouble."

"Probably," Helma agreed.

"Oh, thanks a lot." Ruth drummed her fingers on the dashboard. "Should I confess? Maybe I'd get a lighter sentence."

Helma thought. Promptly owning up to a trespass was the responsible action, and often resulted in an advantage for the trespasser. Lighter sentences, forgiveness. Apologies mitigated the need for complicated explanations.

Acknowledging one's transgressions had been her way of life, all those dark confessions in the back of St. Alphonse's, where the Second Vatican changes had been resisted until the bishop's accomplices arrived to bring the parish into alignment. "Henchmen," her father had called them.

But on the other hand, Helma doubted Ruth would get off

with three Our Fathers, three Hail Marys, and three Glory Be's.

"Did you damage anything?" she asked Ruth. "Anything at all?"

Ruth shook her head. "Roxy left her studio door unlocked. I just walked in and started looking around, that's all. Shut all the doors behind me, didn't break anything. Whatever I moved, I put back in place. I tell you even God wouldn't have known I'd been there."

"If the police ask you, you have to confess. Tell the truth. Immediately, with no equivocation."

"What do you mean, *if* the police ask me?" Ruth asked, the finger-drumming halting in mid-thump as she turned to gaze at Helma. "What if they *don't*?"

Helma would never recommend evasion, ever. "I would never suggest evading the truth if you're confronted," she told Ruth.

Ruth slowly nodded. "Then just exactly what *are* you suggesting?"

"Merely telling the truth," Helma said. "Now, I think we should both get a good night's sleep."

Ruth was halfway out the passenger door when Helma remembered the woman by city hall who'd worn the yellow coat. "Wait," she told Ruth. "Today a woman asked me about your paintings."

Ruth ducked back inside. "That's good. I've been promoting them until I'm blue in the face."

That was true. Anyone who'd ever crossed Ruth's path, which was most of Bellehaven, had probably felt a few twinges when they heard of Ruth's biographical art show.

"She asked which paintings had been stolen," Helma explained. "And I had the impression she didn't want to be seen talking to me."

"So what'd she look like?"

"Middle-aged, quite attractive." Helma described the

woman's careful appearance, her matching shoes and purse.

"Sounds anal," Ruth commented. "I hope she brings her checkbook."

"She wore a bright yellow coat."

Ruth frowned. "Doesn't go with the rest of the package, does it, bright yellow? Can't picture her, but I'll think on it, and keep an eye out for a yellow-coated woman." She got out of the car, and before closing the door added, "If I'm not in jail, anyway. Oh, and thanks for the rescue."

Helma parked in her covered space next to Walter David's motorcycle. It was too late to ask the manager about the For Sale sign. The night was thick with humidity, what some Bellehavenites called "congealed air," and the sky above her was dark and clouded. Bulbs above doors were cushioned in misty nimbuses. She'd left her kitchen light on in 3F; it shone pale from behind the single window that overlooked the parking lot.

Lights were also on in TNT's apartment, beside hers. He was usually an advocate of early to bed, early to rise. Helma paused at the *thump-thump* of his metal exercise contraption, then glanced at her watch. It was nearly midnight, an unusual time for him to work out. The ceiling in the apartment below TNT's must be vibrating. She'd seen the way the widowed Mrs. Patrick smiled at TNT, so she doubted there'd be any complaints. TNT was obviously experiencing a sleepless night.

Helma rarely allowed herself sleepless nights; they simply took away too much energy from the next day.

Chapter 12

Ghosts in the Machine

While Helma fried a single slice of bacon to accompany her scrambled egg, which was just reaching perfection in a second frying pan at the back of her stovetop, she heard the morning issue of the *Bellehaven Daily News* thump on her landing. It was 7:06. The new paper girl was running late.

She forked the bacon and pressed the grease out of it between two sheets of paper towel and was using the spatula to slide the egg onto her plate when she recalled Maggie Bekman and her photographer recording Ms. Moon as she was wheeled from the ambulance into the library. Certainly it wasn't a story that rated more than a paragraph in the local section. Was it?

Leaving her breakfast in mid-state, she wiped her hands on another paper towel and opened the door onto the landing. A sea gull sailed out of the mist, swooped down toward her, cried out once, and rose toward the bay. By the Dumpster in the parking lot, Walter David was sweeping up trash that had missed the container. He looked up at the sound of Helma's door and waved. "Morning," he called. Not very enthusiastically, she thought.

Helma waved. The newspaper had landed six inches short of her doormat, a credible toss from the parking lot. She glanced down—the For Sale sign was still there—then picked up the newspaper and removed the plastic sleeve as she stepped back inside, opening it to the local section.

She didn't realize she was holding her breath until she let it out in relief. There was nothing there. Ms. Moon had called on Maggie Bekman before and the results had been what Helma would call sensationalized.

She set the paper beside her place mat and returned to arranging her breakfast on her plate, eggs and bacon not touching, dry toast on a separate plate, wondering if Roxy Lightheart's call to the police had rated any news space.

Normally, she didn't mix reading with eating, but this morning she perused the local section again, searching until she found the police report. Two car prowls, another subversive tree-planting by Ground Up!, one driving while intoxicated, and a bicycle rider threatening pedestrians on the sidewalk. Roxy's prowler might have been dismissed as simply an unidentifiable sound. Ruth was in the clear.

Helma set the local section aside, opened the front page and gasped. There, on the right edge, in the most eye-catching spot above a story on aborted peace talks in the Middle East, a headline read, LIBRARY DIRECTOR INJURED IN FALL, and in slightly smaller print, *Crowded Building a Factor?*

In the center of the page, managing to appear simultaneously frail and appealing, was a photo of Ms. Moon, a wisp of hair against her cheek, eyes wide, in a foreshortened pose with cast leg protruding toward the reader.

As her breakfast cooled, Helma pored over the article. The accidental fall while helping the mayor. The library's square footage compared to the libraries of other cities of similar size, the failed library bonds and tragic building attempt months earlier. And there were those words at the end of the article. "I expect to make a full recovery," the director vowed. "It's not the mayor's fault."

In the covered parking area, Walter David was cleaning the tires of his motorcycle when Helma unlocked her Buick's door.

"Did you see the sign?" he asked, motioning toward the For Sale sign.

"I did. Do you know the details?"

He squirted an oily-smelling spray on the front tire. "It was news to me. The owner phoned an hour before the sign went up. He's selling off his holdings and retiring to Mexico. That's all I know."

"Has anyone asked to view it?"

"Not yet. I bet it'll be bought for the land," he said glumly. "Why bother upgrading these old apartments, anyway? Not much money in that. It'll become a McMansion or Mc-Condos." He sighed. "I thought I'd retire from this place. I've already put out the word I'll be available to manage another complex."

Walter echoed what Helma had already heard. She told him goodbye and left him rubbing his tires with a rag and muttering to himself.

"We have a poltergeist," George Melville said as soon as Helma stepped into the workroom.

"I beg your pardon." Helma unbuttoned her spring coat. It had been forty-two degrees when she left her apartment but the temperatures would rise by noon, promising a partly sunny, warmish spring day.

"You know, woo woo woo." George waved his arms back and forth. "Some creepy thing slipping through the stacks during the witching hours, undoing all the good that we do."

"George, I have no idea what you're talking about."

"Come see."

Helma reluctantly followed him into the public area of the library, depositing her bag and coat in her cubicle along the way. She could tell from the gleeful expression on George's face that he hoped to surprise her, a state she avoided as much as possible.

The library hadn't opened yet so there was no need to lower their voices. Dutch stood at the circulation desk sorting returned books; two pages pushed carts through the stacks, reshelving.

"Look at that, would you?" he said as he stopped in front of the Local Documents area and swept his hand down an aisle.

Helma *was* surprised. There, on the floor, sat the stack of pamphlets, reports, and studies she'd shelved the day before, the stack Ms. Moon had knocked to the floor in her fall, which Helma had reordered and reshelved.

"Who's responsible?" Helma asked.

George made woo-woo motions again. "Don't know. This is how Dutch found it this morning." He turned his head toward the circulation counter. "Right, Dutch?"

Dutch nodded curtly and went back to sorting books.

"I told him to leave it," George continued. "in case there was a clue to who's messing around with our minds, or if the guilty somebody wants to own up to it. What do you think?"

"This was the work of a flesh-and-blood person, of course," Helma said. "Is Ms. Moon here?"

"You think she did it?" George's eyes gleamed

"I don't believe she's capable in her present state."

"Probably not. Hard to climb around with your leg in a cast. But no, she's not here yet. Harley and Glory just drove off in the bookmobile to pick her up. Oh yeah—and just wait until you see our little Glory."

"Why?"

"I can't do her justice. You gotta see this one for yourself."

Helma briefly examined the stack of materials. Yes, they were the same. Only those she'd sorted and rearranged had been set on the floor. Whoever was responsible had identified them by their conspicuous orderliness.

"Did you catch our daily rag this morning?" George asked, watching her.

"The *Bellehaven Daily News*?" Helma said. "Yes, I did."

"Her fifteen minutes. This isn't the end of it, believe me."

The library phone rang, and a few moments after he answered it, Dutch said, "Excuse me, Helma, there's a phone call for you. I'll transfer it to the reference desk."

She left George musing over the stack of environmental materials, mumbling, "Gaslight," and picked up the phone at the desk.

"I'm still free. No police pounding on my door yet."

"Hello, Ruth."

"I think I got away with it, don't you?"

"The incident only took place last night. It's still early."

"Well thank you for your reassurance. Do you remember Mrs. Budzynskas in Scoop River?"

Helma pictured Mrs. Budzynskas, whom she hadn't seen in over twenty years. The erect, blond woman, exotic compared to the other mothers. Always upright, correct, wearing trim skirts and low heels, smiles sparingly bestowed.

"Well, do you?"

"She wore her hair in a chignon," Helma said.

"Like the yellow-coated woman, right? Not a hair out of place?"

"There was a similarity," she told Ruth, "except I believe she turned the chignon in the opposite direction from Mrs. Budzynskas."

"Okay, okay. But the same aura, am I right?"

Helma had to agree that Ruth was right. "Do you know who she was?" she asked.

"I do. Or at least I think I do. That was Vincent's widow."

"The object of your stolen painting? His *wife*?"

"Well, you don't have to say it like *that*. They were separated, remember? I ran into them on campus once. If looks could kill, I'd be dead meat. He probably confessed every sordid detail of our brief encounter."

"Then this was after your involvement with her husband?"

"There was never any *real* involvement, Helm. Just a little friendly companionship. All was forgiven."

"By whom?"

"By everybody. She's one of those 'keepers.' She wanted to be married to a bigger fish in this small pond and all the nice things that went with it. They hadn't slept together in years."

"He told you that?"

"Well, *she* didn't."

"That's very indiscreet of a husband to divulge that information, Ruth."

"You don't have to tell me. It's a well-used line and I've heard it before."

"Then perhaps it's not worth believing."

"Just part of the game. So tell me again what she wanted from you."

Helma turned her back to Carolyn, the page who had pushed a book truck close to the reference desk to reshelve a volume of the *Dictionary of Music*. "Somehow she knew we were friends and that you'd had a break-in. She asked which paintings had been stolen."

"Hmm. How'd she know that?"

"Ruth Revealed," Helma reminded her. "It's very public that you're painting incidents from your life."

"I'm building a buzz, and the mysterious element packs them in."

"Are you recreating the paintings, like Carter Houston asked?"

"The detectobot? Not yet. I told him to give me back the shred I found on my bed first." She sighed. "Maybe it'll give me some clue. I do this stuff in the heat of the moment. Once it's done, it's gone, out of my mind. Poof. On to bigger and better things."

Helma heard a noise by the front doors and told Ruth, "The library's about to open. I have to hang up."

"Yeah, yeah. Do me a favor, would you? Perform your librarian magic again and look up Mrs. Vincent. I just want to know the public stuff, no big secrets, okay?"

But Helma was looking through the library's plate-glass front doors. There, like the ambulance the morning before, was the oversized bookmobile, backed up to the front doors, blocking street traffic and patrons waiting to enter. Harley opened the rear doors to expose Ms. Moon in a wheelchair and Glory Shandy solicitously tucking a robe across her lap.

She studied Glory, recalling George's remark, "Wait until you see Glory."

Glory wore a short leather skirt with a silver buckled belt. A leather vest with fringes topped a pink denim shirt. And on her feet were tooled blue leather boots. All she needed to complete the picture was a Stetson and a six-gun on her hip.

Chapter 13

Despair in the Deli

Dutch unlocked the library's front doors and stepped back. Ms. Moon wheeled through, with Glory at her side, fringes swaying.

Gone was the green hospital-issue wheelchair Ms. Moon had arrived in the day before. On this day she entered in a streamlined self-propelled chair with a panel of controls on the right arm. The chair was red, and shiny, and obviously brand new. Ms. Moon steered it with such dexterity one might think she'd had long practice, performing subtle turns and shifts around a potted plant, detouring to avoid an upturned mat corner, with a little dip and spin aimed toward Dutch in an electric acknowledgment. And all the time, mixed with a weary frown of pain, was an upward tip to the corners of her mouth that she appeared to press her lips together to dampen.

George Melville tipped his head to one side as he watched Ms. Moon. "Hear that?" he said to Helma, holding his hand to his ear like an ear trumpet.

"What are you referring to?" Helma asked, watching

Ms. Moon halt her chair to acknowledge a woman entering the library who leaned over, her arms laden with books, and patted the director on the shoulder.

"Her motor. Her sneaking up on us days are over."

"She won't be confined to a wheelchair for very long," Helma reminded him.

"I bet you six number-two lead pencils she's going to stretch this one out to the last possible second."

"Why would she want to?"

George shook his head at her. "You just wait and see, oh innocent one. She and her sidekick, Annie Oakley."

Ms. Moon aimed her chair at Helma and George, but six feet before she reached them, with a neat pivot, motored past, saying over her shoulder, "Yes, I'm here. Thank you."

The early-morning library patrons were more thoughtful than usual, eyeing Ms. Moon's progress toward the rear of the public area. A white-haired woman shook her head sadly, and turning to a woman who looked very similar, said, "I've never seen anyone so dedicated."

Ms. Moon's wheelchair paused and smoothly spun around as if on an axis. The director smiled in the general direction of the woman, then whirred through the workroom door toward her office.

"Got an appointment with William Cody, Glory?" George said as Glory flounced to the reference desk, fringes trembling and swaying.

Glory frowned. "Who?"

"Never mind. He's dead, anyway."

"Oh, I'm sorry, George." She pressed a finger into the dimple of her left cheek. "Helma, what did you say that man's name was yesterday?"

"I don't believe I did."

Glory waggled her fingers. "You know, the cowboy you were talking to in the stacks."

"Cowboy?" George blurted. "We have cowboys in *Belle-*

haven? Is that why you're all got up in that getup? You aim
to trap a cowboy? You're in the wrong country, ma'am."
George stretched the word "ma'am" into a drawl.

Glory raised her chin. "You're mean, George, just plain
mean. I *love* cowboys. I've *always* loved cowboys." She spun
on her booted heels and pranced toward the workroom.

"Got you out of that one, didn't I?" George said to Helma,
raising his hands to his chest as if he were snapping invisible
suspenders.

"I don't know what you're talking about, George," Helma
told him.

With Ruth's phone call in mind, Helma looked up Vincent
Jensen's obituary again and read the list of survivors: a
daughter who lived in Seattle, a son in New Jersey, and his
wife Lynnette. There was no photo of Lynnette, of course,
but Helma studied the grainy online photograph of Vincent
Jensen. It was an amateur photo, cropped to a close-up head
shot, with a hint of sky behind his left ear. Very professorial
in a distractedly rugged way. If he smoked a pipe or cigar,
she doubted he inhaled. A broad forehead and wide mouth
tipped up in a relaxed smile, hair rumpled. She imagined
him standing on a rock near Mount Baker when the picture
was snapped.

She tried to picture Vincent Jensen with the woman in the
yellow coat. A simple photograph could portray lies as well
as people could tell them, but the man and woman didn't
appear suited to one another. The woman in the yellow coat
was more . . . well, tense, as well as . . . Helma struggled to
find the right word, absently tapping the edge of her keyboard. Arranged, even careful. Time and attention had been
spent on her appearance. Perhaps the woman in the yellow
coat wasn't Lynnette after all.

She performed a quick search on "Lynnette Jensen" and
found a newspaper article on a new consignment boutique

for women with limited funds to purchase clothing for job interviews. Lynnette was listed as a volunteer "fashion adviser." A photo of the staff and two well-dressed shoppers accompanied the article. Helma zoomed in on the faces and found the yellow-coated woman: third from the end, as beautifully and coolly coordinated as she'd been in front of city hall, every hair in place, face smooth and controlled, but pleasant. Lynnette Jensen.

Had Lynnette believed that Ruth had painted *her* into a picture depicting an indiscretion with her husband? Was she afraid of being embarrassed by Ruth's portrayal? But Lynnette Jensen had asked which "paintings" had been stolen, plural instead of singular. She had either known there was more than one picture missing or she'd guessed.

Helma continued her search and discovered Lynnette was involved in several worthy local causes: environmental, early childhood, the humane society, and several Bellehaven advisory groups. Her name began appearing after her husband's death in December. Prior to that, "Lynnette Jensen" only came up in connection with University Wives, the Nature Protection Group, and the consignment shop.

She printed off the consignment-store article to show to Ruth, standing beside the reference desk printer until it emerged, and tucked it inside her calendar to take to her cubicle. Not that she was using taxpayers' time for personal research. Ruth was a citizen of Bellehaven, legally a patron of the Bellehaven Public Library despite being currently barred for owing $86.32 in overdue fines.

Before the end of her shift, Helma answered two questions about a former president's secret love affair that had been highlighted on a morning news program, caught a woman surreptitiously razor-blading a recipe from the new edition of *Joy of Cooking*, and suggested a new mother change her baby's diaper in the women's rest room instead of on top of the atlas case. She was just stacking a pile of orders before

Glory was due to relieve her when the reference telephone rang.

"Reference. How may I help you?" she answered.

It was a man. "Do you have any books on Ruth Winthrop?"

Helma was rarely without a professional response to patrons, but this time she asked. "Ruth? Ruth the artist?"

"Yeah," he answered impatiently. "I want to see what her pictures look like. Do you have any books?"

Even though the man couldn't see her, Helma shook her head. "I don't know of any books," she told him, "but there was an article written several years ago. It was illustrated."

"With pictures of her paintings?"

"Yes." She didn't mention they were all from Ruth's "Purple Period," a thankfully brief but intense phase in Ruth's career.

"Several years ago, huh?" he went on. "Nothing about the stuff she's doing now?"

"No. You could contact the gallery that's hosting her next show. They might be able to help you."

"Nah," he said, stretching out the word, and then adding, "I don't want anybody to know I'm the one asking, you know what I mean?"

"Not really," Helma admitted.

He laughed shortly. "Then I guess you're not the sort of person who has much to hide, are you?" and he hung up before Helma could agree that no, she wasn't that sort of person at all.

Glory appeared before Helma had replaced the phone on the cradle. "You still use that old thing?" Glory asked as she adjusted her headset on her head, using exaggerated motions that wiggled her fringes, at the same time glancing around the public area as if searching for someone. The headset disappeared into her red hair, except for the barely noticeable mouthpiece.

"I prefer not to impede my hearing," Helma told her, not for the first time. Ms. Moon had urged the staff to participate in a class sponsored by the city titled "Multitasking for Efficiency." Glory and Harley had attended and then playacted multitasking scenarios at the next staff meeting, using props and demonstrating how to provide information to three patrons at once, while simultaneously smiling, smiling, smiling.

"Isn't Ms. Moon supertalented with her new wheelchair?" Glory asked, shaking her head. "She's even thinking of joining the Paralympics."

"Ms. Moon has a temporary condition," Helma said. "She wouldn't qualify."

"Maybe the mayor will help her, like he did with the wheel—" Glory slapped both hands across her mouth, and when Helma didn't respond, she removed her hands and said naughtily, "Ooh, I shouldn't have said that. Nobody's supposed to know." and when Helma still didn't respond, Glory continued, "About the wheelchair, I mean, that he arranged for it."

"It should be a quiet shift," Helma told Glory as she stepped away from the desk.

"I hope I don't accidentally tell anybody else," Glory called after her.

"Want to go for lunch?" Ruth asked. "The walls are closing in. I need a break."

"Aren't you painting?" Helma asked into the telephone.

"I don't want to discuss it. Talking about creative projects dries up the urge, squeezes out the artistic juices. Poof. Gone."

Which probably meant Ruth hadn't wetted a paintbrush all morning long. "I can meet you at five minutes after twelve at Saul's Deli."

"Do we have to go there? Isn't that where the police hang out and talk about criminals over soup and doughnuts?"

"Have the police talked to you?" Helma asked.

"Not even Carter Houston, though I did call him twice to tell him to bring back my strip of paint. What's he doing with it anyway?"

"Examining it for evidence."

"So I guess they haven't connected me to whoever broken into Roxy Lightheart's house."

"'Whoever,' Ruth?" Helma asked.

"You know what I mean."

"Twelve-oh-five at Saul's," Helma told her

"Wait. Do you have the goods on Vincent's wife?"

"I have some information, which I'll share with you at Saul's."

"So *was* it her you saw at city hall?"

"Twelve-oh-five, Ruth. Goodbye."

"You are such a . . . " Helma heard as she replaced the receiver.

Helma raised her head at the sound of an electric whine and then dead silence. Ms. Moon sat in the doorway of her cubicle, her foot six inches from Helma's chair, an adept feat of maneuvering.

"There's no room for a wheelchair back here," Ms. Moon said.

"It *is* very crowded," Helma agreed warily.

Ms. Moon smiled, her eyes not focusing on Helma, and for a moment Helma felt the urge to turn around to see what she was gazing at, until she recognized one of Ms. Moon's *internal* stares, contemplation of forces in the universe few others could imagine. "There are librarians in wheelchairs," she said in the tone of an announcement.

"I know a few," Helma agreed, thinking of her friend Janet at the University of Washington.

"They might want to work here." Ms. Moon nodded to herself, biting her lip. She punched the button on the wheelchair panel and the chair whined to life and backed up, banging into a stack of boxes across the aisle.

"Whoopsie," she said cheerily, hit another button and rammed forward into the walls of Helma's cubicle. Helma leapt up and steadied the shaking walls, grabbing for the calendar that had come unpinned as Ms. Moon careened down the aisle of cubicles toward her office, calling out, "Oh darn it," and, "Oh my but it's crowded," or, "There's no room for my wheelchair," as she jerked and bumped, mysteriously losing her former finesse at steering and aim.

Ruth, who was as likely to be late as early, already sat at a table beside the front window in Saul's Deli. Not only that, she was halfway into a meal of a double bacon cheeseburger, onion rings *and* French fries, coleslaw, and peanut butter pie, plus a chocolate milk shake.

When Helma sat across from her with a tray holding a glass of ice water and a chicken garden salad, dressing on the side, Ruth said around a mouthful of coleslaw, "Let's see what you've got on Mrs. Vincent."

"Her name is Lynnette Jensen," Helma told her as she removed her plate and silverware from her tray, "and she *is* the woman who asked me about your paintings in front of city hall."

"Oh goodie. That answers that question. Maybe she's the one who broke into my house." Ruth made slashing motions with her fork. "Shredded my paintings and left a threat to my life."

"If she was," Helma said reasonably, "she wouldn't have asked me who the subjects of the stolen paintings were."

Ruth shrugged and used her hands to tear off a portion of her cheeseburger. "Could be a ploy to throw you off track."

"Why would she want to throw *me* off track?" A patch of skin had been left on Helma's chicken and she carefully removed it with her knife and fork and set it on the rim of her plate.

"Maybe she hired somebody to steal the paintings and she was just checking on their efficiency. Or maybe she killed Vincent in a belated fit of jealousy over *moi* and is afraid that I implicated her in my paintings." She shook her head. "Weak connections, I know, but still . . ." She wiped her hand on her sleeve and held it out. "Let me see what you have."

Helma removed the *Bellehaven Daily News* article from her calendar and gave it to Ruth, who leaned back in her chair and read it, squinting over the photo.

"That's her, all right. 'Fashion adviser,' eh? It fits. If you like the dragon-queen look." Ruth handed the article back. "Good cause, though, that consignment shop. She gets a 'by' for that."

"Do you think she knew both men?" Helma asked.

"Can't see her hanging out with a chain-saw artist."

"She had other interests, too," Helma said, naming the charities listed in the articles. "Didn't you say that Meriwether Scott was involved in environmental issues? Maybe she met him through one of her organizations."

"Could be, but like I said, I just can't see it. If you'd met Meriwether, you'd know." She squinted at Helma. "*Did* you ever meet him?"

Helma shook her head. "A man called the library this morning, asking for information about you and your paintings."

"Did you tell him about the purple article?"

"He wanted something more recent. I suggested he talk to the gallery."

"Good. Publicity."

"I don't think that's what it was, Ruth. He sounded . . . I can't explain it, but I doubt he wanted to *buy* one of your paintings."

"Then he's afraid of what I might have painted. His life in art, hung for all to see."

Unusual for her, but Helma asked before she thought, "Did you paint impressions of your life with Paul?"

It was as if Ruth had been punched. First she went completely still. Then she pushed her food away and swallowed what was in her mouth. Swallowed so hard that Helma was afraid the food wouldn't stay swallowed. Slowly, she shook her head. "No," she whispered, looking down at her hands.

"I'm sorry," Helma told her. "I shouldn't have said that."

"Nah, it's okay. I just wasn't prepared to hear his hallowed name, that's all. A little pathos becomes me, don't you think?" she asked in a brittle voice, turning her head to the side as if she were posing for a photograph. "Or maybe it's bathos, after the amount of time he and I spent thrashing around. Kinda like you and our beloved chief of police, sitting forever on the cusp of indecision."

"Wayne and I are good friends. Indecision has nothing to do with our friendship."

"Oh. Sorry. I guess I should have used the word 'cowardice.'"

Helma was grateful for the diversion of the squeal of brakes outside and looked through the window to see a small, blue van double-park in front of Saul's. The driver's door flew open.

"Uh-oh," Ruth said, half rising. "Do I run for the back door or surrender?"

A woman with long blond hair so curly and thick it undulated ran toward Saul's front door. One finger pointed at Ruth, her mouth moving soundlessly but intensely.

"Who is it?" Helma asked.

"Roxy Lightheart in all her glory. Prepare yourself to witness an unpleasant encounter." Ruth settled back in her chair and waited as Roxy lunged for the door handle, missed, and then successfully jerked it open, nearly colliding with a man leaving. He raised his hands as if she had a gun. She was a small woman of blockish size, her round face skewed to rage.

"You," she said, finger jabbing toward Ruth. "It was you."

"Hi, Roxy," Ruth said calmly. "How goes the art effort?"

Roxy leaned close to Ruth's face, her hair so wide it nearly touched Ruth. Helma covered her salad with her napkin. "You should know. You were in my studio last night, sneaking around. What were you looking for? I heard a couple of your paintings were stolen. You didn't think *I* took them, did you?"

"I don't know what you're talking about," Ruth said.

"I wouldn't go to those lengths for one of your second-rate paintings, especially paintings about your slutty love life."

"How do you know they're slutty?" Ruth asked. "Could you have seen them?" She picked up a cold French fry and bit it in half.

"Hah," Roxy snorted. She stepped back, the heat of her anger dissipating. "You've been bragging for months about Ruth Revealed. Even eviscerating the dead."

"That's an interesting image but a biological impossibility," Ruth told her, fingering another French fry.

Helma was curious. "Are you referring to Meriwether Scott and Vincent Jensen?"

"Are there more dead ones?" Roxy asked. She looked at Helma. "Doesn't it make you curious about what she had to do with their deaths?"

"Now *that's* absurd, Roxy," Ruth said. "I may leave 'em breathless, but I don't kill them."

"Tell it to the police."

"No thanks."

Roxy smiled. She rubbed her hands together like a silent film villain. "See what I have?" she asked in a deadly calm voice. And she pulled Ruth's red gloves from her pocket and held them out, one in each hand so the threads of the embroidered dragons blazed in the light.

"New gloves?" Ruth asked, glancing at the gloves, then away.

"Very unfunny, I found these in my studio. The police haven't seen them. Yet. Unless we make a small agreement, I'll turn them over to them. Tomorrow."

"How do you know they're mine?" Ruth asked.

"Did I say they were?" Roxy asked sweetly, holding the gloves in one hand and slapping them against the other. "I just said I'd turn them over to the police tomorrow and let them figure out who they belong to."

"What kind of an agreement?" Ruth asked. She sounded only mildly curious, but Helma saw the muscle jump in her throat.

"You convinced Cheri at the gallery to give you *my* show dates because you were jealous about Meriwether." She paused, then leaned forward and demanded, "Give me back my show."

"I can't—" Ruth began.

But Roxy only waved the red gloves in front of Ruth and said, "Tomorrow."

Slapping the gloves against her hand once more, she turned and left Saul's Deli in measured, confident steps.

Chapter 14

A Trip to the Woods

"She's bluffing," Ruth said, watching Roxy Lightheart slam the door of her van and speed away.

"Why did she say you were jealous about Meriwether?" Helma asked.

Ruth bent over the remains of her double bacon cheeseburger and lifted the bun to remove a slice of bacon. "Who knows? She's obviously in her usual agitated addled state of mind," and she popped the bacon in her mouth, chewing with great concentration.

"Ruth."

Ruth tapped her lips as if she were suddenly the sort of person who didn't talk with her mouth full.

"Did Meriwether Scott drop you for Roxy? Is she the woman you said made concrete earrings?"

"That was an exaggeration, the concrete part."

Helma waited and Ruth scrunched her face and said, "Okay, okay. So maybe Meriwether showed a *little* interest in Roxy. That doesn't mean he dumped me for her."

"It does put a different light on your show. Was Roxy seeing Meriwether when he died?"

She shrugged. "I might have miscalculated his interest a teensy. Or maybe he didn't want to change all those initials he carved in the trees. Ruth: Roxy. R:R. Get it? But I assure you, whatever little bit of attraction he felt for her, *she* was hot after him."

"And you were responsible for Roxy's show being canceled?"

"Helma Zukas. I will *not* admit to anything so low. I simply let Cheri know I was working up a new show and she set the date. She said she'd schedule my show in place of a weak one she'd been considering. I never said one word about Roxy. Besides, she's the one trying to stir up trouble, waltzing in here like a soap-opera queen waving those gloves."

"Those were definitely your gloves, Ruth," Helma pointed out.

"That doesn't mean I was in her house—theoretically, I mean. She shouldn't have touched them. Who's to say she didn't pick them up on the sidewalk?" Ruth vigorously shook her head. "Nope. She shot herself in the foot by not calling the cops so they could see them *in situ*. I'm not giving my show to her, not after all the publicity I've done. I've already convinced *Art Trends* to attend the opening."

"From San Francisco?" Helma asked.

"You got it. I told them it was a cutting-edge form of memoir, the painted life. Nobody reads anymore, anyway."

"Our circulation statistics don't support that," Helma told her.

"Weren't you moaning only a few short months ago that people weren't checking out as many books?"

"We're holding steady," Helma said, which was true. After an alarming dip in circulation for the first time in the Bellehaven Public Library's history, the trend had leveled off. "But about Roxy—"

"Not gonna do it. Period."

For some time, Helma had been aware of a small man sitting two tables away watching them, or more precisely, watching Ruth. Since men watching Ruth was a common occurrence, she'd at first ignored him. Ruth's height, her clothes and voice, the *bigness* of her—not in size as much as the amount of space she seemed to fill—drew glances wherever she went.

But his gaze was so intent, Helma had grown uncomfortable. He appeared to be in his late twenties, a slender man in glasses and wearing jeans and a sweatshirt.

"Don't look now, Ruth," she finally said, "but the man sitting to your left two tables over is watching you."

Ruth immediately stood and looked to the left. She briefly frowned, then nodded. "Jet," she called out to the man. "Come sit with us."

He didn't appear startled to be recognized, or embarrassed to have been caught staring, but stood and walked to their table. Not very good posture, Helma noted, although he did push in his chair before leaving his table. He carried a glass of cola with him.

With one foot, Ruth nudged out the chair between her and Helma and motioned for him to sit. He dropped into the chair and grinned. "Hey," he said to Ruth.

"What are you doing here?' she asked him, and then remembering Helma, added, "Oh, this is my friend Helma Zukas. Helma, this is Jet. He was Meriwether Scott's apprentice."

Helma did take special note of him then. He had a thick lower lip, as if in a perpetual pout. His left eye had a bit of "wander" to it, as her mother would say, casting off to the side.

"Hey," he said to her, just as he had to Ruth.

"Hello, Jet."

He turned back to Ruth. "I'm just in town, that's all. There are a few of my tools I didn't pick up after . . . last winter. Doing it now. Or tried to."

"You couldn't get them?" Ruth asked.

Jet shrugged and his left eye wandered even further. "I should have come sooner. Somebody ripped them off. The whole shop was cleaned out. House, too." He shrugged again. "No big surprise when his place is so far out."

Ruth looked at him curiously. "Why didn't you get them when Meriwether died?"

"I was in Peru and then I kept putting it off. My own fault, the vultures saw their chance and took it."

"Who owns his place now?"

Jet shook his head. "Don't know. His mother, maybe. Gorgeous piece of property, though. Nice trees. And that creek with the little falls. He should've taken the offer he had for it. He could have used the money."

"Someone offered to buy his land?" Helma asked.

"Probably more than one someone." Jet drained his cola and shook the glass so his ice rattled. "But this was a developer who showed up a couple of times while I was working with Meriwether. Wanted to build a resort out there. Exclusive."

"A local developer?" Helma asked.

"Yeah, but don't ask me who. I never heard his name."

"What'd he look like?" Ruth asked.

Jet shrugged. "Ordinary. Middle-aged. I didn't pay much attention. Why?"

"Just curious," Ruth told him.

"All I remember is after the guy left, Meriwether grumbled about him trading on Frank Lloyd Wright's reputation."

"*The* Frank Lloyd Wright?" Ruth asked.

"Musta been. I never heard of any other Frank Lloyd Wright." He rocked back on his chair, lifting the front legs off the floor, and Helma held her hands together to keep from pushing his chair flat on the floor. He fidgeted.

"So, why didn't you just come over and say hi?" Ruth asked, eyeing him suspiciously. "Why sit there and stare at me across the room? And don't tell me it was my eye-riveting beauty."

"You eat a lot."

"That's the reason?"

"No, just an observation. I remember when you came out to Meriwether's."

"So?"

"So nothing." Jet shook his head and stood. "It's a coincidence to run into you on my way back from Meriwether's, that's all. It was tough to see his place like that: already moldering into the ground. A house goes to hell fast when nobody's living in it. I'd guess it's been broken into more than once. I'm living in Sweet Harbor now."

"What's your last name?" Ruth asked him. "I don't think I ever knew it."

"Black. Don't laugh. Jet's a nickname. I'm in the book under James P. Or you can stop by my studio on Front Street. It's called Basic Black."

"Are you doing chain-saw art?"

"Mainly carving stuff that'll sell to tourists. Meriwether was a damn good teacher. I was lucky."

He saluted them with two fingers and left Saul's Deli. They watched through the window as he walked down the sidewalk toward a blue Toyota with a dented front fender. He didn't actually slouch, Helma noted; he walked like a man with a bad back.

Ruth squeezed a cold onion ring into a flat shape and shoved the whole thing into her mouth. "Interesting little lunch. First, vile threats from the jealous Miss Roxy. And then Mr. Jet Black. Want to go out to Meriwether's with me after work?"

"What would be the reason?" Helma asked.

Ruth closed one eye, thinking. "Research," she said finally. "Police orders. Remember how Carter Houston asked me to recreate my missing paintings? I think if I hung out at Meriwether's place for a few minutes and soaked up the atmosphere . . ." She licked her lips. ". . . do a little remembering, and I could do a better painting. I'd be inspired. Get it? How late are you working tonight?"

"Five o'clock."

"Perfect. It'll take us a half hour to get there, and it's light until eight-thirty. I'll pack a picnic and pick you up at your apartment at 5:45. What do you say?"

Once Ruth had an idea, she followed it with single-minded intensity no matter how ill-prepared—or ill-conceived. Helma knew that Ruth would go to Meriwether Scott's property whether she accompanied her or not. And she *was* curious about this entanglement of Ruth, Meriwether, Roxy, and death.

"I'll clean my car first," Ruth cajoled. "I'll even fill the gas tank."

"If I accompany you," Helma warned her, "no breaking and entering."

"Nothing illegal," Ruth said, her smile wide. "Absolutely not."

The remainder of Helma's afternoon in the library was quiet. Ms. Moon whirred around the public area, more in evidence than Helma had ever witnessed, accepting wishes for a quick recovery, buzzing past patrons she recognized, but never once pausing to answer a library question. Helma heard her once tell a patron, "Oh, you're so lucky that one of our expert librarians is on duty. She can't wait to help you."

Protruding from the back of a pocket on her wheelchair were two rolls of rubber-banded blueprints that Helma recognized: the aborted plans for the new library, which Ms. Moon periodically altered to suit her changing tastes, employing a ruler and eraser. By now, the staff suspected, the plans had been altered beyond usefulness.

Glory circuited the library several times an hour, flitting from the magazines to the circulation desk to the stacks, fringes swaying, a bright smile flashing and fading each time she paused to peer down an aisle. Helma was positive she heard Glory humming "Happy Trails to You" during one of her passes.

Helma packed her own meal, knowing Ruth's idea of a "picnic" might be two cans of smoked oysters and a package of Nutter Butters, and wasn't disappointed when she climbed into the blue VW Beetle, a gift long ago from Paul, and Ruth said, "Great, I thought you'd bring food so I stopped at the store and picked up dessert and a little liquid."

Helma rested her feet lightly on the floor of the VW. Mysterious things rustled down there. "Did you bring a map?"

"I know the way, Helma. We're not exactly heading into the wilderness. Despite you being dressed for it."

Helma had chosen hiking shoes from the box on the top shelf of her closet, and brought an extra sweater with a pair of cotton gloves in the pocket. Her pants were sewn from a tightly woven fabric, less likely to snag on bushes. Ruth wore pants a curious color of orange and a van Gogh shirt. Her sandals were open-toed.

In her pants pocket, Helma also carried a multitooled jackknife-sized gadget that had been a Christmas gift from her brother, Bruce. A compass was set into one of the handles.

Ruth drove out of town to the east, toward the foothills that climbed to the snowy peaks of Mount Baker and the twin mountains referred to as "The Sisters." Early-evening sunshine slanted through a line of clouds to the west, highlighting the green of spring. Interstice, Helma thought, mentally savoring the word.

"Green," Ruth said, turning her head from side to side. "Feast your eyes on all this green. Every shade of the rainbow is in this green." Her voice caught and Helma glanced over to see Ruth flick her hand across her damp eyes. "Sorry. A broken heart sets me up for getting all emotional. Next I'll be bawling over ads for sleeping pills."

"It takes time to recover from rejection," Helma said. She'd once read a book titled *When Love Fails* so she could better understand library patrons who requested information on the subject. Curiously, one of the chapters had been of assistance in her own life during an unsettling incident.

"Well, thank you for that advice, Dr. Zukas. Just my luck I had to hook up with one of those unusual men who means what he says. There are no options in this little drama. No negotiations. Take no prisoners. Bye-bye." Ruth shifted on her seat and looked at Helma. "I know. I have to learn to accept that this one is my own fault. It ain't easy."

Helma decided not to agree, at least not out loud.

They turned off the main road to the mountains and wove through rolling pastures and fewer homes that gave way to forests of fir and cedar where the shadows deepened to gloom. A sign beside a driveway that disappeared into the trees advertised, FOR SALE: ORGANIC, NATURALLY FELLED FIREWOOD. Here the blackberry and salal underbrush hadn't greened up yet and the early-spring growth was more yellow than green, deeply chartreuse.

"It's just up here," Ruth said. "Look for a driveway with a carved fish on a pole."

"What species of fish?" Helma asked.

"Does it matter? How many carved fish on poles do you think there are in the woods?" Ruth slowed her car, peering past Helma at the roadside. They drove up the road a half mile, then back, passing two overgrown two-tracks into the dark forest. But no carved fish on a pole.

"The fish could be gone," Helma pointed out on their third unsuccessful pass along the stretch of road. "It might have been removed by his heirs, or even stolen when the house was allegedly broken into."

"I know it's here."

Helma was not unprepared. From her pocket she pulled a detailed map of the surrounding area that she'd photocopied at the library, along with a piece of notepaper bearing the address of Meriwether Scott. "The address is 4943 Silver Salmon Road."

"Where'd you get that?"

"From the phone book. Are we on Silver Salmon Road?"

"How should I know?"

"Stop the car, Ruth. Right here, beside this creek."

Ruth stopped in the center of the lane next to a bridge across a rushing creek. Helma opened her window to hear its rush and babble. She shivered at the cooler breeze churned by melted snow draining from the mountains. The fragrance of fresh water and new growth filled the air. Beside the creek a rusted sign shot with bullet holes was unreadable except for the first M of the word above "Creek."

"I believe this is Maple Creek," she told Ruth as she studied her map. "And if this is Maple Creek, then we're on Patten Road, not Silver Salmon Road."

"And your point is?"

"We need to drive to the next road, a half mile to the east."

"Okay, okay, whatever you say.," And Ruth spun her VW in an inefficient U-turn that spattered gravel up from the shoulder of the road.

A half mile down Silver Salmon Road, Ruth braked abruptly. "Aha. Here it is, just like I said."

The wooden salmon on the post sat crookedly beside the driveway, the numbers 4943 etched into its side and filled with moss. The wood had long since turned an uneven gray that shone as if it were wet.

"Here we go," Ruth said, and pulled in.

"Slow down," Helma warned her, pointing to a pothole ahead of them filled with water.

The driveway twisted to the left and they entered a clearing that was invisible from the road. Ruth was forced to stop behind a downed poplar tree that blocked the rough path to the front door of a house the same color as the forest. "It doesn't take long for Mom Nature to reclaim her stuff, does it?"

Before them stood a house of many styles: hand hewn, planked, with gables and bay windows and skylights, yet curiously, it created a whole that would have been pleasing except for its broken windows and mildew-stained walls, or the fresh sheet of plywood nailed over the front door. Had Jet Black done that? Helma wondered.

"I want to look around," Ruth said, opening her door. "And don't worry, I'm not going to do anything illegal, only fire up the creative juices."

Just being there was surely illegal, but Helma got out, too, stepping into the silence of the forest. She heard the distant drone of an airplane and the faint buzz of a chain saw. No traffic or voices, not even a bird call.

Ruth rubbed her arms and looked into the dark woods. "I hope Meriwether didn't want to waft back in as a ghost to get whoever did him in."

If she *did* believe in ghosts, Helma thought, this dreary place with its tall dense trees and deep shadows would be a hospitable location.

"Yeah, yeah, yeah," Ruth said absently. She pointed upward to a gabled window where a jagged shard of glass still clung to the upper sash. "That's the bedroom. Nice view of Summer Mountain from up there. And that's his shop."

A separate building the size of a two-car garage stood across the driveway from the house. Large double doors were closed and a separate normal-sized door was set in the wall that faced the house.

Ruth headed toward the shop, leading Helma around a grayed pile of wood chips and sawdust, gesturing as she went. "He had some nice roses right here, and a kinetic sculpture in the yard, with lots of wood sculptures stuck all over the place. It was a nice place, really." She turned the knob of the single door and it easily opened. The sound of scurrying came from deep inside, and Ruth said, "Squirrels," in an uncertain voice.

Helma followed her inside. There were no windows, and when Helma flicked the light switch, nothing happened. They could only see by the daylight shining in through the open door behind them.

"Cleaned out," Ruth muttered, turning in the dim light. "Not much left but his workbenches."

A dusty baseball cap hung on a nail inside the door, and last year's calendar was tacked up beside it: December, the month Meriwether died. Helma glanced at the numbered squares and in the weak light was able to read a few faded numbers: temperatures and rainfall, plus an appointment for a teeth cleaning with Dr. Frier, her own dentist, which raised her estimation of Meriwether Scott.

"Is seeing this helpful in reconstructing your painting?" she asked Ruth, peering at the unknown shapes in the gloomy interior. She was not comfortable here. More than the fact that they were trespassing. There was the silence, the unknown terrain, the pressing trees.

Ruth shrugged as she walked around inside the shop, then picked up a slab of wood that looked like the rough beginnings of a bird. "Not really. Whatever I painted now wouldn't be as colorful as the original, that's for sure. I'd have to use shades of mildew and dereliction. Come on, let's go look at the spot where he died. That oughta cheer me right up."

"How do you know where he died?"

"He showed me the burl he planned to cut. It's in a maple tree, but he was still fussing over how to get it down when we ended our little liaison. And just a couple of months later . . ." She shrugged. "I'm sure that's where he fell."

"He was up in a tree in December?"

"Yeah. He said because it was a deciduous tree he wouldn't harvest the burl until the leaves fell and it was easier to see what he was doing. Lotta good *that* did him."

Along a faint fern-lined trail behind the shop, they came upon two benches made of thick slabs of weathered wood. Each end of one bench perched on the back of a carved bear. The other bench was held up by a wooden salmon. They had been built in place, one of the bears and one of the salmon carved from the stumps of felled trees. The two benches faced each other at an angle.

"Damn. Why didn't I wear different shoes?" Ruth complained, balancing against one of the carved bears to pull a stick caught in a sandal strap.

Helma wondered the same thing. The path skirted a clearing and wound past several large stumps and smaller trees. Meriwether's raw materials for his carvings, she surmised. Moss grew thick and rich green, covering shaded rocks like pelts.

A glimpse of white beside a stump caught her attention. A single trillium. She paused to study the elusive white flower, so purely white it gleamed. She looked but didn't spot another trillium anywhere.

"Right over here," Ruth said, stopping and pointing up into a large, partially dead tree. Since the leaves hadn't fully emerged, it was easy to make out the table-sized burl that grew at least twenty-five feet up in the tree like a gigantic wart. "He called the wood quilted maple. I remember that because he showed me a piece of it. It was really beautiful. All silvery and checked. I don't know why he didn't just cut down the tree instead of climbing it."

Ruth and Helma stood, both of them silently looking up into the tree where a slash cut into the burl was still visible, as far as Meriwether climbed before he fell or—

"You ladies okay?"

Ruth screamed and Helma spun around to face two men who were calmly watching them.

Chapter 15

Double Meetings

The two strangers were dressed like most men in the Northwest who entered the forest in springtime: in jeans, hiking boots, and button-up shirts layered over colored T-shirts. The man who'd spoken was in his late forties, clean shaven, broad shouldered, longish hair turning gray and tied back in a ponytail. A frown rippled up his forehead all the way to his receding hairline.

The other man was slightly shorter. Thinner and wirier, watchful. His eyes moved between Ruth and Helma and then up into the tree toward the scarred burl.

Ruth was the first to speak. "Of course we're okay. Nice men don't sneak up on people like that. What are *you* doing here?"

He smiled at Ruth. "Just looking at the land."

"*You're* the developer?" Ruth asked. "The guy who came to talk to Meriwether?"

"Developer?" the wirier man asked. His left eyebrow was jagged, as if a scar marred the skin in the brow's very center.

Ruth opened her mouth; she was about to divulge too much to strangers. Helma chose the unusual tactic of interrupting.

"Rumor is," she said, and Ruth, who knew Helma didn't repeat rumors, closed her mouth with an audible click of her teeth.

"Rumor is," Helma continued, "that this property is of interest to several people, perhaps even the Parks Department and a resort developer."

"It'd make a great casino site," Ruth added, getting into the spirit.

"I guess," the man with the ponytail said. "It's not that far out of town, not like people think. Feels like it, though, doesn't it?"

"Then you're from Bellehaven?" Ruth asked.

He held out his hand, first to Ruth, then Helma. "I live south of town. I'm Stu."

"Richard," the thinner man said, offering his hand, too.

Both Helma and Ruth shook their hands but neither woman gave them her name. "We knew the previous owner," Ruth said, being unusually discreet.

"That right?" Stu asked without much interest, and Helma realized she had jumped to an assumption.

"You're interested in purchasing the land?" she asked.

"Nah," he said. "We're just geocachers."

"Geo-whats?" Ruth asked.

Stu reached into his pocket and pulled out a hand-held GPS, a Global Positioning System, the size of a cell phone.

"They search for caches using geographic coordinates posted on the Internet," Helma explained. "When they find a cache, they take an item and leave an item. Someone hid a cache in the 337s once."

At their blank looks, she explained "It's 337.73, to be exact. International economic theory. A less used section of the library stacks."

For a brief time the librarians had rejoiced in the sudden interest of Bellehavenites in world economy. Until Helma grew suspicions and discovered a nest of key chains, cards, and trinkets in the shelf space behind the books. "Aren't geo-caches usually hidden in public places?" she asked. "Parks and public land?"

"Mostly," Rich said. "Sometimes in abandoned places, too." He nodded in the direction of Meriwether's crumbling home.

Helma cast one last look at the burl high in the tree and began slowly but purposefully walking back toward the house and shop. The others followed her, as she knew they would, compelled by human instinct.

Ruth chattered about the various colors of green surrounding them. "Now, I'd call the leaves on that bush verdigris," she was saying.

"Where did you leave your car?" Helma asked the men as they reached Meriwether's driveway. Only Ruth's VW sat in front of the house on the rough driveway.

Stu laughed shortly. "On the next road over. We tramped through the woods when we could have just driven in." He held up his GPS again. "These things will get you anywhere. Better than a compass any day. But mine has coordinates only; it doesn't tell you the details, like roads, rivers, and mountains."

Helma wasn't afraid of these men, not at all, but they were strangers and this land *was* a very long way into the country. The most judicious action was to leave their company. She casually walked to Ruth's car and opened the passenger door, purposely not looking at Ruth in case Ruth tried to signal her to stay.

But Ruth opened the driver's door and waved just as casually to the two men. "Well, good luck."

The men watched Ruth back up and leave. Helma looked in her side mirror as they left the clearing, and saw them turn and head toward the shop.

"Aren't they a little old to be playing games?" Ruth said. "What's it called again?"

"Geocaching," Helma told her. "And no, a surprising number of the geocachers who came to the library were middle-aged." And older, she recalled. "Men *and* women."

"Yeah, I guess your average ten-year-old needs a healthy allowance to buy one of those little gadgets. Do you think those two guys, Stu and Richard, couldn't *really* find their way to Meriwether's driveway?"

"We couldn't," Helma said, to be fair. "Not at first."

"Yeah, but we didn't sneak around and jump out at people."

"They didn't actually jump out at us, Ruth, but you're right, it's unwise to remain in a remote area with strangers." There had been a sense of words left unsaid about the two men, and in that gloomy, shadowy place, her discomfort had been magnified.

Spring grew more evident the closer they drove to Belle-haven. Rhododendrons bloomed, red-winged blackbird song was audible even through the closed car windows. The air felt gentler, less weighted, and the darkness of Meriwether's abandoned home receded. As did the encounter with the two men. Streetlights began blinking on, the mercury bulbs building to brightness, as Ruth pulled into the Bayside Arms.

The For Sale sign swayed gently back and forth in a breeze off the bay.

"For Sale?" Ruth cried. "Your apartment building? When did that happen?"

"The sign went up yesterday. Walter said the owner's retiring to Mexico."

"The land's worth more than the building. Just think what they could build in its place: a posh hotel, or luxury condos nobody local could afford. What will you do if you have to move?"

"Then I will. But the building was just listed. Commercial sales can take months and any changes could take years if a new owner even wanted to alter the current situation."

"Geesh, you've been here forever. Want me to keep an ear out for a new apartment for you?"

"Not yet, but thank you," Helma said, declining to imagine what type of apartment Ruth would think suited her.

"Well, so much for a picnic," Ruth said glumly. "Seeing Meriwether's place morphing into mold was not an art *or* appetite stimulator." She leaned over her steering wheel and squinted up at the top floor of the Bayside Arms. "Uh-oh. Did you forget a date with your mother and Aunt Em?"

"No. I would have remembered that. Why?"

"Because they're standing outside your apartment door."

Helma climbed out of the car and peered upward. Aunt Em and her mother stood in the glow of the photosensitive light over her door, looking as if they'd just knocked and were waiting to be admitted.

"I'm coming, too," Ruth said, and turned off her engine.

"Your car's parked in the middle of the drive," Helma pointed out.

Ruth twirled the car keys around her finger and dropped them in the pocket of her jacket. "Any vehicle that's too big to get around my minuscule vehicle is too big to drive in here."

"Yoo hoo, Wilhelmina," Helma's mother called, cupping her hands around her mouth like a yodeler. "Up here."

Helma waved to her mother and climbed the stairs, carrying their aborted picnic and her extra coat.

"Hello, beautiful ladies," Ruth shouted from behind Helma.

"Hello, Ruth," Lillian said in a voice that carried less enthusiasm.

"Ah, *Ruta*," Aunt Em said, naming Ruth in Lithuanian. Stairs were beyond Aunt Em now. She must have taken the elevator. In the more than twenty years that Helma had lived in the Bayside Arms, she'd never ridden the elevator. Whenever possible, she avoided elevators, disliking the sensation of being trapped in a moving, windowless box.

Helma's mother carried a cardboard carton and Aunt Em clutched a paper bag, a black patent leather purse in her other hand.

"Did I forget a dinner appointment?" Helma asked.

"You know Em," Lillian said, shaking her head. "She got a bee in her bonnet to make *Grybai kiaušiniuose,* so of course she made enough for a starving crowd."

What's that?" Ruth asked. "Do I like them? Is it like *kugelis*?"

Grybai kiaušiniuose was Helma's least favorite of Aunt Em's Lithuanian dishes. "Perhaps your friends at the Silver Gables would enjoy a taste," she suggested.

"It was your mother's idea to bring them to you," Aunt Em said.

"They would've just gone to waste," Lillian sniffed.

Ruth rubbed her hands together. "Okay. Let's go in and set the table. I'm starved."

Aunt Em had even brought her own apron, which Helma's mother had to tie for her. "Shoo, shoo," her aunt said as Lillian straightened the bow behind her. "I have to coordinate on what I'm doing."

"Concentrate," Lillian corrected, and Aunt Em gave a tiny upward shake of her head, glancing toward the ceiling, an expression of irritation Helma had seen her father—Aunt Em's brother—make hundreds of times.

Lillian, Ruth, and Helma sat in Helma's living room while Aunt Em banged and fussed in the kitchen.

"We'll be lucky if she doesn't poison us, the way she's been acting lately," Lillian whispered, turning her finger beside her ear.

"She's sharper than I am," Ruth said, but softly so Aunt

Em couldn't hear, because actually, Helma knew, it was no longer true.

"And what have you girls been up to?" Lillian asked in a louder voice.

"Oh, we just went for a ride," Ruth told her.

"In the woods?" Lillian asked. "You have a sprig of cedar caught in your sandal, Ruth."

"Those cedars cling to you like magnets." Ruth tugged the cedar sprig from her sandal strap and put it in her pocket. "How's life in the fast lane?"

"Were there men involved?" Lillian went on as if she hadn't heard Ruth's question.

"Mother, we went for a ride. We'd planned a picnic but it was too chilly."

Lillian nodded absently and stood, then went to the sliding glass doors onto Helma's balcony and looked out. "I think I'll take a breather," she said, and leaned down to remove the safety stick that blocked Helma's sliding door.

Ruth and Helma watched in amazement as Lillian stepped onto the balcony in the near darkness. Helma's mother was not a woman to spend undue time in the elements. "What *is* she doing?" Ruth whispered.

Her mother walked around the small balcony, pacing really, from one end to the other and then back and forth, pausing at the side of the balcony closest to TNT's balcony. "I don't know," Helma told Ruth.

"I know what she's doing," Aunt Em said huffily from the kitchen, surprising Helma that she could hear their whispers and wondering just how acute her aunt's professed hearing loss actually was.

"You do?" Ruth asked. "What?"

Aunt Em shook her head and went back to her construction of the *Grybai kiaušiniuose,* clattering dishes and muttering. Helma thought she heard the word *mergše,* which was a Lithuanian form of the word for hussy.

Ruth sniffed the air. "It smells good in there," she called to Aunt Em. The rich smell of onions frying in real butter wafted from the kitchen. "Can I help you?"

"No, no. This is all mine," Aunt Em told her.

Finally, Lillian returned, rubbing her arms. She sat in the rocking chair and rocked back and forth several times before asking Helma, "Your apartment building is for sale?"

Yes," Helma told her.

"Where will you move, dear?"

"It's too soon to think of that."

"If you had a family, or if you'd thought to get married . . ." She sighed and shook her head as if there were no point in discussing the subject. "I've just been swamped organizing the spring craft show next week. We need a few more art pieces and then we'll be finished." She looked at Ruth, realizing what she'd just said and quickly added, "I mean art work from *residents* of the Silver Gables, naturally. All the crafts are from residents. There aren't any from outsiders, I mean people who don't live in the Silver Gables."

"Oh darn," Ruth said.

"All ready now," Aunt Em said from the kitchen, and tapped a spoon against a glass. "Come to my table."

Lillian held a hand to the side of her mouth and whispered to Ruth and Helma, "Be nice, now."

Aunt Em had set four places at the table, and at each one sat a *Grybai kiaušiniuos.*

"It's an . . . a . . ." Ruth stood before the table, frowning. "A giant mushroom?"

On each of the plates sat an upright boiled egg on a patch of sour cream. The egg had been sculpted and shaped, with the wide bottom sliced off and replaced on top of the up-turned egg, covered with a layer of sour cream and sprinkled with bits of herb and onion to replicate a mushroom cap.

Aunt Em beamed and made scooping motions with her hands. "Like *Mama* made. I scoop out the *tryn* . . . yolk, and mix it up with the fried onion. You sit and eat now." And she waited for each of them to take a chair before she sat down. "Eat, eat. Enjoy."

Helma's mother picked up her fork and cast warning glances at Helma and Ruth.

Helma never willingly ate slippery food. The egg white was cold and wobbly, the filling warm, the sour cream shiny and thick.

But even more, she would never willingly hurt Aunt Em.

So, keeping her mind firmly on recalling the names of the past four presidents of the American Library Association, she lifted her fork and delicately decapitated the *Grybai kiaušiniuose*, cutting it into four pieces.

Beside her Ruth picked up the egg with her fingers and bit off its top, pausing to add more salt to the already salty filling.

"Is it good?" Aunt Em asked, still not having touched her own.

"As good as you always make them, Aunt Em. Thank you."

"It's great," Ruth said. "Are there any extra?"

"Two for each," Aunt Em said, rising from her chair.

"Do you know Lynnette Jensen?" Ruth suddenly asked, still chewing, apropos of nothing.

"The professor's widow," Aunt Em answered, sitting down again. "She might move to the Silver Gables."

"She's too young," Lillian said.

Aunt Em shook her head, a sage look on her face. "No she isn't. She was older than her dead husband. I heard Thalia on second floor talking about her. She has beauty secrets."

"No," Lillian said, her eyes gleaming. "She had surgery?"

"No, no. Creams. She has secret creams."

"Her husband was a science professor. I'll bet he made them."

Aunt Em shrugged. "Women don't ask *husbands* to make creams for them, women use creams *for* their husbands. It's the . . ." She struggled for the word, not seeing Lillian tuck the remains of her *Grybai kiaušiniuose* in her napkin. ". . . illusion they're looking for."

"I'm all for illusion," Ruth said.

Lillian looked at Ruth, opened her mouth and then closed it.

"Illusion," Aunt Em mused, tapping her fork against her plate. "Like secrets." She slowly shook her head back and forth. "Everybody who knows my secrets is dead."

"How were you acquainted with Lynnette Jensen?" Helma asked her mother.

"Yoga class at the new gym downtown. She came for a couple of months."

"And she volunteered at our Christmas bash," Aunt Em added.

Helma's mother nodded. "I saw her handing out programs at the Parks Benefit concert. She volunteers at the museum, too, and the Marine Center. Busy, she's new-widow busy, so she doesn't have to think."

"Or happy to finally be alone," Aunt Em said, her eyes twinkling. "So she's catching up on what she missed."

"Maybe she's planning on reeling in a new man," Ruth suggested.

"Then she should change her perfume," Lillian said, waving her hand in front of her face as if she'd sniffed a rude odor. "I don't see how *that* smell would attract *any* man."

Helma didn't recall anything but a light floral scent in Lynnette Jensen's presence, but Ruth, whose preferred musky fragrance made Helma's nose twitch, shrugged. "To each her own. I knew somebody who said that if a chemist could develop a perfume that had a new-car smell, they'd make a million dollars."

"I thought your yoga class was at the Silver Gables," Helma told her mother.

"It was. But this one's cheaper. And there are younger people."

Again Aunt Em harrumphed.

Helma helped Aunt Em into her coat. Her aunt's arms had lost their flexibility so it involved complicated maneuvering. Aunt Em whispered as Helma guided her hand into her sleeve, "Ruth is lemoncholy, yes?"

She meant melancholy but Helma didn't correct her. She nodded. "Yes, she is."

"Love," Aunt Em said, shaking her head sadly. "Always love. It breaks our hearts."

Chapter 16

The Developing Mind

On her break, Helma telephoned local developers, beginning with Aggemeyer Homes in the Bellehaven yellow pages. Only six developers were listed.

"I'm looking for a developer who understands the Frank Lloyd Wright concept of design," she said each time, remembering Jet Black relating how Meriwether had referred to a developer interested in his land as "trading on Frank Lloyd Wright's reputation."

"Frank Lloyd Wright?" the woman who answered the phone at Forrest and Gardener said. "He is *so* passé. Nobody here would be doing a Frank Lloyd Wright."

"Too pricey to construct for us," another said.

"Wrong office," she was told at Sustainable Development, the last entry in the book. The way the man said it made Helma ask, "Can you tell me *which* office I should be calling?"

"Sure. That'd be Doug Bogelli, over at Banner and Bogelli." He laughed. "Doug's greatest regret in life is that he was born too late to worship at the man's feet. And you can tell him I said that, too."

"They're not listed in the yellow pages," Helma said as she glanced through the short list.

"That's Doug all right." He laughed again. "Exclusive. He thinks the harder he is to find, the more he can charge."

The telephone number at Banner & Bogelli rang five times before it was answered and a man brusquely said, "B and B."

"Mr. Bogelli, please," Helma said.

"You got him."

"My name is Miss Helma Zukas," she told him, "from the Bellehaven Public Library."

He gave a nervous laugh. "Geez, I'm sorry. I know the books were due three months ago. I've just been so d— so busy."

When opportune moments presented themselves, Helma was not one to waste time pondering the reason while they slipped away. "I understand," she told Mr. Bogelli. "This must be a busy time of the year for you. You're working on a project inspired by Frank Lloyd Wright?"

There was silence. Then he asked warily, "How'd you know about that?"

"I didn't actually. But I recently had the opportunity to speak to a colleague of yours who said you had an interest in Frank Lloyd Wright."

"Well, that's the truth. But I don't go blabbing my work around town. People spot a trend and they break their necks trying to beat you to it. What did you say your name was again?"

"Miss Helma Zukas."

"Thanks, Hilda. I'll get the books back as soon as I can."

On a square of notepaper imprinted with the new City of Bellehaven logo, Helma jotted down the name Douglas Bogelli of Banner & Bogelli, and their phone number, then tore off the sheet and slipped it into a new folder she'd already used the label maker to identify with the words, WINTHROP, RUTH: MISSING PAINTINGS.

George ducked his head into Helma's cubicle. "May Apple Mayhem is afoot," he said in a low voice, holding his hand to his mouth and nodding toward Ms. Moon's office, and then in a louder voice, "Time to gather together for another scintillating staff meeting. Don't be late."

Six of the seven librarians gathered in the staff room. The only one missing was Ms. Moon, who'd abandoned her onetime dedication to everyone changing places at the conference table each meeting in order to "enhance the group dynamic" and now laid claim to the head of the table. Her chair—the only armed chair in the room—had been pulled from the table and a glass of ice water sat beside two mechanical pencils and a yellow pad imprinted with, MS. MAY APPLE MOON, DIRECTOR OF YOUR LIBRARY.

Helma took a chair directly opposite Ms. Moon's, between George and Roger Barnhard, the children's librarian. Glory Shandy sat to George's left, wearing a butterfly barrette in her voluminous hair, perched to the side as if it were about to take flight. Again she wore the fringed vest, but her short skirt had been replaced by a denim gored skirt with a fringed hemline, and a chain belt made of silver interlocking horseshoes.

"How much longer do we have to live with this?" George muttered, gazing at Glory.

When there was a lull in the conversation, Glory swept her eyes around the table and said, "She'll be here in a minute. She had to take her medication."

Harley leaned toward Glory. "Is she in pain? Maybe the sutures are suppurating. People don't think bones feel pain but they do."

"Harley," George said. "Let me tell you about being a pain."

"Shh," Eve said, turning toward the door. "I hear her coming." And indeed, Helma heard the gentle whirring of Ms. Moon's motorized wheelchair. She buzzed through the door, her library blueprints protruding upward from the back of her chair like thick antenna, scraping the chair arm a little against the left jamb, pausing and frowning as if she'd felt the machine's distress.

"Did you see that?" she asked the gathered staff, pointing toward the bruised doorjamb. "That's exactly the issue. Exactly."

The librarians watched her electrified progress toward the head of the table. She maneuvered the chair with remarkable dexterity, but the table was too low for her to tuck her chair arms beneath and she was forced to sit back two feet, her raised foot nearly at the librarians' eye level.

"Here, in our own library." Ms. Moon sorrowfully shook her head. "Here, where we are dedicated to serving the varied population of our community." She touched her heart. "All the community, the able and the unable, the ill and the healthy."

"The nuts and the cranks," George murmured from beside Helma.

Ms. Moon paused and glanced from face to face. "Do you know what I'm talking about?" she asked in a fervent voice. "Do you realize the problem here? What's vital to serve our community?"

"We need to buy more medical texts?" Harley ventured.

Ms. Moon's face reddened. "My wheelchair *bumped* the edge of the door," she said. "It *bumped*."

"I know." Glory waved her hand. "I know! Our doorways aren't big enough."

"That's right," Ms. Moon said, nodding. "Nor are our tables high enough, nor our aisles wide enough. Even our counters are too high. We are not providing proper service to our community."

"And you're suggesting we find better methods of serving people in wheelchairs?" Helma asked, hoping to forestall Ms. Moon waxing any further.

"Oh, Helma. You have named it exactly. Thank you. Isn't that wonderful?"

Helma sat back in her chair, putting more distance between herself and Ms. Moon's enthusiasm. She'd long been aware of the tight spots in the aging library building for wheelchairs. They weren't insurmountable, but traveling through the building could be time-consuming and awkward.

"Don't you all agree with Helma?" Ms. Moon glanced around the table, smiling in encouragement as each librarian nodded that of course he or she wanted to serve every member of the public as best they could.

The director thumped her fist on the table. "I can't wait to inform the mayor that we are *unanimous* that a new library is imperative. Critical. Even an emergency."

George opened his mouth, but Ms. Moon continued. "My fall was a wake-up call. Luckily, it was me and not some unfortunate citizen who could sue the city for being in violation of access laws." She fingered the amulet around her neck. "That's all now. You may go."

Helma stood. "Ms. Moon, I don't believe we—"

"Shoo, shoo," Ms. Moon said, waving them toward the door. "I'm simply too tired to hear another word. Oh," she added like an afterthought. "And the city council should know how fortunate the city was that it was only me who fell, too. I'll tell them."

Helma had just pulled up the local Associations file on her computer when Glory stepped into her cubicle. "You and I don't look a thing alike," she said, gazing at Helma and twisting a red curl around her finger.

"No," Helma agreed. "We don't."

"That's what I told him. I don't know why he made that mistake."

"Who?"

She shrugged. "A patron. He asked me if I was Miss Zukas. 'We don't look a thing alike,' I said. 'She's more . . . mature.'"

"Is there someone in the library who has asked to speak to me?" Helma asked Glory.

She shook her head. "He only asked if I was you, that's all. I don't know why. Nobody would make that mistake."

"Who was it, Gloria?" Helma asked, unaccountably re-calling the young mother at the reference desk that morning who'd placed both hands on her screaming toddler's cheeks and turned his head so his eyes were six inches from her own.

"A man. Kinda old, and not very . . . I don't know. Just a man. He's wearing a leather jacket, a bomber jacket with a sheepskin collar. I bet it's vintage."

Helma left the workroom for the public area, glancing at the tables. No one to match Glory's description—"kinda old" and wearing a bomber jacket—sat at any of the tables. No bomber jacket was draped over a chair. He'd probably already left the library.

As she walked back toward the workroom, Helma glanced down the library's aisles in the stacks, as was her habit, just a cursory glance to be sure nothing was blatantly out of order. Fiction, computer books, social issues. And as she passed the shelves that held architecture, she glimpsed a man run-ning a finger along the spines of books and squinting at their titles. He wore a brown bomber jacket and she judged that by "kinda old" Glory meant early fifties.

Helma approached him, stopping five feet away. "Excuse me," she said in her library voice. "I'm Helma Zukas."

"Hi," he said. He was Ruth's kind of tall and had the rounded shoulders of a man who'd worked too many years bent over a desk. His face was pocked with small marks like old chicken pox scars and his eyes were dark, with startlingly dark eyebrows beneath thick white hair. "I returned my books, even paid the fine. I'm clean."

"I'm sure that feels satisfying," Helma said.

"As good as a well-made confession," he said, smiling so his eyes nearly disappeared.

"You're Mr. Bogelli?" she asked.

He nodded. "I'm curious. How'd you know about my interest in Frank Lloyd Wright? I thought which books the public checked out was a secret."

"It is," Helma confirmed. "Completely confidential. I spoke to a colleague of yours who mentioned you were influenced by Wright." She took a deep breath. "Also, your name came up as someone who was interested in property east of Bellehaven."

"Is that right? Which property?"

"The owner is deceased. Meriwether Scott."

He shook his head as people did over a hopeless case. "I was. Maybe once the estate is settled I will be again. It's a gorgeous spot, have you seen it?"

Helma nodded. "It felt gloomy for a development."

"A lodge is what I had in mind. It *is* gloomy near the house, but that could be cleared out and brightened up." His voice rose in enthusiasm and his eyes took on a faraway cast. "There's a beautiful rise at the back of the acreage with views of Mount Baker and the Nitcum River. Parts of it were logged a few years ago, but that only makes it more desirable."

"Why?" Helma asked.

"You create bad feelings when word gets out you plan to log a place. Slows things down. You stir up bad enough feelings and the whole process grinds to a stop." He shook his head. "But Meriwether Scott's place is perfect. Already cleared. Even a little near-virgin timber way in the back.

Great nature-walk site. Heck, you'd hardly have to rearrange the dirt. What a waste. A lodge there, that close to the ski area and hiking. The views. It's worth millions."

"He wasn't interested in selling?" Helma asked.

Doug Bogelli rubbed his chin and looked away. "Nope."

"Did you know Meriwether very well?"

"The word 'know' isn't even in the vocabulary. I went out a few times and tried to coax him into selling. Oohed and aahed over his sculptures, tried to take him fishing. He wasn't interested."

"He was solitary?" Helma asked.

He narrowed his eyes and crossed his arms; she'd gone too far. "You're asking a lot of questions. In fact, you sound like the police."

"The police talked to you?" she asked.

"Why would they?" he retorted, taking a step backward. "Nice chatting with you."

And Douglas Bogelli turned and walked out of the library. Helma watched him, regretting only one thing: that he'd left without checking out another library book.

Chapter 17

The Bartender's Reminder

"Get this, Helma," Ruth said, cutting off Helma as she picked up the phone and said, "Miss Zukas speaking."

"Ruth, I'm in the midst of conducting research for a patron." She was, too, searching for the name of the U.S. Secretary of the Interior during the Dust Bowl.

"What on?"

"Our patrons' research topics are confidential," she replied, glancing toward the patron who'd asked the question and now perused the magazine stand while he waited.

"Haven't you heard, *nothing's* confidential anymore. But anyway, I found an interesting little tidbit. You know Lynnette Jensen, grieving widow of my dear friend, Vincent?"

"Yes?" Helma said, flipping open the *World Almanac* to "U.S. Cabinets." Sometimes the simplest reference sources provided the fastest answers.

"Well," Ruth sighed dramatically. "I heard that not only was good old Vincent playing during their separation, but so was she, can you believe it? All that uptight, holier than thou, sleekness? And she had the nerve to give *me* the look. And you'll never guess whose heart she was toying with."

"You're correct, I couldn't," Helma told her.

"Well, you should. But this is the good part: she was fooling around with . . . ta da . . . " The name blasted into Helma's ear. "Meriwether Scott."

"Is that gossip?"

"Definitely not. Carol Deckert saw her talking to Meriwether at Joker's, and get this, they left the bar *together*. Now it's obvious Lynnette asked you about my stolen paintings because she's afraid I'd splashed her face all over my portrait of one or both of the men, and that tied her to the deaths of one or both of them."

Helma held her finger to the name of Harold Ickes, Secretary of the Interior, 1933–1945, and considered Ruth's assertion. "There was a significant difference in age," she mused.

"You're saying older women aren't attractive to younger men, Helma Zukas?"

"Not at all. I'm logically looking at the situation. On the surface, they seem to be very different personalities."

"Who knows what lurks behind closed doors? Maybe she liked what he could do with all his tools. Her husband strayed and she found out. So she fooled around with Meriwether to get even, but then he found out and killed Meriwether. Then she found out and gassed her husband in his lab. She switched gunpowder for his sulfur or something, then lit a match. See, it all makes sense. End of story."

"Then who stole your paintings?"

"She did," Ruth said with certainty. "I'm going to call the detectobot and tell him to bring the handcuffs."

"Ruth . . . "

"Or maybe I should check out her house first, see if I can find the remains of my paintings."

"You already illegally entered Roxy Lightheart's, remember?"

"I'll be more careful this time."

Ruth's voice raced; her words tumbled. She sounded manic, frantic. Helma had heard her sound this way before. "Are you drinking, Ruth?"

Silence. Then, "Maybe a little, to clear the cobwebs, why?"

"Don't do anything, Ruth. Stay home. I'll stop by as soon as I'm finished with work, and we'll figure this out."

"You know you can't stand to come here. Let's meet at Joker's. That's where I am, anyway."

Helma looked up at the clock. It was only 1:46.

"I called him, Helma," Ruth said in a ragged voice. "He asked me not to call him again."

"Oh, Ruth, I'm sorry."

"Yeah, me too." She gave a harsh laugh. "What time will you get here?"

"I'll be there by five-fifteen."

"Got it. We'll crack this case, you bet."

After Helma hung up, she checked a legal tome on Washington State law before looking up Joker's bar in the Bellehaven phone book and dialing their number. She'd had occasion to visit the establishment and recognized the voice of Kipper the bartender.

"This is Miss Helma Zukas," she told him. "I would like to remind you of the responsibilities of bartenders to limit a customer's excessive alcoholic intake."

"Are we talking about anybody we know?" he asked her.

"I believe we are."

"Got it," he said, sounding like Ruth.

Helma heard the whisper of wheels and rose from her desk, expecting to see Ms. Moon whisking through the workroom. But instead a man in a manual wheelchair came from the direction of the staff entrance off the loading dock.

He was in his thirties, square-jawed and broad-shouldered, with the well-muscled upper body of a man who'd been in a wheelchair for years.

He nodded to Helma, wheeling close to her cubicle. His chair was low slung and sleekly lightweight, its wheels tipped inward. "Are you May Apple Moon?" he asked.

"I believe she's in her office," Helma told him. She wouldn't normally have offered, but she was frankly curious. "Can I tell her who's here?"

"Russell Bell," he said. "with High Wheelers. We have an appointment. I'm a few minutes early." He wore tight-fitting leather gloves that snapped across the backs of his hands, and easily maneuvered his chair, backing up to allow Helma to exit her cubicle.

"I'll tell her you're here," Helma offered. "Are you waiting for someone else to join you, or are you alone?"

"I'm it," he said, grinning at her. His legs were strapped together below his knees. "It's crowded in here, just like she said."

Ms. Moon's office door stood open. The metronome on her desk ticked an andante beat, and Ms. Moon sat in her electric wheelchair in front of her desk, her head swaying in time to the soft ticking, the volume that held Chapter 49 of the *Revised Code of Washington*, the chapter on disability rights, on her lap.

"Helma," she said with such pleasure that Helma froze mid-step. "Isn't it a beautiful day?" Ms. Moon's curtains were closed, her office lit only by two desk lamps, one in the shape of a pyramid. Not one inch of the "beautiful day" was visible.

Helma judged the question to be rhetorical and told the director, "Mr. Russell Bell from High Wheelers is here to see you. He said he has an appointment but he's early."

"Oh," she sang out. "The lawyer." She reached out to turn the setting of her metronome up to allegro before she switched on her motor and swung the chair to face the door. "Send him in. I'm ready."

Russell Bell had followed Helma, and Helma stepped aside to allow him to enter. The two wheelchairs stopped inches from one another, and Ms. Moon stuck her hand out toward the handsome man, both their faces bright with anticipation.

Helma raised her head at the hiss of excitement.

"He's here!"

She set the new staff-meeting agenda on the reference desk and spotted Boyd Bishop walking past the circulation desk toward her. He was grinning, his eyes locked onto hers. As she had in the past, she marveled at the narrowness of his hips, for such a tall man. And his shoulders were far broader than one would expect. It was curious how being physically disproportionate could be so visually pleasant.

And that's when Glory Shandy stepped in front of Boyd so abruptly the two collided.

Glory squealed. She teetered on her blue boots. Boyd reached out to hold her upright, and she collapsed against him in a flurry of fringes and giggles

Heads turned, the line of people at the circulation desk silenced, even a toddler screaming for his "Pookie" stopped, all turning to the tableau in the center of the library.

Helma had work to do and she stepped back and headed for the workroom, glimpsing, as she walked away, Boyd Bishop's eyes on her and his mouth moving.

At five o'clock Helma drove directly to Joker's bar, not even stopping at her apartment to change clothes. She wasn't sure what she'd find when she entered the bar and expected anything, but was shocked to see Ruth at a table in the corner, an empty glass and a can of ginger ale in front of her, seated across from Lynnette Jensen.

Ruth waved and beckoned when she saw Helma. Lynnette turned stiffly and watched Helma approach, her posture impeccable, her face unreadable. Every blond hair was smoothly tucked into the coil at the back of her head, and Helma was struck anew by her resemblance to Mrs. Budzynskas in Scoop River, and found herself fighting that sensation of childhood uncertainty.

The table in front of Lynnette was bare. Her hands were folded in her lap. She did not greet Helma.

"I invited her," Ruth announced cheerfully.

"You coerced me," Lynnette corrected icily.

Ruth shrugged. "You help us; we'll help you."

"I don't see a possibility in either option," Lynnette said. She turned to include Helma, only a hint of accusation in her voice, "You're both aware of my questions regarding the paintings."

"Because you were having an affair with Meriwether," Ruth said, leaning forward, eyes agleam.

"Hardly," Lynnette told her, a flash of disdain crossing her face.

"But you knew him?" Helma asked, sitting in the other chair at the small table.

"I knew of his hobby."

"Hobby?" Ruth said. "Chain saws can be tools to create art, just like welding torches. Do you know who stole my paintings?"

"I do not."

"Then why—" Ruth began, but Lynnette held up her hand. Her nails were rosy colored, short and finely shaped.

"I'll tell you what I do know," she said. "I know you and my husband had an affair while we were separated. You weren't the first, and it barely mattered to me, except you were less discreet about it than others."

"Oh, me and my big mouth," Ruth said, shaking her head. "So you were interested in my paintings because you thought

I'd spill the beans to the whole world about your unfaithful husband? And your . . . whatever you want to call it with Meriwether. Funny how they're both dead, isn't it? And now both of their paintings are missing from *my* studio."

Lynnette only gazed at Ruth, her face as bland as if Ruth were talking about a boring novel. Helma sniffed, searching for the perfume her mother had described as "that smell," but still detected only a floral scent.

"The police are looking for a connection between the two men," Helma said. "And you knew both of them."

"As did Ruth," Lynnette countered. "And so did many people in this area. We're not exactly a metropolis."

"But you going out of your way to ask questions about the paintings might be significant," Helma said. "The authorities are trying to establish a connection between your husband and Meriwether Scott. You could share your knowledge with the police."

Lynnette's composure faltered. She swallowed. "I prefer not to speak to the police any more than I already have."

"Don't we all," Ruth said.

Lynnette folded her hands on the table. "You have every right to tell the police I asked about the paintings. But I will tell you this: my involvement, for what it's worth, has absolutely nothing to do with an affair, or either man's death."

Chapter 18

Willows Weep

"That was a totally useless endeavor," Ruth said, nodding toward Lynnette Jensen as she pushed open Joker's door, her back as straight as Dutch's, head held high. Not hurrying or faltering, smoothly exiting as if she were on her way to a not very vital appointment

"I don't agree," Helma told her. "We learned she does have a connection to both men. She knew about your stolen paintings and she has knowledge of Meriwether's art. Could the key be art—yours and Meriwether's? Was her husband an artist, too?"

"Vincent? Not that I know of. He taught at the college." Ruth shrugged. "But I was never inside his house, so he might have had a little art studio tucked away in the attic somewhere. See, I really should take a peek."

Helma ignored Ruth's reference to her latest interest in breaking and entering and took a sip of her cola. Joker's was quiet, although half the tables were taken. Since the ban on smoking in public places, the rowdier establishments, which Joker's had once been, had either closed or shifted their emphasis to games, large-screen televisions, or dining. After floundering, Joker's mounted its recovery by increasing its prices and painting their walls a deep moss green. It now ranked as a popular Bellehaven "in" spot.

"How did you convince Lynnette to meet you here?"

Ruth swallowed from her can of ginger ale and her nose flared. Helma leaned closer and sniffed. It wasn't ginger ale. "I just told her that her secret was out, and if she didn't, I was going to share it with the biggest gossip in town."

"Which secret?"

"Beats me, but everybody has at least one they don't want the world to know. I myself have several."

"I'm sure," Helma said, and Ruth tut-tutted at her.

A small thin man with a moustache and wearing a baseball cap bustled into Joker's, his arms laden with plastic boxes similar to the boxes of Christmas ornaments Helma stored beneath the bed in her back bedroom. He glanced around Joker's, frowned at a table where two couples sat chatting, and carried his boxes to the table next to Ruth and Helma's.

"Hi, Spud," Ruth said. "Is this a poker night?"

The man glanced at his watch and nodded. "You bet. Six-thirty. You wanna play?"

"Not tonight."

He nodded and pulled two tables together, then placed a U-shaped hinged board across the two tables, arranging and rearranging the chairs until each was equidistant from each other and the table.

"So what do we do now?" Ruth asked, downing the last of her drink. "My paintings are gone, men are dead, wives are hiding secrets. I've been dumped and threatened. Oh, and I forgot to tell you: Roxy Lightheart phoned me with another friendly threat."

"What did she say?"

"That woman talks longer than I can listen. She just can't

drop the subject of my gloves. I said she could keep them if she liked them so much, but she has absolutely no sense of humor."

The man called Spud arranged multicolored chips in the center of the table, each pile of equal height, leaning and eyeing them, nudging a stack to one direction or the other until he'd created a symmetrical multicolored star design. He nodded at it and smiled.

Helma set a dollar bill on the table and stood. "Are you going to let Roxy have your show dates at the gallery?"

"Not a chance, would you?"

"I never participate in blackmail," Helma told her.

"I'm not telling her it's a no-deal. If she's true to her word, I could end up spending my opening in the local slammer. I'm betting she wants her show more than she wants to see me in jail, so she won't turn me in, at least not until the last possible second. Good luck tonight, Spud."

"Thanks, Ruth. Come on back if you change your mind."

Ruth waved to Kipper as they left. "Thanks for the prop," she told him, nodding to the ginger ale can. He looked at Helma and shrugged.

The wind blew from the west, off a low tide. Bellehaven was protected from the open sea by the San Juan Islands, and only a few times a year did the winds grow strong enough to splash waves into an actual surf. The sky hung gray, not a rainy-day gray, but in sunless density. Two hours of daylight still remained. A car door slammed.

"Uh-oh, here comes my favorite art critic," Ruth said.

Helma turned to see the rounded figure of Detective Carter Houston. Behind him was parked a plain blue police car. His dress was so standardized it constituted a uniform: dark suit, perfectly pressed; tie knotted and hanging straight if slightly curved over his roundness; polished wing-tip shoes. His face was carefully set, as usual, especially when he and Ruth came face-to-face.

"Maybe I was wrong about Roxy and she's already turned me in," Ruth said quietly to Helma. To the detective, she said, "Hey, Carter. Care to join us for an off-duty drink?"

"How's the new painting progressing?" he asked her. With a touch of maliciousness, Helma thought.

"When are you giving me back my little strip of canvas?" Ruth retorted.

"Hopefully, tomorrow," he answered seriously. He squared the front of his suit jacket, which was already perfectly aligned.

"Did you find fingerprints?" Helma asked.

"I'm not at liberty to discuss it."

"Then what *are* you at liberty to discuss, Carter?" Ruth asked.

Carter's nose twitched. "Are you driving, Miss Winthrop?"

"Of course I'm driving," Ruth began, waving toward her blue VW parked crookedly next to a pile of banded and flattened boxes.

"She's with me," Helma hurriedly said. "I'm driving her home."

Carter nodded, Ruth grunted, and Helma led the way to her Buick.

"I can drive," Ruth protested. "Didn't you see the ginger ale on the table?"

"If you turned on the engine in your car, what do you think Carter Houston would do?"

"Nab and breathalyze me, the little Nazi." She raised her hands in surrender. "Okay, okay, lead me away. I'll come back tomorrow for my car."

"Do you know Lynnette's address?" Helma asked her.

"Sure," Ruth said as she made an elaborate show of fastening her seat belt. "There's something suspicious about every-hair-in-place Lynnette, don't you think?"

"She's very cautious," Helma agreed. "Which direction?"

"To where? Oh, Lynnette's. It's on the slope with all the other academically employed. Head up Knot Avenue. I'll tell you where to turn."

The Slope contained late nineteenth-and early twentieth-century craftsman homes. Wide porches, complementary color schemes, huge old trees with erupting roots, and careful green lawns. Ruth lived on what she called the "hard-scrabble end" of the Slope. They passed two spandexed and helmeted bicyclists pedaling up the steep hill, one directly behind the other. "Crazy," Ruth muttered. A young family pushed a double stroller brimming with identical blond boys.

"Turn left," Ruth said. "It's the gray one with the double garage."

Helma turned and slowed in front of a wide-porched, two-story house with wooden gingerbread along the roofline. The house was painted a color gray that functioned as camouflage on foggy days. A padded swing was attached to the porch ceiling, two empty wicker chairs with bright cushions opposite. The lawn was freshly mowed, but horsetails and ragweed had invaded the flower beds.

"Vincent Jensen was a gardener?" she asked Ruth.

"Yeah, how'd you know that? Okay, slow down. Looks like nobody's home, doesn't it? Lynnette must have run off to one of her clubs."

No lights shone from inside the house. On such a gray day, most people kept a few lights turned on inside. Helma didn't see any open doors or anyone working in the yard, either. "Where was his lab?" she asked.

"You mean where he died? In the back of the garage, off the alley. You can't see it from here."

Helma turned up the street and drove into the alley behind the Jensen house.

"I don't want to confront the Ice Woman again, Helma," Ruth said. "We don't really *know* she's not at home."

"The alley is city property," Helma told her. She braked next to the garage, letting the Buick's engine peacefully idle. The garage was the same color gray as the house, but long irregular patches of charred wood blackened the walls. Two windows were boarded over with plywood so new they looked like scars, and the door had a rectangle of plywood covering its window. She was surprised; from Lynnette's appearance, she would have expected the lab and garage to be repaired by now. It had been four months since her husband died. The burnt garage had to be a daily reminder to her.

"Creepy, isn't it?" Ruth asked as she stared out the window. "You just know something very bad happened inside."

"Were you ever in his lab?"

"I told you I didn't . . . well, actually, I guess I was, but only once. He had this stuff that . . . never mind." She looked gloomily at the charred garage. "It can end just too damn quick sometimes, can't it?"

Helma agreed. "Did you notice any woodworking tools inside? Any wood at all?"

Ruth shook her head. "You mean, like if he and Meriwether carved little wooden duckies together? Nope, never saw anything in there but chemistry stuff. Beakers and scummy petri dishes, Bunsen burners, jars of nasty chemicals, one of which obviously did him in."

Wayne Gallant hadn't said the hydrogen sulfide was confidential information but Helma decided to treat it that way. "Do you remember the names of the chemicals or gases?"

"Definitely not. Some only had symbols. Remember the chemistry lab we had in high school? It was about like that, except without the graffiti on the lab tables. And a slide rule hanging on the wall like a piece of art." She slid her fingers back and forth as if she were working one of the ancient rulers.

"Did he work with lignins or resins?"

"You mean the stuff in tree wood? How would I know? Is that another angle for the woodsy connection between him and Meriwether?"

Helma gazed at the scarred garage. A man had died inside it. She remembered the story in the newspaper, the spot on the local news. Overcome by gases, a fire. Trapped inside. She closed her eyes and opened them at the sound of high-pitched barking.

Lynnette Jensen stepped around the corner of the garage, a pale and fluffy big-eyed tiny dog cradled in her arms.

"I suppose it's too late to squeal our tires and peel out of here," Ruth said. "Especially when she's carrying an attack dog."

Lynnette walked calmly to the car, her lips thinned. She hadn't changed clothes from their meeting at Joker's but she wore a pale blue smock over them. A black smudge darkened one arm. She stopped two feet from Ruth's window and waited.

"Roll down your window, Ruth," Helma told her.

"Do I have to?" Ruth said, but dutifully rolled it down.

The little dog yapped fiercely, but when Lynnette touched its nose, it stopped as if a switch had been thrown. "May I help you?" Lynnette asked.

"Just passing by," Ruth said. "Nice day, isn't it?" Lynnette sniffed delicately, but pointedly, and Ruth clapped her hand over her mouth. "Whoops. Bad breath."

But Helma opened her door and stepped out of her car. "I'm sorry," she told Lynnette. The little dog growled, and again that silencing touch on the nose. "Frankly, after you left us at Joker's, I was curious about your husband's death."

Lynnette said nothing; she watched Helma without a twitch of movement in her face. Helma knew that tactic: the police used it, too, and actually, hadn't she as well? After five seconds people couldn't help it; they said more than they intended. "Is this where it happened?" she asked, and without waiting for Lynnette to answer, continued, "I'm curious why you haven't had the garage repaired."

"Insurance," she said curtly.

"May I look inside?"

"No, you may not. It's boarded up, anyway. Inaccessible." She shifted the little dog in her arms; it didn't take its bulging round eyes off Helma.

Helma glanced at the side door to the garage where the window was boarded over. A metal hasp attached between the door and jamb stood open, a padlock dangling from the eye of the bolt. Lynnette followed her glance toward the door but said nothing.

Helma noted the blackened sleeve of her smock and guessed Lynnette had been inside the lab when she and Ruth drove up. She carefully breathed in the air through her nose and caught the faintest whiff of something burnt, similar to the odor when people burned trash in the fireplace, a particularly unpleasant habit, in her estimation.

"If that's all . . . " Lynnette began, and looked past Helma to include Ruth, too.

"Hi, Mrs. J. Sorry I'm late." A young woman in shorts and a sweatshirt strolled up the alley, an ear bud in one ear with a wire that led to a device fastened to her upper arm.

"That's all right, Brianna. I left instructions on the kitchen counter."

The young woman stopped beside Lynnette and Helma. She was in her late teens or very early twenties. "Hi. Don't I know you?" she said to Helma.

It was a comment that Helma heard often. People recognized her *in* the library but seeing her out of context mystified them. "I work at the Bellehaven Public Library," she told her.

"That's right. You helped me find the *CRC* when it was misshelved. Thanks again."

Helma didn't remember the incident but she did know the *CRC*, the *Handbook of Chemistry and Physics*. "You're a chemistry student?"

Brianna nodded vigorously, both in assent and in time to something on her earpiece. "Yeah, I was in Dr. Jensen's class." Her smile drooped and she bobbed apologetically to Lynnette. "He was just the best. Hi, Tutu," she said to the little dog, and rubbed its ears so hard it squeaked like a squeeze toy.

"They were just leaving," Lynnette told Brianna.

"Oh. Didn't mean to slow you down. Bye."

"Goodbye," Helma told both of them and returned to her car.

She drove slowly out of the alley, watching in her rearview mirror as Lynnette and Brianna stood behind the garage talking. Lynnette didn't glance after them.

"You know what Lynnette was wearing, don't you?" Ruth asked.

"A smock," Helma said, waiting for a bicyclist who was zipping downhill on the sidewalk, coasting too fast to stop.

"Vincent's lab coat. I recognize that baby blue."

"She was in his lab," Helma said. "There was soot on her sleeve and the garage door was unlocked."

"She's finally started to clean it up. I bet she hired Brianna to label deadly little bottles with skulls and crossbones. Her and Tutu, too. Do you think little Tutu was named after Desmond or ballet apparel?" She mused. "When did people start naming their kids Brianna? Who thought that one up?"

"I believe it's a traditional Irish name, the feminine form of Brian."

"News to me. I don't know anyone over seventeen named Brianna."

"Whatever Lynnette is hiding," Helma said, "it's important enough that she consented to meet you at Joker's, an establishment I doubt she frequents."

"That's refreshing. Most secrets aren't big enough to keep." Ruth pointed out her window. "Looks like Ground Up!'s struck again."

A giant vine maple along Fourteenth Street had fallen in last winter's wind storm, the stump recently bulldozed and carted away. Two thin saplings had been planted in its place. They stood like stalks, still leafless, the fragile trunks protected by Ground Up!'s signature pink tree tubes.

"Aren't those willows?" Ruth said, pointing to the smooth yellow bark. "Can you believe it; they planted weeping willows on the *street*? Weeping willows shouldn't be allowed inside the city limits. Every blade of grass under them dies; the branches fall off; they take up too much room." Ruth waved her arms behind her toward the twigs they'd already passed. "They get buggy."

"Maybe the city will replace them with something more suitable," Helma offered, remembering her father chopping down the weeping willows behind their house after they invaded the sewer and water lines. It was an event she'd overheard from the safety of her bedroom; her father, her uncles, her grandfather, arguing in Lithuanian over which way the tree would fall, who had the better eye, the better axe, and where the beer was.

"Not likely. Willows are only nice from a distance. And the god-awful color of their tree tubes. It's . . . I don't know. Call it coral fuchsia. Somebody oughta grind up Ground Up!"

"I'm surprised you know the habits of trees," Helma said.

"I'm a woman of many surprises. You want to come in?" Ruth asked, only rhetorically, of course.

"I'll talk to you tomorrow," she told Ruth, who had just realized why her car wasn't in her car port.

Chapter 19

Feeding the Kitty

At the Bayside Arms, Walter David stood outside the manager's apartment, talking to a man in a well-tailored suit. Helma slowed her car. The man nodded to something Walter said and wrote in a leather-encased notebook. The Faber Realtor? Or a potential buyer?

An unmarked police car was parked against the curb, no one inside. She parked her Buick squarely in her covered space, and after assuring herself that the doors were locked, spotted Wayne Gallant descending the stairs of the building. Walter David and the man were so deep in conversation they didn't look up.

"Hi," Wayne said, smiling but not touching her. So this was a business call, then. "I was afraid I'd missed you. Do you have a minute?"

"Certainly. Come up to my apartment."

He followed her up the stairs. As they reached TNT's apartment, just before hers, TNT's door opened and he leaned out. The sounds of a sportscaster's voice and cheering came from his television.

"Hi," he said, looking from Helma to Wayne. "I

think we're in trouble." He nodded toward Walter and the stranger. "Somebody's here to look at the place already."

"Has he looked inside the apartments?" Helma asked.

TNT shook his head. "Just walked around outside so far. That's all." He raised his hands in a gesture of helplessness. "What can you do?"

The chief said, "There'll be a lot of interest, but these transactions go slow. Don't worry, yet."

"Yeah, but a guy can't help it. Good to see you, Helma. Chief, call me to set up a little sparring at Goodwin's, okay?"

"Will do," Wayne told him. "Don't expect me to be up to your standards, though."

TNT tugged a lock of his gray hair. "Hah, you can pummel an old man like me into the mat." He looked beyond Wayne and Helma toward the parking lot. "Well, have a good night, kids."

Wayne saluted TNT and when the door was closed shook his head. "I've sparred with TNT before; *I'm* the one who got pounded into the mat. Have you ever seen him fight?"

"I've never attended a boxing match," Helma said as she unlocked her door.

"You should drop by Goodwin's Gym on a Tuesday or Thursday afternoon. He's good."

Helma swiftly surmised that all was in order in her apartment, just as she'd left it. Since she hadn't come home after work, Boy Cat Zukas paced her balcony, glaring in at her. His mouth opened wide in a yowl she gratefully couldn't hear through the glass doors.

"How about if I feed him for you?" Wayne asked, nodding toward the cat. "He looks famished."

"He usually does. His food's in a plastic container in my dishwasher."

"Where else would it be?" Wayne asked as he opened the machine.

While Wayne let in Boy Cat Zukas and fed him, Helma hung her coat and put away her bag, hearing him talk to the cat, something she never did. She was curious at the unaccustomed feeling in her apartment: of . . . well, of domesticity. It wasn't completely unpleasant. In fact, listening to the cat's teeth crunching kibble before his bowl was even filled, she realized it was actually quite pleasing.

"Would you like something to drink?" Helma asked. "I have tea or wine. White only, though."

"No thanks. Could we talk for a few minutes?"

It was always surprising how her apartment shrank in Wayne's presence, as if her furnishings weren't on a scale large enough to accommodate him. Or that the walls had suddenly squeezed in a little tighter.

"Does this relate to Ruth's stolen paintings?" She sat on her sofa, and Wayne chose the chair opposite her, across the coffee table.

"I suspect, indirectly, it does, but you'll have to tell me."

Helma sat up a little straighter. "If I can help you, of course I will."

One corner of his mouth lifted. "I understand you and Ruth spoke to Lynnette Jensen."

Helma glanced at her watch. "We only left her house ten minutes ago. How . . . " Then she realized her mistake.

"Her *house*?" Wayne asked, frowning. "I understood you met her at Joker's."

"We did," Helma said, and added hurriedly, "Ruth arranged it. Lynnette had asked me about the missing paintings."

But he was not to be diverted. "Her house?" he repeated. "You and Ruth went to her house, too? She invited you home after meeting you at Joker's?"

"No," Helma admitted. "But I *was* curious about where her husband died. And she happened to be home. We drove up the alley. That's all."

Now it was as if he'd heard her earlier statements. "Why did she ask you about Ruth's missing paintings?"

"I think she knew I was a friend of Ruth's." Helma didn't add that she suspected if a woman knew her husband was having an affair with another woman, she'd probably learn everything she could about the other woman, including *her* friends.

He nodded, obviously aware of Ruth's connection to Lynnette. "What did you learn from Lynnette?" he asked. "Or from seeing the damaged garage?"

"Are you asking me as a policeman?"

"And as a friend." He leaned forward as if he were about to reach across the coffee table and touch her.

"I think Lynnette was acquainted with both men. She only admitted to being familiar with Meriwether's art. It was a sense I had, the way she spoke."

"People sometimes reveal more by what they don't say than what they do say." He picked up last week's *Time* magazine from her coffee table and rolled it as if he were going to rubber-band it. "Did you go inside the garage where the professor's lab was?"

"There was a padlock on the door," she said, and under his gaze, admitted, "However, the padlock was open and Lynnette was wearing a smock—Ruth said it was her husband's lab coat—with black smudges on the sleeves."

"She'd been inside the lab?" he asked, rolling *Time* in the opposite direction.

Helma was about to say that yes, Ruth had been inside Vincent's lab, when she realized he meant Lynnette. "I didn't see her enter or exit the building."

Wayne nodded.

"You don't see anything suspicious in Lynnette being inside her husband's lab, do you? She may have been cleaning it out."

"She may have been," he agreed.

"Do you suspect her in the robbery? Or the deaths of the two men?"

"I haven't seen any evidence to suggest that," he said evasively.

He looked across the room at Boy Cat Zukas, who now sat in his basket rudely licking his bottom and purring in a rackety rumble. "There's something I've been meaning to ask you for a while."

"And that is?"

He considered Helma, glanced at Boy Cat Zukas, then gave a slow smile and shook his head. "Another time." He stood. "Thanks for giving me your view of this. It's very valuable to me."

"Do you believe Ruth's in danger? That the slashed painting was meant to be a threat?"

He shrugged. "I wish I knew. Whoever stole Ruth's paintings might have left the strip behind accidentally, not as a warning to her."

"But you don't believe that?" She walked with him to her door, and there he did hug her. When they separated, Helma released her breath to silence the ringing in her ears.

"I'll talk to you soon," he said as he left.

As Helma straightened the *Time* magazine and set her unabridged dictionary on top of it to reflatten its pages, she realized that in the midst of their embrace he hadn't answered whether he believed the strip of Ruth's painting had been a warning.

Chapter 20

Speculation in the Library

"Since our meeting, she's being veddy, veddy quiet," George Melville was saying as Helma entered the staff lounge for a cup of tea. "This does not bode well for us peons."

"It might be the pain pills," Harley, who was pouring soy milk into an earthy-smelling drink, offered. "I've had pain pills. You'd be surprised at what they can give you while they're relieving your pain: nausea, dizziness, constipation. Once my whole chest itched like fire for twenty-four hours. I can ask her," he offered, even turning to face the door, his pale cheeks flushing.

"Contain yourself, man," George told him, holding his hand out flat in front of Harley's chest. "I've been in this asylum longer than you and this is *not* a side effect; it's a full-blown syndrome. She's up to no-goodery and trying to hide it from you, me, and the public. Keep your head low and your eyes open so you don't get sucked into it." George piled two doughnuts on top of his coffee cup. "Hi, Helma. You heard it here first: the Moonbeam's on the prowl."

Helma would never have called Ms. Moon "the Moon-beam," although the rest of the staff and some people outside of the library did. "Is she already here?" Ms. Moon often didn't arrive at the library until it opened to the public.

"Rolled directly into her office an hour ago, and get this, she shut her door." Ms. Moon was inordinately proud of her "open door" policy. George raised and lowered his brows in Groucho Marx fashion. "I don't know why I don't just retire and get out of this place."

"Because you wouldn't have anybody to pick on," Harley answered in unusual insightfulness.

At the reference desk, Helma had just finished helping a man find information on where hair plugs came from—a question for which she had to contact her friend Beulah at the hospital, who faxed over a medical article—the only reassurance the man would accept that hair plugs didn't actually come from pubic hair. A disturbance near the circulation counter made her rise.

A line of wheelchairs rolled into the library. Not part of the line, but to one side watching from his own wheelchair, was the lawyer Russell Bell, the head of High Wheelers. Maggie Bekman stood next to his chair, along with her photographer from the *Bellehaven Daily News*. Three motorized wheelchairs and six standard models advanced through the library, one after the other, some alone, some being pushed, others being followed by what Helma took to be supporters.

There were no banners, no signs, no speeches, only nine solemn people of varying ages in wheelchairs circling peacefully through the reference area past Helma, then around the magazines and past the rows of computers, and finally up and down the library stacks. Slowing at tight turns, trying to avoid but inevitably bumping chairs and kick stools left in the aisles. Patrons stepped aside and silently watched the procession.

And once the procession had covered the entire library, the woman in the lead wheelchair led the others out the front door.

One of the walking members of the line stopped in front of Helma. "Hi again," she said.

Helma didn't recognize her at first, and then she spotted the electronic device on her arm and the tiny speaker in one ear. "Hello. Are you with this group?"

"Kinda. My friend Sheila's in one of the chairs."

"And the purpose is?"

"Oh, they're all part of High Wheelers, they do this once in a while. Nothing rude or demanding. It's just for public awareness."

"I see. You're Brianna, aren't you?" Helma said, recalling the meeting behind Lynnette Jensen's garage.

She nodded. "You've got a good memory. Brianna Bogelli. I forget your name."

"It's Miss Zukas," Helma told her, then seeing Brianna's frown, she added, "Helma." Bogelli?

"I like that, Helma. Is it short for Wilhelmina?"

No one had ever made that connection without knowing her given name. Helma was surprised. "Yes, it is. Are you the developer Douglas Bogelli's daughter?"

"*Mm hmm*. Do you know my dad?"

"We've met."

"You're not one of his clients, are you?"

"No," Helma said, and Brianna looked relieved. "But I do admire the work of Frank Lloyd Wright."

"Well, that would make you one of Daddy's new best friends, then."

She turned as if to walk away, and Helma asked, "And you were a student of Vincent Jensen's?"

Brianna twirled the cord of her speaker wire around her finger. "For the Chem series: 201 and 202, and then 218, too. He was one of those teachers who make you think. We did really hard stuff but it stuck with you, you know what I mean?"

Helma's Readers' Advisory instructor had been that way. What you figured out yourself you were more likely to remember. "Then you did a lot of experiments?"

"Yeah. It was hard to go into the lab after . . ." She faltered.

"After he died in *his* lab," Helma finished for her. "You might loosen that cord; the end of your finger's turning purple."

"Oh. Thanks. It's easier now, though. In fact, on Saturday I'm helping Lynnette clean Dr. Jensen's lab."

"Isn't that dangerous? There may still be hazardous chemicals."

"She hired a Hazmat company to take out the dangerous materials first. She's turning it into her studio."

"She paints?" Helma asked. A light flashed and Maggie Bekman's photographer rose from a crouch in an aisle where a kick stool had been knocked over by a wheelchair and had yet to be righted.

"Sculpture. With clay. She's going to install a kiln and replace the sink and maybe even give lessons." Brianna's expression turned doubtful.

A red-haired young woman in a wheelchair swung around the end of the circulation desk. "Bree, are you coming? We're going to that matinee next."

"Coming. Bye, Helma. I think you should go by the name Wilhelmina; it's more musical."

Helma watched Brianna, her walk turning to skipping as she joined her friend, both of them talking over each other as Brianna grabbed the wheelchair handles. She imagined the nine wheelchairs attending the matinee at the theater, wondering if they'd circle through the theater and the rest rooms, maybe order popcorn and drinks at the too-high counters.

And during all this, there'd been no sign of Ms. Moon. The workroom door remained closed, the telephone quiet. No sign of Glory Shandy, either. The library settled back into its accustomed bustle. Dutch sent two pages through the stacks to restore order. "Be sure the kick stools aren't blocking the aisles," he told them.

Glory entered the public area, carrying a box of file folders. She wore plain black shoes and a childish pink dress with a pinafore. No fringes or silver buckles. No blue cowboy boots or denim.

"Hi," she said in what Helma thought was a desultory fashion.

"Hello, Glory."

"You know that guy? He wasn't *really* a cowboy. He was from New Mexico."

"There are cowboys in New Mexico," Helma told her. A toddler raced past, no mother in sight.

"Well. He didn't act very interested in cowboys. He didn't even know who starred in that Wyatt Earp movie." She swayed back and forth, then wrinkled her nose at Helma. "But he talked to *you* like he was interested in—" She stopped and shook her head so her red hair swung. "No, he wasn't a real cowboy," and continued toward the circulation desk.

Carolyn, the older page, approached Helma. "Miss Zukas," she whispered, and rolled her eyes toward the stacks. "There's a man in the Botany section doing something."

"Yes?" Helma asked, already moving her hand toward the phone. The Bellehaven Public Library was too small to justify its own security guard, although that was the trend in many libraries. "We're just across the street from the police station," Ms. Moon had reminded them. And it was true; the rare times the staff *did* have to call the police for assistance, they arrived within five minutes.

"I don't think what he's doing is *illegal*," the page added hurriedly, "but I'm sure it's against library policy. I didn't say anything to him; Dutch is on break so I decided to tell you."

"In the Botany section?" Helma asked. "Five eighty?"

Carolyn nodded. "He's a tall man with a ponytail."

Helma walked down the aisle next to the Botany shelves and saw that the page was slightly off; the man was near 580 but actually in the 570s, the Ecology section. He stood with his back to her. She pulled a book from the shelf, and from her peripheral vision, which was acute, watched him remove a book from the shelves, tuck something into it, return it to the shelf and pull the book next to it from the shelf and do the same thing.

Carolyn was right: it wasn't illegal, but it *was* against library policy. People with their own agendas often tucked flyers and bookmarks into books that either mirrored or opposed their own agendas: religious tracts in books on sexuality and women's rights, racist materials in equal-rights books, creationist pamphlets in books on evolution, even beauty-salon advertisements in grooming books.

Stepping up behind the man, she pulled the last book he'd touched from the shelf and opened it, pulling out a *Ground Up!* leaflet. It was identical to the pamphlet she'd found in the Local Government materials that had toppled from the top shelf when Ms. Moon fell.

"Excuse me," she said in her silver-dime voice. "What you are doing is a form of vandalism."

The man spun around, his eyes easy, narrowing slightly, as if he'd been rudely interrupted, a stack of *Ground Up!* pamphlets in his hands.

"Hi," he said.

Helma held the pamphlet toward him. "You may take this, and remove the others from the library's books as well."

He reluctantly took the pamphlet, and Helma saw a flicker of recognition cross his face. He knew her. She peered more closely at him: his broad shoulders, the graying hair and receding forehead. He was dressed like a college student, in jeans and a sweater. On his feet were worn brown hiking boots, and that solved the puzzle.

"You're Stu," she said. "We met in the woods two days ago, at the property of Meriwether Scott."

He frowned. "Meriwether Scott?" he asked. "I don't know who that is."

"Are you a member of Ground Up!?" she asked.

He held up the pamphlets. "Well, yeah," he said as if she'd missed a fact that was blazingly obvious. Then, as if he'd gone too far, he smacked a hand against his forehead and said in a warm voice, "Right. Now I remember. You and the tall lady were at that property where I was geocaching. I didn't recognize you. Your friend is more . . . visible." He shrugged. "I didn't expect to see you in the library. Are you a librarian?"

"I am. Is there a contact number on those pamphlets?"

"Yes." He hesitated. "Want one?"

"I'll take one of these," Helma said, and pulled one of the pamphlets from another book on the shelf. "Please remove all the others from library property. You may speak to the director about leaving them on the public-information shelf."

Without waiting to see if he'd comply, Helma turned and left the stacks. At the reference desk, she found the contact number on the bottom of the *Ground Up!* pamphlet and dialed it. A woman answered with the words, "Ground Up! Come join us."

"This is Miss Helma Zukas at the Bellehaven Public Library," she said into the phone. "May I speak to the head of your organization?"

"He's not here right now. Can I have him call you back?"

"Yes, please." She gave the Bellehaven Public Library's phone number to the woman. "May I have his name, please?"

"Sure. It's Stu, Steward Arbor."

"Stewart?" Helma asked.

"No, Steward, like caretaker. Isn't that cool?"

"And Arbor, as in tree?" Helma asked.

"Right."

"I see. Very clever. Would Mr. Arbor have gone to the library?"

"I don't know. I think he was delivering some pamphlets."

Helma hung up and hurried back to the Ecology shelves. The *Ground Up!* pamphlets still protruded from the ecology books and Stu—aka Steward Arbor—was nowhere in sight. She walked through the stacks, the magazine section, checked the tables, and finally went to the front doors.

There, walking on the sidewalk, she spotted him, ponytail swaying. A man nearly as tall, thinner, walked beside him.

"And Richard," Helma said softly to herself, recognizing the thin man who'd been with Steward Arbor at Meriwether Scott's property.

Richard aimed his hand at a blue sedan—a remote key, she guessed—and opened the driver's door. Steward climbed in the passenger side. The car pulled from the parking place and headed north.

After she'd removed all the *Ground Up!* pamphlets she could find, Helma sat down and read one from beginning to end. After the second sentence, which read, "Nature has it's priorities," she picked up a red pencil and marked all the grammatical and spelling errors, of which there were a surprising number. She had no intention of returning the edited pamphlet to Ground Up! so they could revise their next effort. It was only an exercise, a way of mentally not letting the errors pass. Any organization that was *truly* serious, she felt, would certainly take pains to assure their message wasn't deterred by faulty grammar.

Ground Up! was dedicated to "replacing the trees butch-
ered by America's greed for condos and concrete." They
claimed to replant "lost local varieties." She remembered the
willow tree and did a quick search in the *Western Garden
Book*.

"Weeping willows," the book advised in typical Northwest subtlety, "are best used as single trees near stream or
lake." Invasive roots "subject to tent caterpillars, aphids,
borers, and spider mites." Ruth was right.

But for an instant Helma recalled her grandmother pressing *suris*, the dense white Lithuanian cheese, in cheesecloth
between boards and weighting it with rocks, leaving it to
drain under the giant willow tree on their farm.

She returned to Ground Up!'s brochure. Their signature
and the protection of their newly planted trees was the biodegradable pink circlets of plastic tree tubes manufactured
by Earth's Sheath.

She tapped the Web-site address of Earth's Sheath into
her computer and was rewarded with a graphic of a field
of trees, trunks encompassed by a rainbow of plastic tree
tubes. The tubes degraded in twenty-four months: photos
showed them fading, weathering, and finally dissolving into
the earth. More photos depicted healthy grown trees, busy
smiling employees in the Earth's Sheath factory, each Web-
site page holding a quote from Henry David Thoreau or Lao
Tzu.

On the back of the brochure, Steward Arbor's name was
listed as the director of Ground Up! but there was no photograph. She was sure he was the same man. His excuse
that he and Richard had trespassed on Meriwether's land
during a geocaching game wasn't true. They'd been exploring Meriwether's land for some other reason. To purchase?
Or to replant in one of their stealth activities? The developer, Douglas Bogelli, had claimed the land was partially
logged.

Helma dialed Banner & Bogelli's number. His office was obviously small since he answered the telephone himself again.

"Do you know the name of the Realtor handling Meriwether Scott's land?" she asked after she'd identified herself and he politely but warily agreed to talk to her.

"Why?" he asked bluntly.

Always acknowledge the patron's knowledge, she'd learned in a course on handling the difficult library patron. "The property came up as a topic recently in the library," Helma told him. "And you seemed like the most knowledgeable source."

"As far as I know, the ownership is still tied up in the courts," he said, his voice softening slightly. "The guy didn't leave a will."

She waited, and finally he said, "Give Joyce DeLouise at Faber Realty a call. She keeps track of things like that. Her nose is out there sniffing around for loose property before anybody else hears of it." He paused. "You don't need to tell her I gave you her name."

Faber Realty, the same realty company that was listing the Bayside Arms.

Helma had a knack for recalling numbers. She appreciated their shapes, their neatness of expression, and the stability of their definitions: Two meant two, six was six, and 112 meant 112. She liked that.

She closed her eyes for a moment and the telephone number from their sign, in a bold sans serif font, scrolled across the blackness behind her eyelids. She didn't doubt its correctness, and dialed the number, rewarded after the second ring by a voice that sounded so professional that at first she thought it was a recording. "Faber Realty. How may I direct your call?"

Helma matched the tones. "Ms. Joyce DeLouise, please."

The call was put through without question, and when the

woman answered, Helma heard a radio being switched off and the windy sound of an automobile. Ms. DeLouise was answering on her cell phone.

"This is Miss Helma Zukas with the Bellehaven Public Library," she said. She couldn't help it that she coughed as she said, "Public Library," and perhaps slurred the words. She didn't give Ms. DeLouise time to request clarification. "I have a question about the land on Silver Salmon Road owned by Meriwether Scott."

She paused to give the woman an opportunity to recall the property.

"Has the parcel been cleared for sale yet?" Helma asked. "We have someone interested in its disposition."

"Still in probate," she said briskly. "At least as of yesterday. Which company did you say you're with? And who is it who's interested?"

"Thank you very much, Ms. DeLouise. I realize you're speaking on your cell phone while driving, which is very dangerous, so I won't take up any more of your time."

Helma glanced at the wall clock as she hung up. There was just enough time if she took an extended lunch hour. But first she stood and approached three young boys snickering around an Internet computer. According to the rules, they should have been using the filtered computers in the Children's Room.

"Excuse me," she said, standing to the side so she couldn't view the screen.

The boy at the keyboard jumped. "I ain't doin' nothing," he said, his forefinger hitting the Delete button. The other two boys slipped away toward the steps that led down to the Children's Room.

"Could you assist me with a Web site I believe you can manipulate better than I can?" Helma asked.

"What do you mean?" he asked suspiciously, wiggling on the chair as if he were about to launch himself from it. He was fair-haired and pale, in clothes that were too big. Helma judged him to be eleven or twelve, suspended between two age groups and not very happy about either.

"I'd like to know if there is a geocache planted at a particular site."

The sullenness shifted to cautious eagerness. "What'll you give me if I do it?"

"My appreciation," she told him.

His eagerness won out, and he turned back, expertly poising his hands over the keyboard and already typing in an Internet address. "Yeah," he said in a bored voice. "What's the coordinates?"

"I only have an address, along Silver Salmon Road," she told him.

It took the boy about thirty seconds. "There's one at the Maple Creek Bridge, about a mile away, but nothing on Silver Salmon Road," he told her.

"Thank you very much. I appreciate it."

"Aren't you going to ask me if I'm sure?"

"No," she told him. "You appear to be very knowledgeable. I believe you."

He shrugged. "Want me to look up something else for you?"

"No thank you." She paused. "I did notice no one is waiting to use this computer, so you may use it for fifteen minutes more before you join your friends."

"Sweet," he said, turning his full attention back to the screen.

Helma returned to the desk and dialed Ruth's phone number.

Chapter 21

Back in the Country

Helma leaned forward to peer out her windshield. "Look, there's an eagle."

Ruth slouched in her seat so she could see the raptor from the passenger-side window. It soared over the road and without flapping its wings turned toward the Nitcum River, hidden behind a line of trees, and disappeared.

"So enlighten me again. The guy we saw at Meriwether's yesterday is actually the ridiculously named Steward Arbor, head of Ground Up!, right? So why were they hanging out at Meriwether's?"

"They lied. They told us they were geocaching, but a local geocache expert said there isn't a cache listed for those coordinates."

"A geocache *expert*?" Ruth said, "What was he, a ten-year-old computer nerd?"

"Of course not," Helma told her, thinking that the boy had been at least eleven. "But if Steward and Richard weren't geocaching, their true intent involved either the land or Meriwether."

"What's that got to do with my missing paintings?"

"Your paintings are related to both men's deaths. And that makes activities to do with either man of interest."

"Still doesn't compute. You're reaching."

"The Ground Up! people are planting trees, yes, and trespassing to do it. They've also been inserting their brochures into library books."

"So that makes them art thieves, art slashers, and murderers?"

"Not automatically." Ruth turned on her seat and pointed her thumb at herself. "Or they followed *us* to Meriwether's. *Me*." Her voice rose. "They were the guys who broke into my house, and if you hadn't been at Meriwether's too, they'd have finished me off. They could have hidden my body out there and it wouldn't be discovered until the developers began bulldozing. If even then . . ."

As usual, when an idea came to Ruth, she embraced it. "But *why*, Ruth? What is it *you* know or have that could incite men to violence?"

"Now there's a loaded question." She settled back into her seat, tugging on her seat belt. "Honestly, I've been trying to figure that out. I even made lists—you'd have been proud—trying to find a common link between Meriwether, Vincent, and me." She shook her head and absently unrolled her window a few inches, then rolled it up again. The wind whistled. "But all I keep coming up with . . ." Her voice trailed off.

"Is you," Helma finished for her.

"Yeah," Ruth said glumly. "But like you say, why? Who knows why people do what they do? Why do people leave the water running when they brush their teeth? Why do we open our mouths when we put on mascara?"

Since Helma practiced neither habit, she didn't answer.

They drove silently past a Christmas-tree farm. Ruth studied it out her window, then snapped her fingers. "Trees.

We're going to Meriwether's because you suspect Steward Arbor's gang is planting little pink trees all over Meriwether's property."

"It *was* logged a few years ago."

Ruth tapped her fingers against the dashboard. "I could almost buy that, except Meriwether's place is too far away from the populace. Most of Ground Up!'s projects have been very in-your-face. Highly visible, on street corners, in parks, and in front of public buildings, not tucked away on some backwoods acreage. Unless you could see those coral fuchsia tree tubes from the road, they wouldn't bother."

"Douglas Bogelli, a developer in town, expressed interest in turning the property into an upscale lodge," Helma told her. "If he *did* purchase the property and apply for permits, it's bound to be very controversial."

"So if Ground Up! did their stuff, they'd already have a claim on the land, right? Stir up emotions. Don't kill the new baby trees. And so on. But murder and art thievery over *trees*? Uh-uh."

As they reached Meriwether's driveway, Ruth pointed out the window. "His carved fish is gone,"

Ruth was right, the weathered fish had been taken; fresh saw marks still marred the rough-cut post it had perched on. "Someone stole it."

"Grave robbers," Ruth said. "Where are you going? You missed the driveway, Helma."

"I think I'll enter the property another way."

"What do you mean, 'another way'? How do you know there's another way?"

"The library has an up-to-date collection of local maps: topographical, aerial, USGS, trail maps."

"Skip the public service announcement. Just say you looked at a map."

"I looked at *detailed* maps."

"You're hoping we can catch them busily digging baby-tree-sized holes," Ruth said, rubbing her hands together.

"That's a possibility. If tree planting is their goal, there should be indications, and I suspect they'd choose to enter the land in a less public way than drive up to Meriwether's front door."

"It's not as if Meriwether lived on a main road."

"It would still be blatant trespassing."

A quarter mile past Meriwether's driveway, a two-track led into the woods on the same side of the road. "See," she told Ruth, "those are fresh tire tracks."

"Just look like tracks to me."

Helma shifted her car into first gear and turned into the trees, driving so slowly the speedometer didn't register. She steered her tires precisely in the two ruts. The two-track narrowed a hundred feet into the woods. She stopped the car and opened her door.

"What are you doing?"

"I don't want to scratch my car. I have a tool in my trunk."

"A tool? What, a machete? This I gotta see," Ruth said, and joined Helma at her trunk.

Next to an emergency bamboo rug for picnics, a hefty tire iron, a thick sisal rope, a first-aid kit, bottled water, an umbrella, and extra batteries, was a pruning tool she'd bought on sale after a miscalculation along the Nitcum River. Now she removed it from the trunk and lopped off two branches that hung near enough to the two-track to scrape the side of her car.

"You can carry these," she told Ruth, handing the pruners to her.

"What for? Put them back in your trunk."

"If you walk ahead of the car, I won't have to keep stopping."

Ruth snapped the blades of the pruners open and closed.

"Like the faithful bearer, you mean? I'll clear the way by the sweat of my brow while you ride all warm and safe in your car?"

"If you don't mind. You do have the proper footwear."

Ruth looked down at her feet. Instead of the sandals she'd worn the last time, she wore bright blue rubber Wellington boots that reached halfway up her shin. "My new Wellies," she said. "I saw them on a BBC comedy. It's too soon to get them all dirty."

"We only need to go a hundred feet further to be completely invisible from the road."

"I can't see the road now. We may as well be in uncharted territory it's so damn thick in here."

But Helma was already behind the steering wheel, putting her car in gear. Ruth stomped ahead of the Buick in her Wellies, cutting branches in unnecessary exaggeration. In fact, she took pains to lean into the trees and cut branches that couldn't possibly reach Helma's car. The third time Ruth stepped into the trees to cut a branch, Helma turned off her engine and got out of the car. "Ruth, what are you doing?"

"I'm doing exactly what you told me to do: I'm cutting branches."

"You're cutting more than is necessary."

"I'm participating in what is called malicious compliance."

"Give me the pruners, and I'll put them back in the trunk."

"Heck no. These things cut through branches like butter. I'm taking them along for protection."

Which, Helma conceded, wasn't an unreasonable idea. She tested all her doors to be sure they were locked and glanced a last time at her car. Then they walked in the ruts of the two-track, moving in a direction Helma judged was parallel to Meriwether's house, although she couldn't see it. Water, either from rain or condensation, still clung to leaves and moss in the deepest shade. At the edge of the track she spotted a tuft of grass with bent and broken shoots, and then another three feet away. "They came this way," she told Ruth. "So we leave the two-track here."

"Why? I don't see anything."

Helma pointed out the crushed grass, the faint trail across a damp mossy area.

Ruth grunted. "You're like that fictional character in *Butch Cassidy and the Sundance Kid*. Remember? In the white hat? Butch kept saying, 'Who are those guys?'"

"Actually, the character was based on an actual tracker, Joe LeFors, who was a deputy U.S. Marshal."

"If I want facts I'll go to the library. Lead the way. Have you ever seen those spiked steel things they use to plant trees? They're like those poles our dads used to break the ice for ice fishing."

"Ice spuds?" Helma said, remembering.

"Yup. Deadly."

They walked out of the denser trees into the open area that had been logged. Someone, Meriwether probably, had burned the slash. The open area was less scarred than most logged-over land. It had a meadowy feel. Instead of replanting with evergreens, Meriwether had removed the slash and stumps. Less moss grew there, displaced by thready grass.

"Wait. Listen."

Helma stopped, tipping her head. In the distance she heard the sad song of a mourning dove. They topped a small rise.

"Great place for a lodge," Ruth commented. "Look up there."

Mount Baker hung above them in the distance, only the top few thousand feet visible, its white peak glistening like a mirage. Water babbled to their left.

"Sign me up for a room and a massage." Ruth spun around in a circle. "I don't see any newly planted trees, do you? No blazing hot coral fuchsia tree tubes, either. I bet you don't know where the word fuchsia came from, do you?"

"I don't," Helma admitted.

"A Mr. Fuchs, or *Herr* Fuchs, a German botanist. Blame him for those messy, gaudy flowers."

They wandered the property, Ruth swinging the pruners, Helma holding her multitool with its compass in front of her to make sure they didn't get lost. The land had been groomed and mowed, with brush removed, branches trimmed, and toppled trees sawed up and hauled away. A few neat piles of split logs waited to be carted for firewood.

"Did Meriwether plan to develop this himself?" Helma asked Ruth.

"You mean because it's parked out? No, he just liked it that way. He enjoyed putting the world in order. You'd have liked him." They paused beneath the fatal tree with its intact burl, both of them helplessly gazing upward. "Nothing here," Ruth said. "So I'd say Ground Up! hasn't bothered with this place."

"At least not yet. As long as we're this close to the house, let's look around there."

"All right with me." Ruth led the way, swinging the pruners haphazardly. Helma stayed back, out of their range. "I think my heart is beginning to heal," Ruth was saying. "No place but up for me now. Up, up, and away."

She halted and Helma nearly ran into her. She jumped to the side, away from the sharp implement. "Who's that?" Ruth whispered.

A white BMW sedan sat in Meriwether's driveway. The boarded house seemed to brood. Helma surveyed the scene with the same piercing awareness she used to scan her apartment. The day was silent, still. She detected no movement, no other person. But the door of Meriwether's shop stood open.

She held up her hand for Ruth to remain quiet and stepped ahead of her, heading toward the shop, her multitool in her right hand.

"Wait," Ruth whispered shrilly. "It's them. The Ground Up! guys."

Helma hadn't seen Steward's car but doubted that he owned a white BMW. "I'm going to discover who it is."

"You need a weapon," Ruth said, shoving the pruners at her. "Take these. I'll cover your back."

Helma slipped her multitool into her jacket pocket and pointed the pruners in front of her, one hand on each handle, holding them the way she'd seen water witchers in an illustration from the Dust Bowl years. Anyone coming at her, from the front at least, would have to deal with the sharp end first. The owner of the BMW had surely heard her and Ruth's approach, but she detected no movement anywhere near the white car. Was it Douglas Bogelli, the developer? Or perhaps the interest of the Faber Real Estate woman, Joyce DeLouise, had been piqued by her call.

One silent step after another along the mossy driveway toward Meriwether's shop. The door stood open into the shadowy interior, and again Helma wondered that an artist—even a chain-saw artist—didn't require more natural light. But maybe working with chain saws was different.

A narrow beam of light flashed from inside. A flashlight, and then the sound of metal scraping against metal.

Helma never underestimated the clichéd but crucial element of surprise. She stopped in front of the open door, standing carefully to the side in case there were weapons. Holding up the pruners and straightening her shoulders, she asked, "Do you have permission to be on the premises?"

A screech came from inside. A woman's voice.

It was too dark to see the interior so Helma stepped farther back from the door and said, "Come out into the light. I have a weapon."

"She really does," Ruth said, joining Helma.

After another scrape of metal against metal, then a soft thud, the woman stepped from the garage.

It was Lynnette Jensen, dressed in dark pants and sweater, her hands in fashionable black leather gloves. A cobweb clung to an old-fashioned blue kerchief tied over her hair and under her chin. The fearful look on her face vanished the instant she recognized Ruth and Helma.

"Do *you* have permission?" she asked, untying the scarf and shaking it, then picking off the spiderweb with two gloved fingers before she folded the scarf into a square. Not a hair strayed out of place. "Or did you follow me?"

"Why are you here?" Helma asked. Aside from the flash-light, Lynnette didn't appear to have a weapon.

"And what are you looking for in Meriwether's shop?" Ruth added.

Lynnette glanced over her shoulder into the dark interior. "Nothing."

Ruth snorted and Helma walked to the old-fashioned double doors and tried to pull them open. After a few inches, one of the doors scraped and thumped to a standstill against the ground. The other wouldn't budge.

"Let me," Ruth said. "I'm brilliant with stubborn objects." She grunted, lifted the stuck door and slid it open two feet, rested and pushed it another two feet. The other door wouldn't move but there was now enough light to see inside.

"Nothing?" Ruth repeated. All three women stepped into the shop. Helma had heard metal against metal, and now she spotted freshly disturbed dust on a workbench. At the rear of the bench's surface, against the wall, stood a small metal cabinet with drawers, the size of an old-fashioned card catalog. One of the drawers stood partially open.

"Meriwether had something of mine, that's all," Lynnette said. "I wanted to find it."

"But you didn't," Helma supplied. "What was it?"

"It was private."

"Love letters?" Ruth asked, but Lynnette only gave her a withering glance.

"Do you know Steward Arbor?" Helma asked.

Lynnette pulled off her gloves finger by finger and then folded them together, finger to finger, before she answered. "The Ground Up! director? Only by name. It's obviously an adopted alias. I've never met him."

"Alias," Ruth pondered. "Does he have a police record?"

"I'm sure I don't know," Lynnette said. "Are we finished here? I'd like to go home now."

"I wish I'd had gloves like that a few nights ago," Ruth said, nodding to Lynnette's black gloves. She idly poked around the shop. "I wonder what you're looking for. Not love letters, but private. A receipt for one of his carvings you plan to donate for a tax write-off?"

Helma walked to the metal cabinet and pulled open the drawer six inches. Three loose screws rolled around inside. There were six drawers. The next two were empty, the fourth had a sticky residue in the bottom, and the fifth drawer held small plastic containers nestled inside one another. A stack of screw-on caps in the last drawer obviously fit on the plastic containers.

Helma turned to see Lynnette intently watching her. The remains of an apparatus were bolted to the bench, partially rusted. Helma touched it, trying to recall what was familiar about it.

"Were you here the day Meriwether died?' she asked Lynnette.

"I understood the authorities weren't exactly sure which day Meriwether died."

"They figured it out, give or take a few hours," Ruth said in the casual way that meant she didn't know what she was talking about. "Did you come here with your husband?"

"That's absurd."

"Or maybe Vincent came here and whacked Meriwether out of the tree because you two were having an affair."

"There was *no* affair," Lynnette said, her cheeks flushing. "Why do you keep bringing that up? There was *no affair*."

"Meriwether was my friend," Ruth continued.

She ignored Lynnette's arch, "Him, too?"

"This isn't productive, Ruth," Helma said. "We may as well go back to town." She continued walking around the shop. Someone had removed nearly everything. Only a few odds and ends and the rusted apparatus remained, and that probably because it was bolted down.

Why was it bolted? She returned to the apparatus and nudged it. For stability?

"Why are you futzing with that old Bunsen-burner stand?" Ruth asked. "If you really plan to leave Mrs. Professor to rummage around in a dead man's chest, let's go."

"Bunsen burner?" Helma repeated. That's why it looked familiar. It was outdated and rusted, but very similar to the equipment in their tenth-grade chemistry lab. A pipe extended beyond the stand. She glanced around the shop for chemistry equipment, but didn't see any, just the lone stand.

"What did Meriwether use it for?" Helma asked.

Ruth shrugged. "Maybe to keep his coffee warm, I don't know. I never saw it in action, but then I didn't spend a lot of time out here in his shop."

Lynnette brushed at something Helma couldn't see on her pants. "Do you know?" Helma asked her.

"I have no knowledge of his personal habits," she said primly.

Ruth opened her mouth to speak and Helma gave her a warning look until she closed it again.

"This is interesting," Helma said, tapping the Bunsen-burner stand again. "Could Meriwether have been involved in chemistry as well, like your husband? Perhaps even a student of his? Is that how you met him?"

"This is tiresome." Lynnette said. "I'm leaving."

"We are, too," Helma agreed. "My lunch hour is nearly over. I do have time to stop by the police, though."

Lynnette froze, her lips pursed.

"I wonder if they noticed the stand."

Ruth, always ready to jump in and assist, said helpfully, "They didn't mention it to me. Well, actually, they never talked to me about Meriwether's death, at least not then. I might be able to fill in a couple of blanks for them. What's that detective's name, Helma?"

"Are you speaking of Carter Houston?" Helma asked.

Ruth snapped her fingers as if she hadn't spent the last five years bedeviling Carter at every opportunity. "That's the one. Do you have your cell phone? We can call him right now."

Helma didn't own a cell phone, but she said, "Let's go back to my car. Goodbye, Lynnette."

She had just stepped from the shop, followed by Ruth, when Lynnette called after them in a weary voice, "Wait. I'll tell you the truth."

Chapter 22

The Truth of Time

"You'll tell us the truth about what, exactly?" Helma asked, looking back at Lynnette, who stood in the open door of Meriwether's shop, composed except for her mouth, as if she were biting the inside of her lower lip.

"About Meriwether."

"I knew it," Ruth cut in.

"I recommend you don't take action on what you think you know," Lynnette said coolly.

"I've just been insulted," Ruth said, and paused. "Haven't I?"

"Come outside," Helma told Lynnette. "We can sit on the benches behind the shop."

Fresh saw marks marred the base of one of the benches, the end of which had been carved into the likeness of a bear. Helma thought of the stolen fish marker at the end of Meriwether's driveway. The only reason the bear bench and the salmon-carved bench next to it hadn't been stolen was because they'd been carved from standing stumps. But it wouldn't be long before someone figured out how to take them as they had the fish. She removed a clean tissue from her left pocket and brushed off the seat of the salmon bench. "Sit here," she told Lynnette, then sat down beside her, saving the tableau from resembling an interrogation.

Lynnette squared her shoulders and adjusted the scarf and gloves on her lap. Ruth sat on the other bench and draped her arm over one of the carved bears, her face bright with expectation.

"You visited several times while Meriwether was alive?" Helma gently asked.

Lynnette nodded, her eyes on her lap.

"Did your husband know?"

She shook her head. "But not for the reasons you think. I was *not* having an affair with Meriwether."

"But Meriwether and your husband were acquainted?"

"I honestly don't know. They may have been. Vincent and I sometimes lived separate lives. Most of the people we knew mutually were connected to the college." She cast a dark look at Ruth. "I didn't meddle in his other liaisons."

"Can we just hear about Meriwether?" Ruth asked irritably. "*Why* were you here several times?"

Lynnette refolded the gloves and scarf yet again. She took a deep breath, then said, "I'm older than I look."

Ruth's eyebrows rose and her mouth opened. Helma shot her another warning glance. Ruth shrugged and patted the bear's head.

"I'm actually several years older than Vincent. It was very important to me—and to him—to maintain the facade of an ideal couple. I've kept myself in good shape. I exercise. I buy tasteful clothes."

Ruth tapped her fingers on the bear's left ear.

"And Meriwether?" Helma asked. "Meriwether helped you? As a personal coach?"

Lynnette raised her head and looked at Helma with wet

eyes. "You don't know what it's like to grow older faster than your husband."

"My aunt says we all grow old together, all of us at the same time," Helma offered.

"Yeah, I guess it's all relative," Ruth said gloomily. "How did Meriwether help you? He taught you chain-saw art? Gave you a new lease on life?"

Helma recalled Aunt Em saying that Lynnette had a "beauty secret" to keep her young. And her mother had mentioned Lynnette's malodorous perfume. "Did Meriwether create a . . . potion for you? Some kind of chemical mixture? Is that what the Bunsen-burner stand is for? A component of a formulaic process?"

"An extract," Lynnette whispered.

"Drugs?" Ruth said, sitting up straight. "I don't believe you. Not Meriwether. I'd swear to it." She looked upward, a little more uncertainty on her face. "Although some of these guys way out here—"

"Not drugs," Helma said.

"Yeah, and how do you know?" Ruth challenged.

"It was a skin cream, wasn't it, Lynnette? What was it made from?"

"He didn't tell me. Only that it was a process he developed from a particular type of tree burl. It was very rare, he said."

"You bought it from him?" Helma asked. "In small plastic containers," she added, remembering the containers in the metal cabinet.

"It was very expensive. But it worked." She stroked her cheek as if she couldn't help herself. "I used up my supply and I didn't know what to do. So I drove out here to see if he'd left any in his shop."

"Were you the only person he sold this cream to?"

Lynnette shook her head. "No. There were more, but I don't know who. It was kept very secret. I only heard about it through a woman who goes to my beautician. She made me promise not to tell."

"That devil," Ruth said. "What a racket."

"It wasn't a racket," Lynnette insisted, raising her chin. "It worked."

Helma had seen other people who'd paid too much for a product swear that the product was worth every penny, rather than admit they'd been duped. "Did the concoction have an odor?"

"That was its only drawback," Lynnette said. "I tried to cover it with perfume but I'm not sure it always worked."

"So wait a minute," Ruth said. "Did you steal my paintings?"

"No."

"So when you asked my good friend Helma about my missing paintings, you thought I was going to give away your *beauty* secrets?"

"I knew you'd been to Meriwether's house. You drove past me one morning not far from his driveway and I recognized you from . . . from your attachment to my husband."

Ruth smacked her forehead. "You thought I'd gone to Meriwether's to buy some secret rejuvenator, too, and my painting might expose everyone who bought it from him? Like maybe he'd given me his client list?"

"That was a possibility."

"Well, it didn't happen. I never knew what the guy was up to besides his carvings."

"Did Meriwether concoct any other kind of products?" Helma asked. "Lotions, sprays, cleaning supplies?"

Lynnette shrugged. "I don't know. He had rudimentary laboratory equipment but I wasn't aware of other products. But then, I wouldn't be."

"Did he ever mention where he bought the lab materials?" Helma waved a buzzing fly from her face.

"No. I didn't know him that well, can't you understand that?" Her voice cracked.

"Could he have bought them from your husband?"

"I doubt it."

"From the college? Isn't outdated and obsolete equipment sold at auction every year?"

"That's where my husband obtained some of the equipment for his personal lab," Lynnette said. She absently drew circles on the bench seat with her fingertip.

"And perhaps they'd met at a surplus auction?"

"You're reaching, Helm," Ruth said. "What? You think the two boys were planning to build a cosmetics empire together? Give Estée and Lizzie a little competition?" She clapped her hands. "I know! The Revlon empire caught wind of his remarkable but foul-smelling skin cream and sent out hit men to do him in. Picture them: all dressed up in little black suits like Lynnette here, blowing up labs and knocking guys with chain saws out of trees."

"Meriwether and my husband may have been aware of each other, but I have no knowledge of that," Lynnette said, looking at Helma, not Ruth.

"And now you're transforming your husband's lab into an art studio," Helma said.

Lynnette didn't appear surprised that Helma knew. "Most of his equipment was ruined. The kiln will be delivered next week."

"You're not a friend of Roxy Lightheart's, are you?" Ruth asked.

"I'm not familiar with that name," Lynnette said.

"That's one detail that's in your favor. There's a lot of competition in the art field in this part of the world," she warned Lynette. "Don't count on fame and acclaim."

"I don't care. Sculpture is my passion. I always intended to sculpt when I had the time."

"When you had the time," Ruth, who'd always *made* art her time, repeated, her face darkening.

"Meriwether may have kept a supply of the cream in the house," Helma suggested to Lynnette.

"I already looked," Lynnette told her. "I didn't find any. What'll I do?"

"A cream is only one minor aspect of proper skin care," Helma advised her. "Clean skin and a pleasant attitude can take years off a person's face. And don't forget to drink plenty of water and exercise daily."

Lynnette stared blankly at Helma, and Ruth said, "Don't get her started or she'll be recommending dietary fiber next."

"Fresh fruits and whole grains are sufficient," Helma said.

"See, I told you."

Chapter 23

Skin Deep

They followed Lynnette's white BMW back to Belle-haven from Meriwether's. Lynnette drove at a steady pace and Helma trailed her by four and a half lengths, one length for every ten miles per hour, just as she'd learned in driver's training.

"If Meriwether was selling miracle creams, why didn't he give *me* any?" Ruth asked.

"Perhaps he didn't think you needed them," Helma said tactfully.

Ruth shook her head. "I knew he was struggling to make money, just like every other fool who hears art's siren song. When he said he had a few irons in the fire, I thought he sold firewood or painted houses, not that he was developing his own beauty line."

"We only have Lynnette's word that's what he was doing," Helma reminded her. She turned her windshield wipers on low as they entered a misty rain. Opposing cars had their headlights on.

"I'm not sure I believe her, do you?"

"It fits. Lynnette isn't a woman who'd tell a story on her-self unless she was forced to."

"Because we talked about going to the police. That's the last thing she wants." Ruth pulled a half-eaten chocolate bar from her pocket and took a bite. "Because she's hiding something worse."

"Or she's afraid of the publicity. When Meriwether fell from the tree, he was removing the burl for his skin cream formula."

"'Fell' isn't the operative word. He was pushed or knocked out, something nefarious like that."

"He still *fell*," Helma clarified, "no matter how he *began* the descent."

"All right, already, you win: he fell. But cooking up lig-nins and resins; that explains the smell your mother men-tioned. Like burnt pine trees."

Helma found the odor of burning wood soothing, and the smell of freshly cut wood just as pleasant.

In Bellehaven, Lynnette turned off first, stopping at an upscale hair salon that occupied its own building of steel and glass. Helma slowed her Buick as they passed. The shop was called Le Hair.

"I'll take you home," she told Ruth, "and go back to the library."

"No need. I'll go with you. I'm famished, so I'll run over to Saul's Deli and grab a sandwich. The only thing in my refrigerator is a half-dozen eggs I'm saving to make my own tempera. Gotta keep stretching these artistic muscles."

Helma pulled into the library's staff parking lot, aiming her hood ornament at the flag pole so she was squarely in the center of her assigned spot. She hesitated when Ruth accompanied her toward the staff entrance, but Ruth stopped and held up her hands. "Don't fret. I won't trod into the inner sanctum."

The staff door opened, held by George, and Russell Bell wheeled past him onto the ramp, tires whispering on the concrete. The handsome man had a thoughtful look on his face. "Keep it in mind," George called after him.

"Hey, Russ," Ruth said.

Russell Bell looked up and his smile widened. "Ruth. What are you up to?"

"I could ask you the same thing," she said, leaning down and hugging him. "You realize that's some kind of an honor to come and go through the library's back door? What's the matter, is the front door too narrow?"

"Varying my scenery, that's all," Russell said with law-yerly smoothness. "Are you on your way in for a book or do you have time for coffee?"

"I'm starved. How about we go to Saul's so I can replenish my strength?"

"You got it."

"Lead the way," Ruth said, and as Russell Bell fluidly turned his chair toward the street, she leaned back toward Helma and whispered, "Want me to find out why he's here? I'll be subtle."

Helma had experience with Ruth's "subtlety." "No thank you."

Ruth shrugged and wagged her fingers, following after Russell Bell. "Ta ta."

In her cubicle, Helma dialed her telephone.

"Le Hair," the voice answered. Soft unidentifiable music played in the background. "Danielle speaking."

"An acquaintance mentioned a beautician in your estab-lishment," Helma began, and then stopped. She wondered if beauticians had a privacy policy like librarians did.

"Who would that be?" Danielle asked.

"I'm sorry, I'm not sure of her name, but your client was Lynnette Jensen."

"Oh, Lynnette was just here. You mean Katarina, who does her hair."

"Yes, Katarina. May I—"

"She's usually booked *solid*, but Lynnette . . . we just had a cancellation." There was the sound of rustling paper. "Katarina has an opening at three today or . . ." More rustling. ". . . at ten-fifteen two weeks from Tuesday. Unless you want more than a cut and style. In that case, we're looking at three weeks out."

Helma had worn the same becoming hairstyle since she was sixteen years old and had frequented the same Bellehaven beautician, Clare, at Hair Design, for nineteen years. It had been six weeks since her last haircut; it was time, but . . . She scanned the day's schedule and made the most sensible decision.

"I can be there at three today," she told the receptionist.

"Excellent. Katarina dislikes gaps in her day so this is perfect."

Helma hung up. Once she was in the salon chair, she'd simply question Katarina about Meriwether's magic cream and skip the haircut. She'd pay Katarina for her time, of course, but surely the stylist wouldn't expect the complete price of a cut and style for only a few minutes of conversation.

"I have an appointment at three o'clock today," Helma told Ms. Moon, who'd hurriedly turned over papers on her lap when Helma tapped on the doorjamb.

Ms. Moon sat in her electric chair by the window, a brown clasp envelope between her thigh and chair, the return address almost readable.

Helma did not consider herself a prying woman, definitely not. But she *did* move three steps closer to Ms. Moon, so neither of them would have to raise her voice. The envelope had a Bellehaven return address. She recognized the zip code.

Ms. Moon moved her arm and the address disappeared beneath her elbow. "Three o'clock?" she repeated. Her eyes were distracted.

"Yes," Helma told her. "I'll be back afterward to finish a project I'm working on."

"Mm hmm," Ms. Moon said, and simply sat in her wheelchair, waiting for Helma to leave.

The same unrecognizable soft music she'd heard over the phone was playing when Helma stepped through the glass door of Le Hair. A lulling melody with gently tapped piano keys, or maybe electronic, she thought. The young woman at the counter, who wore a smooth cap of magenta hair, waited without comment until Helma gave her name.

"Oh yes," she said, gazing at Helma's hair. "Katarina will be *thrilled* to work on you."

Helma seated herself on the corner of a leather love seat in the plush waiting area. Only hair and fashion magazines sat on the low table in front of her, so she pulled a book from her bag that she'd checked out from the library, titled *Today's Beauty Industry*.

"Is it Helma?"

She looked up to see an astonishingly thin young woman, her silver hair only an inch long, critically eyeing her. She wore tight black jeans and a black smock. "Come back, please."

Helma followed her into a tiled room with four chairs, all but one holding women in various stages of beautification. Her nose pinched at the chemical odor of hair treatments. The light was low, the walls rosy. A young man busily cleaned up hair from around the chairs with a nearly silent vacuum, reminding Helma of the efficient but ear-splitting vacuum cleaner at the back of her coat closet. If she decided to buy a new one, she'd ask the people at Le Hair the brand of theirs.

Katarina pointed her to the empty chair, and as if the stylist were Ruth sweeping one of her capes over her shoulder, she swept a black cape over Helma's clothes and snapped it at her neck, never taking her eyes from Helma's reflection in the mirror. "You should have come in long ago," she said. A tiny ruby was studded into her left nostril.

"I don't really want a haircut," Helma began.

"That is only the *first* step of what you want, I promise you." She tipped her head this way and that, then turned the chair in a slow circle, eyeing Helma's head in the mirror.

"Only a trim," Helma told her. "There's someone else I usually go to for haircuts."

"Well, it's time for her to choose a new career," Katarina said cheerfully. "She's way out of date." She squinted into the mirror, cupping her hands on either side of Helma's head. "Your hair has great body." With two fingers she lifted the stubborn curl on the left side of Helma's head. "We can use this wayward hair so it becomes part of your hairstyle. I bet you put a curler in it every night trying to tame it down, right?"

Helma nodded, surprised Katarina could tell. As long as she could remember, she'd struggled to tame that particular lock of hair.

"And by the end of the day it's springing out again, right?" She clicked her tongue. "It'll be a lot easier to keep in order if you let me style it."

"It wouldn't spring out?" Helma asked.

"If it did, it wouldn't be noticeable."

Helma considered it. What was it Ruth said? "When people are fussing with personal parts of your body, they're ripe for spilling their secrets."

"All right," she said carefully. "But nothing dramatic."

"No way. Let's wash."

They chatted about the weather and the new grocery store being built on the edge of town while Katarina washed and combed Helma's hair. "Have you ever thought of having your eyebrows shaped?" Katarina asked.

Helma was about to say no, and definitely not, when she

realized Katarina had presented her with an opportunity. "Do you think they need it?"

Katarina arched her own thin brows at Helma in the mirror. "It would bring out the more youthful details in your face."

Helma swallowed, thought of Lynnette and her story, and said, struggling to sound truly concerned, "It's my skin that worries me. It seems to be . . ." She thought furiously; what was that ad she'd heard during the evening news? ". . . prematurely aging."

Katarina stopped separating Helma's hair into sections and studied Helma's mouth and the corner of her eyes. "Actually, it's in quite good shape. What do you use now?"

She named the product she'd seen on her mother's dresser when she was a girl, and Katarina's eyebrows rose. "Do they still make that? My mother used it a million years ago."

"I know," Helma said. "I need something more up-to-date, a cream with more . . . dramatic results. Perhaps you could recommend something new?"

Katarina bit her lip as she worked.

Helma could tell she was considering what to say, so she added, "Or perhaps an old product? Or even a product that's not very well known."

Snip snip went Katarina's scissors.

Helma relaxed. It didn't *look* like very much was coming off. "Expense isn't a concern," she added helpfully.

Katarina combed out another section of hair and took her scissors to it. "Well, a few months ago I would have suggested a particular cream, but it isn't available anymore."

"It's been taken off the market?"

"It was never actually on the market. But the man who had the formula died."

"I'm sorry. And no one else has the formula?"

"Not that I know of. People swore by it." She wrinkled her nose. "It cost a fortune, but the smell was pretty repulsive."

"Oh," Helma said as if she'd just recalled a detail. "I believe I've heard of it. It smelled woodsy."

"That's a kind description. It was made by some guy out in the county and we kept a few jars in the back room for a while. I told some of my customers about it." Her flying hands paused and the scissors stilled. "But I got nervous."

Helma tried to turn and look at Katarina's expression, but the stylist swiveled the chair around so Helma faced the entrance to the waiting room. "Why did you get nervous?"

"Honestly, I didn't think he was careful. Women swore by it, but the quality was uneven, know what I mean? He'd bring in a few jars that smelled like it came out of a nice pine tree and then jars that smelled like a swamp. Sometimes it was runny and other times it was hard as wax. He charged a super-high price and I was afraid a customer would develop a reaction to it and then *we'd* be in trouble."

"He didn't have good quality control?" Helma asked.

"If any. My real feeling, if you want to know, was— Whoops, I think we're ready to blow dry."

Once the blow dryer was turned on, the conversation would end. "Could you make the back slightly more tapered," Helma said, not having a clue what the back actually looked like.

"Only a little or we'll upset the balance." Katarina began snipping away again, and Helma had to remind her of the conversation. "Your real feeling was . . . ?" she asked.

"Oh, Meri—the manufacturer, I mean. He wasn't serious about creating a really *good* cream. He wanted to make money, so he whipped up this soup, put a high price on it, and sold it to the gullible." She slapped her free hand over her mouth, her eyes wide. "I can't believe I said that, when I turned some of my own clients on to it. You won't tell anybody, will you?"

"I certainly don't intend to," Helma assured her.

"Good," Katarina said, and turned on the blow dryer.

Helma closed her eyes while she worked, feeling the warmth of the heated air and the pull of the brushes. Katarina was finished sharing her thoughts about Meriwether's cream.

So Lynnette had told the truth. Whether the cream had any efficacy was debatable. But he'd been sloppy, Katarina believed, not caring about a good product, just money. Had there been other "products" he'd used the Bunsen burner for? Had money really been his only concern?

The blow dryer switched off. "We're finished. What do you think?"

Helma opened her eyes and stared at herself. She blinked. "That's not my usual hairstyle."

"Definitely not. Here, look at the back with this mirror." And she turned Helma in a circle so she could see every side of her creation. "See this area here? Don't comb it after you wash it; just run your fingers through it."

"It's not as smooth."

"It needed a little interest. See how the stubborn part fits right in?"

"And the wisps by my ears?"

"That'll just happen with this cut. Let it."

"My forehead shows more."

"Mm hmm, it makes your eyes look larger."

Helma stared. It wasn't *that* much shorter, yet it was very different.

"Do you like it?"

She tipped her head to the left and the right, then looked at the back again in the mirror. "Yes," she finally said. "Yes, I believe it's quite suitable."

Chapter 24

A Hint of the Southwest

Helma entered the library through the front door and passed Dutch pulling books from the book return. Curiously, he glanced at her and past her as if he hadn't recognized her. Her mind still played over the strange scene with Lynnette.

The book she'd taken to Le Hair hadn't provided any detailed information about cosmetic formulas, since most formulas were proprietary information. But she did discover that tree lignins served as binders and emulsifiers in creams and gels. And wood oils were used in fragrances. Next, she'd research if it was possible to process lignins in a home laboratory.

The staff was leaving for the day, and Gloria, in a pink quilted jacket, a bag in the design of a cocker spaniel over her shoulder, passed Helma as she stood in the stacks, glancing through the index of a book titled *Powers of Wood*. Just as Dutch had, Glory glanced at her and past her, obviously deep in thought of her own. But ten feet past Helma, she emitted a squeak and spun around.

"It *is* you," she said. "Your hair." She pulled a strand of her own red hair as if Helma might not understand the word.

"It's been cut," Helma told her.

"It's . . ." Glory's wide eyes returned to normal. "It . . . you . . ." Now her eyes actually narrowed. "It's a very good haircut." And Glory stood there, eyes still narrowed as she studied Helma's hair.

Helma banished the urge to touch her new hairstyle. "Thank you," she said.

"You look different," Glory continued. "More . . ."

"Thank you," Helma repeated. "Excuse me, please."

She copied five pages from *Powers of Wood* and took them to her cubicle to tuck into her bag. As she entered the workroom, she heard the staff door close as one of the other staff left. The room was silent, lights in the individual cubicles switched off. Ms. Moon's office light was still on, but then she frequently forgot to turn it off.

Helma pulled out the reading list she was developing on personal accounts of World War II. It wasn't all that difficult for patrons to find the books by using the library's online catalog, for what Ms. Moon called "resource discovery," but it sometimes confused people. More and more of the dwindling number of World War II men—and women—asked for stories of their comrades. Next, she thought, she would begin a reading list of the Korean War.

Even as she worked, first glancing at the clock and ascertaining that thirty-five more minutes would make up for the time she'd spent at Le Hair, she turned Lynnette's story over in her mind, searching for its weaknesses. Could anyone *really* covet a product so much and believe it was their only option, be so desperate they'd plunder an abandoned building to find it? Risk embarrassment and possible arrest?

But then, Ruth had broken and entered Roxy's house on a whim of suspicion.

She clicked on the book title, *A Flier Remembers*, and

heard a thump at the other end of the workroom, then a scrape and another thump. She was sure the room had been empty when she'd sat down. Warily, she stood and peered over the walls of her cubicle.

Ms. Moon hobbled toward the large table where books were processed, head bent and a roll of blueprints hugged awkwardly between her chin and neck. Helma had once declined to play a pass-the-orange game that used that same stance.

No electric wheelchair, only a pair of aluminum crutches that she swung clumsily with each tiny step. With a wheeze of exhalation, Ms. Moon dropped heavily into a chair and leaned her crutches against the table. They clunked. Then she began unrolling the blueprints: the director's often-altered dream plans for a new library.

Helma sat down again and made a few more entries before she heard Ms. Moon hum an Andrew Lloyd Webber tune. When Ms. Moon began to sing "Zipadee Doo Dah" in a loud contralto, she realized Ms. Moon believed she was alone in the workroom.

Helma avoided embarrassing people during vulnerable moments, so she packed her bag, and when Ms. Moon loudly warbled "Everything's going my waaaaay," soundlessly exited her cubicle and left the workroom, holding the door so it wouldn't click on her way out.

Turning the corner onto First Street, Helma recognized Ruth striding along the sidewalk toward home, arms swinging, her gait . . . light, in a way Helma hadn't seen since Paul left Bellehaven. She stopped her Buick by the side of the street and Ruth waved and opened the passenger door.

"Hey, thanks. Oh my God, Helm, your hair! When did you get that done?"

"This afternoon. It was the only way I could think of to talk to Lynnette Jensen's beautician."

"Well, *you* certainly benefited from the experience. When do you see the man again?"

"Tonight."

"He'll fall to his knees, you watch. It's good, Helma, really good. In fact, it's absolutely brilliant."

"Thank you."

"So what did the gifted beautician say?"

Helma told Ruth about Katarina—"That has to be a bogus name," Ruth said—and her assertion that Meriwether made and sold face creams strictly as a money maker, that his products weren't carefully manufactured, or even standardized.

"But he put a good one over on a lot of women. That's why he had the Bunsen burner: for his witch's-brew cosmetics. I wish I'd paid more attention—his own little cosmetics lab."

"The lab is his connection to Lynnette's husband."

"Lynnette could have *really* been sneaking around Meriwether's shop to destroy any connection to Vincent, not for the magic elixir."

"I believe her story about the creams," Helma said.

"Yeah, I guess I do, too." Ruth raised her empty hands, "The quest for youth and beauty trumps common sense every time."

"Where's your car? You're not just heading home from your lunch with Russell Bell, are you?"

Ruth turned to look out her window at the progress of the new condos on First Street. "Oh," she said lazily. "We went to his apartment for a sandwich and stuff."

Helma knew better than to delve into what Ruth meant by "stuff." "He must have been a tall man," Helma said.

"He still *is* a tall man, Helma Zukas," Ruth said. "Just not on a vertical plane. But if you lay him out flat, he remains a very satisfying six feet four inches."

* * *

A slip of paper was taped to Helma's door, fluttering in the breeze. Her first thought was that Wayne Gallant had canceled their date. Her second thought was that Wayne Gallant certainly wouldn't leave a *note* to cancel a date with her.

She gently edged up the tape, careful not to pull off Walter David's most recent coat of green paint, and unfolded the paper.

I was here, ta ta!! the note read, with two explanation points. Helma recognized her mother's handwriting. They hadn't had an appointment; her mother did have a key to her apartment, "Just in case of emergency, dear. Don't you think it's a good idea?" But when Helma stepped inside, there was no sign anyone else had entered her home.

Boy Cat Zukas wasn't in his usual place on her balcony, but a movement caught her attention and she spotted the swish of a white-tipped black tail from the roof eave above her sliding glass doors, one of his favorite spots to sit and consider life beneath him, particularly small flying things.

She tapped out her mother's phone number, and when Aunt Em answered, asked if she and Lillian had been to visit.

"Not me," said Aunt Em. "I went with the Sunset Ladies to the pool. On the Silver Gables bus."

"You went swimming?" Helma had never known Aunt Em to swim.

"No, no. It was a free class." Her words failed her. "You get in the water and jump around."

"Water aerobics? You went to an aerobics class at the pool?"

"Only a little jumping. Water came up my nose. Do you want to speak to your mother?"

"Yes, please."

"I'll get her. She's in the bathroom." Aunt Em's voice dropped. "She's dyeing her hair again. 'Autumn sunset.' You tell her to stop before it gives her old-timer's disease. That dye eats into the brain."

"Mother has never listened to me," Helma said.

"She *hears*, she just doesn't *do*. They are two different things. Here she comes. She has a plastic bag over her head. *Mylieu tave*."

"Mylieu tave," Helma answered. *I love you.*

"Yes dear?" Lillian asked.

"I found your note on the door."

"I was just in the neighborhood and stopped by. And you know what, when I got there, a man was walking around with your manager, taking pictures."

"Did you recognize him?" Helma asked.

"No, but he wore one of those old coats like your uncle Mick used to wear."

"A bomber jacket?" Helma asked. "Brown leather with a sheepskin collar?"

"Mm hmm. It gave me a start for a second. He was tall like Mick, too."

Uncle Mick had been one of her father's brothers; Aunt Em's brother, too. And her cousin Ricky's father. He'd been the first of that overlarge, overloud family to die. One by one, until only Aunt Em, the oldest, remained.

"Did he have white hair?"

"He did. Do you know him?"

"He may be a local developer." Helma opened her sliding glass doors and the sounds of children filtered inside her apartment.

"I can't imagine who else would buy your apartments. Have you solved Ruth's stolen paintings yet?"

"No, but I'm sure the police are working on it."

"You do know Ruth is all over town telling people about . . . well, all her most personal secrets, don't you? That show she's putting on: Ruth Revealed. If I didn't know she was your friend, dear, I'd suspect she was trying to draw attention to herself." Her mother paused, waiting, Helma knew, for her daughter to fill in the blanks.

"Do you actually know Lynnette Jenson, Mother?"

"Of course I do."

"On a personal level? She'd recognize you if you met?"

She didn't answer right away. "Maybe not. I'm sure she'd recall meeting me at our events if I reminded her, though. Why? Is she important to your case?"

"I don't have a case, Mother. I was just curious, that's all."

"I *did* hear," Lillian went on—cautiously, Helma thought—"that her husband and Ruth . . . well, you know. They may have been interested in each other for a while. But I don't suppose you want to hear gossip, do you?"

"No, Mother, I don't."

"You miss so much by not, dear," her mother said, and sighed.

Wayne Gallant arrived at 6:15, precisely on time. Helma sat at her table when the doorbell rang. She had just opened a labeled folder from the "Personal" portion of her file cabinet. It was thick with reports and columned pages. She closed it and answered her door.

Wayne glanced at his watch. "Ready?" he asked, smiling at her. And then stopped, his expression turning quizzical. He frowned, but his eyes remained warm and he leaned toward her. "Helma, you look . . . I don't know. Beautiful," he said, and he ducked his head as if surprised at his own words. "You always look beautiful," he amended hurriedly, "but, you look different-beautiful tonight. I'm not sure what it is."

She simply nodded and said, "Thank you, Wayne."

Their date wasn't for dinner, but a travelogue about the Southwest United States, followed by a light meal at a new Irish pub in Bellehaven.

The chief had once been offered a position in New Mexico, which he'd declined, but Helma had detected a certain melancholy longing when he spoke of the Southwest.

The travelogue was scheduled in the building of a defunct social club from the 1920s, now refurbished and rewired for the modern world.

"Have you seen these?" the chief asked as they entered the foyer, pointing to a bulletin board between the double doors.

Helma didn't need to look twice to see what he was referring to. Stapled smack dab in the middle of the cork board, half covering a Parks Department yoga class ad, was a ten-by twelve-inch poster.

RUTH REVEALED. COMING SOON, it read. No date, no time, no gallery name. The only illustration was a perfectly rendered painting of red gloves with dragons stitched onto their backs: the gloves Roxy had threatened to turn over to the police. Helma recognized Ruth's "realistic" style, which she rarely employed. The gloves looked like they'd just been pulled finger by finger from warm hands and dropped onto a tabletop, the curl of fingers still imprinted, the bend of a wrist. Shockingly sensual.

"This is the first one I've seen," Helma said, watching Wayne's face, but he gave no sign that he recognized the red gloves.

"They began popping up around town last night," Wayne told her. "The city could use her skills to promote itself."

Only twenty to twenty-five people sat in a room big enough for 150. If it had been a rainy afternoon in November instead of heading into Bellehaven's glory days of spring, she thought, there would have been standing room only.

A portable movie screen sat slightly askew at the front of the room, the only sign of the impending event. Helma and Wayne sat in the fourth row from the front, both of them receiving glances and nods of recognition from citizens who read or who'd dealt with the police.

Seven o'clock arrived, then 7:10. It was Helma's personal policy to never wait longer than fifteen minutes—for anyone or anything.

At 7:11 someone sat in the chair next to her. "Howdy, Helma. Chief."

It was Boyd Bishop, the long and lean western writer. He touched the air by his forehead as if tipping a cowboy hat.

"Boyd," Wayne acknowledged, and Helma felt him stiffen beside her.

"Mind if I sit here?" he asked.

"Go ahead," Wayne told him in a surprisingly cool voice. Helma wondered if the two men had met another time in less friendly circumstances, at least from the chief's viewpoint. Boyd acted no different than he ever did: easy, relaxed, and slightly amused.

"I got waylaid before I could say hi to you in the library the other day," he told Helma.

"It was a busy day," she said noncommittally, recalling Glory's crash into Boyd.

"Buttons and bangles," Boyd said, grinning. Then he turned to Wayne. "Hey, Chief, I saw you going a few rounds at Goodwin's Gym last week. Good left."

"You box?" Wayne asked.

"No way. Not me."

Wayne looked disappointed.

"Excuse me, folks." A gray-haired man in glasses walked to the front of the room and stood before the screen, his shadow blooming behind him. "Unfortunately I just had a call from our presenter, who's stuck in traffic north of Seattle. We apologize but we have to cancel tonight's entertainment. I hope we can reschedule."

"Darn," Boyd said to Helma. "I was looking forward to a peek at my old home country."

"Too bad," Wayne commented.

"How about if you two join me for a drink," Boyd asked, making a lazy hand motion between Helma and Wayne. It was an awkward moment, saved when Boyd laughed and said, "No problem. I can see you have other plans."

Boyd walked with them to the street. "Need a lift?" Wayne asked him.

"Thanks," Boyd told him, "but I only live a couple of blocks from here. I'll be seeing you. G'night, Wayne." He paused and nodded. "Helma." He smiled and touched the air near his forehead again. "Your hair is very becoming. Very."

Wayne was uncharacteristically quiet during the drive to the pub. Finally, as he stopped at a red light, he turned to her and asked, "Did you change your hair?"

"Only a haircut," she told him.

"I see. It's nice."

"Thank you."

The pub was quiet, lit by small table lamps. Penny-whistle music played low enough that it didn't disturb conversation. Helma ordered a glass of white wine and Wayne settled on a glass of foamy dark beer in a British pint glass. They shared a plate of vegetables and an order of roasted potatoes.

"I had an interesting conversation with Lynnette Johnson," Helma said as she cut a slice of roasted potato into pieces.

"No talk of murder, mayhem, or stolen paintings tonight," he said, smiling at her. "Carter's in charge of this one. He's the man who has the answers."

"I would think you'd want to assess the—"

"*Shhh,*" he whispered, and Helma's arms prickled. He leaned back in his chair. "I've wanted to talk to you." He took a deep breath, his eyes never leaving hers. "About us."

"Us?" Her voice squeaked and she cleared her throat. "Us?" she repeated.

He nodded. "I care about you, Helma. I have for a long time. Years. I think it's time we planned a future together."

She gazed into his warm blue eyes, felt her heart pound slow and deep in her breast. The Irish music faded.

"A future," she repeated helplessly.

"A future," he said, and gently plied her fingers from her wineglass to hold her hand. "This can't be a surprise. Don't you agree it's time?"

Helma Zukas's hand responded to the pressure of his fingers. Her mouth felt like the one time as a child when her cousin Ricky had tricked her into tasting peanut butter.

She couldn't speak. This was the natural consequence of their long association. It was the circuitous route they'd been following for years. Forward, as she'd reminded Ruth, the only direction available. It was what she'd wanted, the outcome she'd hoped for since he first questioned her during a murder investigation years earlier.

Helma could not understand why her mouth wouldn't open. She tried, truly.

And no words came.

The chief blinked. His grip on her fingers relaxed. "Helma?"

She swallowed—hard. Where did they come from, the words she was shocked to hear herself say?

"I want . . . I want . . ." She paused to breathe. He leaned closer. She felt his breath on her cheek. She leaned back, but only a few inches. "But I'm not ready. Not yet. I need more time."

He gently released her hand, saying lightly, "Is this a brush-off?"

"If you know me at all," she told him, "you know I would never 'brush you off.'"

"I *do* know that. I'm sorry."

Now *she* reached out and took his hand in her own. "I

mean exactly what I said. I need a little more time." She
squeezed his hand. "And I'm surprised that I do."

He smiled and touched her cheek. "Then time is what
we'll allow. We've waited long enough already, a little more
can't hurt."

"Thank you," she said.

In her apartment, during the darkest of the night, Helma did
what she often did during puzzling times. She Cut Things
Out. Using a pair of imported Scherenschnitte scissors that
Ruth, who had discovered her habit, gave her for her birthday
two years ago, Helma began with last month's *Smithsonian*
magazine. So precise that not a fraction remained of the surroundings or was excised from the illustration. She cut out
two leopards, then the letters of the word "Smithsonian."

She opened the magazine and cut out the editor's head,
then excised the colorful figures occupying a South American landscape. A llama, two girls weaving, an ultramod-
ern hotel, storm clouds, palm trees, rare flowering orchids,
a kitten without eyes, rubies found in Egypt, a mummy, a
double rainbow. The pieces grew on her coffee table, each
perfect image after the next. She did not think, she did not
muse, she Cut Things Out.

And so intent was she that she didn't notice Boy Cat
Zukas creep onto the back of her sofa and lurk there, only
inches away from her head, his eyes burning on every move
her hands made.

Chapter 25

Saturday Reflections

Saturday morning dawned cool. Helma packed a cardboard box with last year's towels and rugs to deliver to the Salvation Army. After doing that, she planned to walk along Bellehaven's waterfront for forty-five minutes. When she donned her light jacket, she discovered that in her haste to avoid Ms. Moon in the workroom the evening before, she'd left her gloves at the library.

"Oh, Faulkner."

She had other gloves, and by noon she wouldn't need them anyway, but the forgotten gloves best complemented her pale green jacket. She'd simply drop by the library and pick them up. It would only take a moment.

A quarter mile from the Bayside Arms a fire truck blocked both lanes of the street. The bay was flat; a flock of sea gulls fought over something unfortunate in the water. The sky to the west was clear, the San Juan Islands dark against the morning sky. She knew it would be a mostly sunny Saturday.

A wooden barricade with a mounted flashing yellow

light had already been erected, so whatever had happened was old news. Helma parked along the street and walked up to the fireman standing beside the barricade. The air was filled with the grinding of heavy machinery and the beep, beep, beep of trucks backing up.

"What's happened?" she asked. "And how extensive an area does this affect?"

"Burst water line," he said, nodding in the direction of the fire truck. "It'll be an hour or so. Take one of the side streets over the Slope." He gazed more closely at her. "You're from the library, right?"

"Yes, I'm a librarian," Helma assured him.

"Didn't recognize you at first."

Helma kept her hands at her sides, despite, once again, that curious urge to touch her hair. She'd awakened that morning and discovered the new hairstyle to be as . . . in order as it had been after Katarina had cut it. Even the stubborn curl had melded into the hairstyle, just as Katarina had promised.

Helma drove up the hill of the Slope, which bordered the bay, intending to turn onto Fourteenth Street to circumvent the blocked road. Lynnette Jensen's house was only two blocks farther up the street. There certainly wasn't any harm in passing her house, and as long as she was doing that, it certainly didn't make any difference whether she drove past the house on the street in front of it or on the alley behind it.

She chose the alley, and was forced to stop twenty feet before reaching Vincent Jensen's lab and soon-to-be Lynnette's studio. Two green plastic garbage cans were positioned next to the lab. One of them had fallen over.

Charred wood and distorted equipment—probably from the heat of the fire—spilled into the alley. A blackened chunk about a foot across lay in the center of the alley, definitely large enough to scrape the bottom of her Buick.

She could have backed out to avoid the chunk, but Helma rarely reversed the direction she was heading. Leaving her engine running, she stepped from her car and, using a paper towel from beneath her seat, picked up the lump of material. It wasn't as heavy as it looked. She'd place it in the standing garbage can and be on her way.

But at that moment a nearby door slammed and she straightened, the wad in her hand, to see Lynnette Jensen and her helper, Brianna, exiting the rear of Lynnette's house. They were talking, their heads turned toward one another.

Naturally, Helma wasn't about to drop trash into Lynnette's garbage can in front of Lynnette and complicate her presence. They hadn't seen her, so she returned to her car, its door still open, set the wad on the floor of the passenger seat and gently closed her door, taking just enough time to tear open a disposable wipe she kept in her glove compartment and clean the soot off her hands before she put her car in gear.

Lynnette and Brianna had reached the lab door when Helma drew even with them. They stopped and stared at her. Helma gave a friendly wave and smoothly continued down the alley, back into the street, and on to the Bellehaven Public Library.

The library was open on Saturdays but only manned by a limited staff, and those only in the public area of the building. On Saturdays the workroom was usually dark and empty, the door from the public area closed and locked.

Helma entered through the front doors, stopping at the circulation desk. Dutch, who now took Mondays off and worked on Saturdays, nodded to her, his hands paused on the computer keyboard as he glanced at the wall calendar that held the staff schedule. "Good morning. You're not scheduled to work today."

"No. I just stopped by to pick up a personal item."

He nodded again and turned his eyes to his screen. Harley

Woodworth sat at the reference desk, eyeing her approach, the expression on his face so morose it appeared his eyes drooped.

"She's done it now," he said, shaking his head.

"Who?" Helma asked.

"I told her she'd end up back in the hospital."

A young man stepped between Helma and Harley. "It's jammed again," he said in frustration, waving an arm toward the bank of computers and printers. "This is the third time. Can't you guys buy better printers?"

Harley pushed back his chair, and Helma told the young man, "New printers purchased by the Friends of the Library will be installed next week."

"That doesn't help me today."

"But it does," Helma corrected. "The organization purchased them, through fund-raising; therefore, it's no money out of your pocket by way of higher taxes."

"That's my parents' problem, not mine," he said and stalked after Harley, toward the offending machines.

The workroom door easily swung open, and at first Helma thought Harley had forgotten to lock it. But as she stepped inside, she caught sight of the desk light over the processing table and smelled the spicy odor of garlic and basil. She stepped past the cubicles and approached the table.

Ms. Moon sat in the same spot as she had the evening before, when Helma left work. The director hunched over her library blueprints, a pencil in her hand and several others scattered around her. A cup and four diet soda cans, their tops popped, sat on the table next to a pile of crumpled napkins and a cardboard pizza box. It was empty except for a stack of pizza crusts.

Helma cleared her throat and Ms. Moon looked up. Her eyes were bagged, her blond hair untidy, as if she'd been running the pencils through it. And she still wore the same suit skirt and blouse as yesterday, although now the blouse was untucked and wrinkled. Her broken leg was propped on the chair across from her.

"Oh. Hi, Helma," she said, her expression distracted, a smear of red pizza sauce on her cheek.

"Ms. Moon. Have you been here all night?"

A look of surprise crossed her face, then a smile, unguarded and somewhat sheepish, brightened her eyes. She glanced at the wall clock. "I believe I have. Take a look at this, would you?"

Helma braced herself for another of Ms. Moon's sweeping modifications to her fantasy library. Would it be floor-to-ceiling pillars? More windows in her office? A wing devoted to psychic phenomena?

"Your hair's very attractive," Ms. Moon said, and Helma stiffened. Praise from Ms. Moon was not normally a good sign.

"Thank you," Helma acknowledged. She waited for a comment to counteract the compliment, but when Ms. Moon didn't say any more, she asked, "May I ask you a question about the site of your fall?"

"Go ahead."

"The materials that fell . . ."

"They made an impressive mess, didn't they? All those brochures and floppy bindings?"

"Is that why you were on a kick stool in the Local Government area? To help the mayor? Or to make the most mess?"

Ms. Moon laughed. "Helma, you *are* a suspicious one." But she didn't deny it.

"You're not using your wheelchair."

The director tapped her pencil against the aluminum crutches and they clunked hollowly. "The doctor said I could graduate to crutches." She shrugged as if she'd said something naughty. "Actually, he said I could have used crutches from the very beginning."

"But you chose a wheelchair."

"I was trying to make a point."

"And did you?"

Ms. Moon frowned and said with unusual candor. "*Using* a wheelchair made a point. Take a look."

She touched the pencil to the blueprints of the main floor of her dream library. Helma leaned closer and saw the dotted lines beside the original blue lines. "You're altering the library's layout?"

"Widths. The aisles between stacks, outside the rest-room doors. The location of trash cans. And an alternative to kick stools. More low shelves. *This* is the plan our voters are going to love. They'll vote for it, I'm sure of it."

"I understood the plans already met ADA standards," Helma said.

"They do." Ms. Moon was thoughtful. She scrunched her eyebrows and drew another dotted line. "Sitting in a wheelchair was meant to accomplish one thing, but, I don't know, I didn't realize what it *felt* like." She looked up at Helma, not the scheming or la-la Ms. Moon, just someone who'd had a thoughtful moment.

"A wheelchair is not very convenient," Ms. Moon said before she bent back to her blueprints.

Helma found her gloves beside her container of M&Ms and paused to choose a plain brown candy

Her phone rang.

"I knew you'd be there," Ruth said. "Where else on a Saturday morning, but at work. Geesh."

"And what were you doing before you called me, Ruth?" Helma asked, tucking her gloves into her purse.

"Hah, you thought I was going to say, 'Painting,' and then you'd say, 'That's work, isn't it?' thereby negating my disgust with your bondage to that place. Well, you're wrong. I was out in the real world picking up a couple of new canvases, blank ones, and surprise, surprise, my beloved blue beetle, which I'd only left for a minute, just a frigging minute in front of the store, was towed."

"Why, Ruth? You don't have to pay the parking meter on the weekends."

"There wasn't a spot in front of the store, so for just sixty seconds I double parked and ran in. Wouldn't you know the other guy complained? I got to see my car's tail end going around the corner on State Street. I was only gone a minute, two at most."

"And now you'd like a ride to the impound lot? I believe it's out near the airport."

"Nah. That can wait, but I've got all these canvases to cart home. Can you do a friend a favor and give me and my load a ride? They should fit in your backseat, no problem."

Helma hesitated, remembering the box of towels for the Salvation Army.

"I'm on a roll," Ruth said. "This'll save my life. If I can finish these up, I'll have enough for the show. Forget my car for a few days."

Helma glanced at her watch. "All right. I'll be there in five minutes."

It was fortunate it wasn't raining because Ruth stood in front of Benny & Strom's Art Supplies with a stack of already stretched canvases wrapped in brown paper propped against a parking meter. Helma wasn't at all sure they'd fit in her backseat.

"Then let's put them in the trunk," Ruth said when she voiced her doubts. "Old cars like this have trunks big enough to house a family of four."

She was right; the canvases fit more easily when they were slid flat into the Buick's trunk rather than angled into the backseat. Ruth hummed an irritating song that had only three notes while she fussed over the canvases and then gently closed the trunk, saying, "Ta da! Let's go."

"So how was the date last night?" Ruth asked as she sat in the passenger seat. "Ouch. What's this?" She leaned down and retrieved the chunk of fused materials, holding it up.

"I found it in the alley behind Lynnette Jensen's. It's from her garbage can."

"*You* went digging through her garbage can?"

"It must have fallen out. The can was tipped over."

"So what were you doing there?"

"Broadway was blocked this morning by repairmen so I had to drive up and over the hill."

"And through the alley we go?" Ruth sang out. "Clever, clever. What else did you reconnoiter?"

"Nothing. It's big enough to damage the underside of my car so I picked it up."

"And decided to keep it as a souvenir?"

"Lynnette and Brianna came out of the house at that moment. It seemed easier to simply take it with me."

Ruth played with the wad, turning it this way and that, her hands growing blacker. "Do you know how many criminals have used that for an excuse: 'It just seemed easier, officer.'"

"Well, it did. Will you be able to finish all these canvases before your show?"

But Ruth was holding up the misshapen blob in the light. She set it on the dashboard and turned it. "Feels like plastic."

"It has soot on it," Helma warned her.

"I know this color," Ruth said, ignoring her.

"It isn't a color. It's burned and melted."

"No," Ruth said, pointing at a crack. She turned it toward her and Helma winced at the way it scraped across her dashboard. "See it?"

"No. It appears colorless to me."

"You don't have my artistic awareness," Ruth said. "It's pink, a specific shade of pink. Oh, geez. Stop the car."

Helma did, so abruptly that the driver of a car behind her blasted his horn twice. "What's wrong?"

Ruth had pressed her hands to her head and was leaning over the blob as if to protect it.

Helma motioned for the car behind her to go ahead and pulled into the driveway of a computer repair store. "Ruth," she said again.

"I know what it is," Ruth said. "I know what it is. It's all coming clear to me now."

"Tell me what you are talking about, please."

"The pink. Coral fuchsia. It's the color that ties the two men together. Meriwether and Vincent. Woodsman and professor. I know what it is." Ruth was making no sense, repeating herself in woeful tones. "I know what it is. Why didn't I see it? It's everywhere. How could I have missed it? What an idiot."

"How are they connected by pink?" Helma asked, beginning a logical series of questions.

"I saw it at both their houses—well, not exactly *in* their houses but in Vincent's lab and at Meriwether's." She pushed the mass closer to Helma as if that was answer enough.

Helma peered intently at the dirty colorless blob, failing to see anything but a tiny blush of pink within the mass. "What is it?" she asked.

"A melted tree tube," Ruth said. "The same tree tubes that Ground Up! hangs around all those trees they plant under cover of darkness. Coral Fuchsia."

Chapter 26

The Trouble with Color

"Tree tubes?" Helma repeated. "Are you saying that both Meriwether and Vincent had Ground Up! tree tubes at their residences?"

"Yes, that is exactly what I'm saying. I saw them. God, why didn't I make that connection sooner? Coral fuchsia. That distinctive, in-your-face color. You know how I get when I paint; I throw whatever's in my head on the canvas, and I bet you a million dollars I included coral fuchsia in both paintings."

Helma touched her finger to the crack, trying to see the Ground Up! shade that Ruth claimed was there. She closed one eye. Maybe, if one could see past the haziness of dirt and other products, there *might* be a tinge of Ground Up! coral fuchsia. "If the tree tubes are the connection that the thief . . ."

"And murderer," Ruth interrupted.

". . . was aware of," Helma continued, "then he or she had to be very familiar with the tubes himself. Or herself."

"Like someone from Ground Up!"

"Ground Up!'s been radical—planting trees illegally—but is that so radical that Meriwether and Vincent would hide any affiliation with them?" Helma asked.

Ruth made a face. "Vincent probably would choose a low profile because of all the college connections; extremism wouldn't benefit his career, I bet. I don't know about Meriwether. He was a little on the fringe himself. Chain-saw art and Ponce de Leon cold creams? He probably wouldn't *condemn* a little radical environmentalism."

"But you didn't know about the creams, either."

"True. I did not know about the creams. Let's go see Carter Houston. I want to see that strip of painting he took. It's important. Trust me."

Helma drove to the police station and snugged her Buick up next to a handicapped space, where there was always more room on either side of her car than in a normal space, room to open and close car doors without risking dents.

The receptionist looked up when they entered. "Oh, Miss Zukas," she said when she saw Helma. "The chief's not here today."

"Then is Carter in his office where *he* should be?" Ruth asked.

"Detective Houston?" the receptionist asked.

"The very one," Ruth said. "Is he still imprisoned down this way?" She pointed down the hall to the left where a series of small offices lined the corridor.

"Let me call him for you," she said, lifting the receiver.

"That's all right. I want to surprise him."

As Ruth led the way toward the corridor, Helma saw the receptionist punching buttons as fast as she could.

Carter Houston had the phone to his ear when Ruth tapped out "Shave and a Haircut" on the jamb of his partly open door. He nodded, both to the telephone and to Ruth, then stood.

"Miss Winthrop, your car was legitimately and legally towed. There's nothing I can do about it."

"Why, Carter, you don't think I'd come here on a Saturday asking you for special favors, do you? I'll take care of my car later, all by myself."

He squinted suspiciously at her. "Then why are you here?"

"Don't be so scared. Nice to see you in your casual week-end clothes."

Carter wore the exact same clothes he wore during the week, right down to his spotlessly shiny shoes.

"I just want to see what's rightly mine."

Helma was sure that Ruth was the only person who could make Carter Houston take a step backward. "And that is?" he asked.

"That little strip of painting that was left on my pillow the night my house was broken into, what else? You said you'd return it but I haven't found it sitting on my doorstep yet."

"We're not finished examining it."

"Then can I visit it?"

"Why?"

"Carter. *You* asked me to recreate my stolen paintings, remember? I need a clue as to what they looked like. Come on, give me a break. My show's coming up pdq."

He considered Ruth, then Helma, rocking back on his wing tips and straightening his blue striped tie.

"Carter," Ruth said softly, drawing out his name, and his cheeks pinked.

"Wait outside for a second and I'll see what I can do," he told them, pointing toward his door.

They waited. Ruth put her back against the corridor wall and pushed her shoulders and the small of her back into it, sliding up and down the wall as if doing posture exercises. Helma remained next to Carter's door, hearing Carter speak into his telephone but unable to make out the words.

"If only I hadn't been so wrapped up in my own broken-hearted little drama," Ruth muttered. "I may as well join a convent."

"You're not Catholic."

"I'm being rhetorical, Helma, just like my life."

Finally Carter emerged from his office, his composure restored. "If you'll follow me," he told them, and walked off down the corridor without actually waiting to see if they were behind him.

He led them to a door with a sheet of paper crookedly taped to it. LAB 2 was printed on it in black marker, and he held it open for them. A young woman in a lab coat looked up. "Jerry's bringing it," she told Carter.

The lab felt temporary: file cabinets askew, folding tables, a scarred desk so at odds with the rest of the furniture that it had probably been pulled from storage. The room reminded Helma of the library workroom. Not enough space, and not enough money for new space.

A few moments later a gray-haired man in a lab coat emerged from a back office carrying a long plastic box covered in clear plastic. He set it on the desk and took a stiff backward step, as if guarding expensive jewels.

"You're in my light, Carter," Ruth said, and the detective stepped to the side so Ruth could peer into the box. Helma joined her.

The strip of canvas lay on a piece of heavy white paper. It appeared as intact as the last time Helma had seen it at Ruth's house. Ruth bent low, bumping the box with her elbow. "Sorry," she told the technician, who'd leaped forward with his hands out to catch it.

"See here, Helm," Ruth said in a low voice, perhaps too low for Carter to hear. "Just beneath that black leek-shaped object. Coral fuchsia. Both paintings had it, I swear. I remember mixing in a little blue to capture just the right shade."

Helma studied the pinkish shade. She couldn't have sworn it was the same pink as the Ground Up! tree tubes but there was definitely a similarity.

Carter had inched closer to them, and Ruth straightened, raising her voice. "Looks good, Carter. I like the way you're keeping it all safe for me. Did you find any evidence on it?"

"It was cut with a box opener," the technician said, and Carter shot him a reproving look. He shrugged.

"That's not news," Ruth said, although Helma suspected it was, and she was only trying to irritate Carter. "I already told Carter that." She smiled sweetly at the detective. "Thanks, Carter. Now I'm going right home to begin those new paintings for you."

When they were back in Helma's car, Ruth tapped her finger against the block of material Helma had picked up behind Lynnette's house. "This contains at least part of a tree tube. So what do we do now? Should I have shared my little revelation with him? That Meriwether and Vincent were covert members of Ground Up!"

"I'd like to ask Brianna a question first," Helma told her. "I'm sure she's still at Lynnette's house."

"What? Whether Brianna shared face cream with Lynnette? Maybe the face cream was an excuse. Lynnette delivered messages between the two men. Or tree tubes. We should have tricked her into opening her trunk to see if it was full of coral fuchsia tree tubes."

Helma turned up First Street, toward the Slope, and said to Ruth. "I saw your gloves poster last night."

"You did? What do you think, will it stir up curiosity?"

"Probably. It's a realistic execution of your gloves."

"That's what I thought." She wiggled her fingers. "Oh, these magic hands."

"But why paint the gloves that tie you to Roxy's prowl?" Helma asked. She stopped to allow a woman with three toddlers to cross the street.

"I'm defusing her. If she really does turn in the gloves, half the police force will have already seen the posters. She'll be late for the party and less believable."

Vincent's lab door stood open and the trash cans had been righted, one of them overflowing with more charred unrecognizable objects as well as items that made Helma's heart lurch: swollen and ruined books, some spiral bound, others the size and thickness of textbooks.

"Are you going in?" Ruth asked.

"Yes."

"What will you say to her, Helma? 'Where's your stash of tree tubes?' I don't want to face that woman again. Honest. She'd like to rip out my eyes."

"I understand that," Helma said, using the paper towel to reach for the blob. "You can wait here."

"Not likely. Maybe I can assist you with one of my sharp verbal comebacks."

Sounds of banging came from the lab, and when Helma's eyes adjusted to the interior, she recognized Brianna. Lynnette wasn't present.

"Hi," Brianna said, pulling off a paper mask and grinning. "I love your hair." She wore jeans and a sweatshirt, her hair tucked under a baseball cap. Her clothes, her flesh, were smeared with ash and dirt. And in her hand she held a hammer she was using to break apart a half-burned shelf attached to the wall. The rest of the lab was empty, stripped, reminding Helma of Meriwether's lab.

"Thank you," Helma told her, taking two more steps inside. "You have a big project ahead of you."

"Yeah. My boyfriend's coming to help tomorrow, but I think I'll have most of it done by then." She said this with a slight raise of her chin.

Helma held up the melted block. "This was in the alley this morning and I picked it up so I wouldn't run over it. Did it come from the lab?"

Brianna frowned at the mass, then took it from Helma with gloved hands. "Oh yeah. I threw it out yesterday. I saw the dogs had been fooling around with the cans."

"What is it?"

Brianna turned it toward the light. "Looks like a bunch of plastic that got melted together in the fire." Her face saddened as she remembered.

"But you don't recognize it as a specific object?"

Brianna shook her head. "I've tossed out a lot of stuff like that. It was probably from one of his experiments."

"What was he experimenting on?"

"*For* class experiments, I mean. Assignments. I cleaned out some shelves of ingredients I recognized from our class projects. Not the lethal chemicals; those are gone. He was a real hands-on professor."

"Can you tell me about some of his assignments?" Helma was aware of Ruth shifting impatiently in the doorway.

"Soil microbes, photodegradation, lysines, kinetic studies." She shrugged, looking far away. "Lots of stuff."

"Did he provide you with the material to do the experiments?"

"He did, for standardization. Otherwise it would be hard to tell if we got the answers right."

"Do you know if Professor Jensen was interested in environmental causes?"

"Some. We talked about chemical effects on the environment, but that was part of school." She paused, remembering him. "He wanted us to defend our findings, like he was training us to face skepticism. And he didn't talk much about his private life. Most of what I know came after he . . . after I started helping Lynnette."

"Where *is* Lynnette?" Ruth asked.

"She had a meeting with the mayor." Brianna dropped her voice and said to Helma. "*You* probably know what that's about."

"No, I don't," Helma told her, puzzled.

"She wants to be appointed to the library board."

"Thank you, Brianna. May I have that back?" She nodded to the chunk.

"This? Oh sure."

"Oh. One more thing," Helma said as she turned back in the garage door. "Have you ever been to Meriwether Scott's property out in the county?"

"Not me. But I know he's dead. Lynnette told me. She cried when she talked about it."

Ruth's attention perked up at that. "Like she was broken-hearted?"

"I don't know. I just saw tears in her eyes, that's all."

"She must have seen a wrinkle in her future."

Ruth guffawed and Brianna gazed at her blankly.

"They were rabid tree planters," Ruth said to Helma, waving to Brianna, who stood in the lab doorway watching them leave. "Vincent and Meriwether, sneaking around together in the dark, shoving trees in the dirt, hiding their passion from wives and lovers."

"Then why were they killed?"

"Another one of the Ground Up! people didn't like how Meriwether and Vincent were taking over. Maybe Vincent proposed running the organization by *Roberts' Rules of Order* and they saw their power being eroded. Mr. Steward Arbor even changed his name to support his cause. If he wasn't in control of Ground Up!, he'd have to spend his life pruning ivy. Or maybe a landowner caught them planting Douglas firs where he wanted to build a chicken coop, I don't know. Let's go share this with your chief of police."

"He's not in, remember?"

"Then how about Detective Houston, my very own personal favorite? He could benefit from a little career assistance."

"It would make more sense to return to Meriwether's property one more time and find tree tubes in his trash or on his property. That would firmly tie the two men together."

"You're saying that my sense of color isn't proof enough?"

"Maybe not to other people."

"Are all librarians like this?"

"Like what?"

"Always having to nail down every last detail before they make their move."

"Only the best ones," Helma assured her.

Chapter 27

Boots and Art

"Okay. Fine. We'll go to Meriwether's, but we have to swing by my house so I can drop off my canvases and pick up my Wellies." Ruth held up a foot encased in a strappy sandal. Her toenails were painted so deep a shade of red they at first appeared black.

"That's reasonable," Helma told her. Ruth's house was only three blocks out of the way. "And I need to pick up my shoes at my apartment."

"Slow down, would you?" Ruth said irritably. "Oh damn. I've got company. I wonder who that is."

A blue van was parked in Ruth's driveway. "I believe it belongs to Roxy Lightheart," Helma said as she parked in front of Ruth's house. "I recognize it from her arrival at Saul's Deli."

Ruth groaned. "There she is, and she's seen us."

Roxy sat on the steps of Ruth's small front porch, watching them. Her bushy blond hair was plaited into two fuzzy braids.

"This is between you two," Helma told Ruth.

"Yeah, yeah. And you don't want to get involved. So

just get out and stand by so you'll be a witness when she confesses—or the shooting begins."

Ruth wearily climbed out of the car and walked toward her house. Helma got out, too, and followed, staying far enough back so she wouldn't interfere. Roxy sat very still, her eyes on Ruth. She held an object in her hands. And as they approached the porch, Helma recognized Ruth's red gloves. She stopped near a new garden plot Ruth had dug but would probably never plant, close enough to hear them.

"So are you going to turn those over to the police?" Ruth asked Roxy, nodding toward her red gloves.

The frenzied anger was gone. Roxy's eyes were red, her expression still and resigned. "No. I'm bringing them back to you."

"Why?" Ruth asked. "Because you've got a more diabolical plan?"

Roxy looked down at the red gloves, which she'd folded together as Lynnette had folded hers, finger-to-finger. "No," she said. "I don't."

"Because you already did the worst: you stole my paintings."

"No. I don't know who stole your paintings."

"Then, second worse: you killed Vincent and Meriwether."

A corner of Roxy's mouth twitched and she looked away. "I cared about Meriwether," she said in a soft voice. "Very much."

"Sorry," Ruth told her gruffly.

"I realized I can't compete, that's all."

Ruth stood with hands on hips. "What's the punch line here?"

"There isn't one."

"This is not computing," Ruth said, frowning down at her.

"I gave up on having a show," Roxy said. Her voice caught. "You're a better artist than I am."

"Now who told you that?" Ruth asked, sounding genuinely insulted.

"It's true. I've tried for years to convince one of the galleries to give me a show. I've sold at every crafts fair and every bazaar in three counties. I've even sold on the Internet. I thought this show was going to be my big break. But really, it was a pat on the head so they could fill space." Roxy shrugged. "You came along, and poof—my show was canceled for yours."

"I thought yours was just postponed," Ruth said.

Roxy shook her head. "Cheri has no intention of giving me a date if she can get a . . ." She made quotation marks in the air. ". . . *real* artist. I'm her last-resort crafts peddler."

Ruth leaned against the porch railing and considered Roxy, who was wringing Ruth's red gloves like wet laundry.

"Listen," Ruth said to her, and waited until Roxy stopped wringing and looked up. "I was just going to call Cheri. I've had a . . . family emergency come up and there's no way I can finish enough paintings in time for the opening."

Helma had to look away from the naked hope on Roxy's face.

Ruth shrugged. "I'll just mention that you're ready to step in. Whatever happens after that is up to you guys."

"That's—" Roxy began.

"I've gotta go," Ruth said, taking the red gloves from Roxy's hand and grabbing her blue Wellies from the porch, where each boot lay on its side.

On their way to Helma's apartment, Helma said, "That was very generous of you, Ruth."

"I just wanted my gloves back before she ruined them," Ruth said.

"Your canvases are still in the trunk. If you want, you can leave them in my apartment until we get back."

Ruth considered the offer, then nodded. "Good idea. I don't want them bouncing around back there while we roam the backwoods of America."

TNT was stretching against the outside wall of the Bayside Arms, one foot precariously close to a bed of irises. He stepped away from the wall when he saw Ruth pulling her canvases from Helma's trunk.

"Let me," he said, reaching for the big rectangles.

"Gladly, sir," Ruth said, relinquishing them.

He took the building stairs two at a time, rhythmically, like an extension of his exercise routine, and waited for them to join him at Helma's door.

Helma unlocked the door and asked him, "You used a word a few days ago, and I've been unable to find the definition. 'Darnik.'"

He laughed and repeated it, rolling the *r*. "Darnik. The bane of my younger years." He leaned the canvases against Helma's kitchen wall. "It's a frozen piece of cow manure. My brothers were keen to throw darniks at me. You can be sure I aimed a few in their direction, too."

"I like that," Ruth said. "A darnik."

"Roll the *r* more," TNT advised her. "Give it authority."

"Darnik," Ruth said, savoring the sounds.

Helma's hiking boots had been cleaned and returned to their box in Helma's closet, shelved between HEELS—BLACK and HIGH TOPS—RED, left from a long-ago canoe outing.

She sat on her bed to change her shoes and returned the empty box to her closet. She was ready.

In Helma's kitchen, Ruth stood beside the table, her lips moving, the folder Helma had been studying the evening before open in her hand.

"Oh boy," she said, looking at Helma with wide eyes. "Holy Toledo. Stars and Mars. Double Darnik. Is this *yours*?"

"That's private information."

"It *is* yours." She held up a columned balance sheet. "How'd you do this?"

"The library maintains an array of excellent investment sources, several updated daily. Compound interest is also very powerful."

Ruth gazed at the sheet, shaking her head. "Investments. You've been investing?"

"Yes, I have."

"You could buy the Taj Mahal. How'd you do this?"

"You're repeating yourself, Ruth." Helma gently removed the sheet from her hand and returned it to the manila folder, then closed it. "It's private information," she repeated. "Let's leave now."

Ruth followed Helma to her car, repeating a series of soft expletives punctuated by her newly learned word, "Darnik."

Chapter 28

Interrupted Silence

"This sunny day won't last much longer," Ruth said, looking at a spreading bank of clouds in the western sky as they drove, the leading edges as defined as the ribboned binding of a gray blanket.

She sat back and picked at a blot of green paint that had dried on her pants. "So if we don't find any tree tubes at Meriwether's, what does that mean?"

"Where did you see them at his house?" Helma asked.

"I wish I could remember. I'm a color junkie and that's what attracts my attention, more than the situation. That coral fuchsia is an attention grabber. It's at least a visual blight on the environment."

"If you noticed the color, it had to have been in a prominent place or you wouldn't have included it in the paintings," Helma said, attempting to keep Ruth on track. "In his shop?"

"Maybe." Ruth's forehead scrunched as she thought. "I also think other places. Maybe in the woods, or the house. Oh hell, let's just wait until we get out there.

Now that I know what I'm looking for, my mind will engage when I'm standing on the land itself. But Helma, about those investments of yours—you could quit the library. Live a life of financial abandon. Buy a new car. Play forever."

"They're private, Ruth."

"They're private, Ruth," Ruth mimicked. "But really, what are you going to do?"

"I haven't decided yet."

"Well, if you need ideas, I'm available."

Since this was the third time she'd visited Meriwether's property, Helma had no difficulty finding the driveway. She drove into the quiet clearing and parked close to the shop.

Helma stood outside her car for a moment and listened. The world was rarely ever quiet, truly quiet. An airplane buzzed somewhere out of sight. A breeze whispered in the upper reaches of the firs, And from far away she heard the sound of a semi gearing down.

"What are you doing," Ruth asked, "communing with the spirits?"

"Just listening. I believe we're alone."

"I sure hope so." Ruth peered around her, then looked over her shoulder and shuddered in an unnecessarily exaggerated manner. "Okay, so let's strut and fret our hour on *this* stage. Where shall we begin?"

"The shop, I think."

"We've already been through the shop, with Lynnette."

"Yes, but now we know what we're looking for," Helma reminded her, leading the way. She'd slipped a small spiral notebook and pencil into her jacket pocket, prepared to jot down anything that appeared significant. Her multitool rested in her other pocket.

When they'd pushed open one of the double doors and allowed the light inside, Ruth circled the shop's interior. "I don't see anything that color. Not even a hint."

Helma peered upward but the rafters were empty. Nothing stood out on the walls. With the toe of her hiking boot, she pushed aside sawdust on the wooden floor near the workbench legs but didn't find any pink scraps. "Somebody's been here," she told Ruth.

"How do you know?"

Helma pointed to the small cabinet where she'd found the jars and lids. "The bottom left drawer isn't properly closed."

"Maybe you just didn't close it all the way."

Helma gazed at her and Ruth amended, "I guess you probably did."

Helma didn't touch the drawer but peered inside. "The lids are misaligned," she informed Ruth.

"Kids maybe," Ruth said. "Or squirrels. C'mon. I don't see anything here. Let's go look in the woods, around the tree of his fatal fall."

"Just a minute," Helma said as she noted the open drawer in her notebook. And when she raised her head, she realized the calendar that had hung near the door was gone; only the bare nail remained. "His calendar's gone," she said, pointing toward the bare nail.

"Why would anyone take an outdated calendar?" Ruth asked, bending low and looking around the shop's floor. "It's useless."

"Unless Meriwether had jotted down incriminating information."

"Dates with Lynnette?" Ruth asked. "Sorry. Probably not."

"But I'm sure it was here when we encountered Lynnette," Helma said, wishing she'd taken a closer look at the calendar. Temperatures, she remembered, a dental appointment. But what else?

"Lynnette could have taken it. We left her here, remember? And wasn't it a little odd how fast we caught up with her? She should have been home before we trudged through the jungles and you backed out to the road."

"Maybe," Helma allowed.

They crossed the meadow toward the scene of Meriwether's death, and then examined the tree and the area around it. Helma was surprised to uncover a beer can when she pushed aside a hump of matted leaves.

They checked mounds of brush, behind trees, followed what looked like trails that only circled back to Meriwether's shop, but discovered nothing extraordinary. Or coral fuchsia.

"None of this is ringing a bell for me," Ruth said, throwing up her hands. "I wouldn't have been wandering around out here. Let's go back to the house."

Ruth stalked back toward the house and Helma followed, still casting her eyes in every direction.

"We can cut across here," Ruth said, motioning to the still little meadow.

But no sooner had Ruth entered the meadow than she yelped and fell flat on her face.

Chapter 28

Facing Unpleasant Facts

Ruth sprawled on the ground holding her right shin. Leaves and needles clung to her pants and elbows and a twig stuck out from behind her ear like a pencil on an old-fashioned librarian. Her cursing was creative and fluent enough that Helma judged her to be not seriously injured.

"You tripped."

"No lie," Ruth said, rubbing her shin with her palms. "I'm lucky I didn't break my leg. I'm not meant for this woodsy life. Give me a stuffy, smoke-filled room any day."

Helma helped her stand, then, out of curiosity, nudged the protruding spot Ruth had tripped over. Ruth walked on ahead, muttering.

It was a pyramid of dirt about a foot high, appearing to have been mounded, not formed by nature. Helma brushed at the debris on the top of the pile and touched a hard object. She brushed away more dirt, then called, "Ruth."

Ruth turned around. "Now what?"

"Come look at this."

Ruth rejoined her and looked down. "That's it! A coral fuchsia tree tube. But that's weird. Where's the tree?"

Helma used a stick to push away the remaining dirt from the tree tube. It emerged ten inches from the ground, straight up, as if it had once protected a small and vulnerable tree. But there was no trace of a sapling.

"There's writing on it," Ruth said, kneeling on the damp earth.

Helma had already noticed the black writing, obviously done with a reliable permanent marker. She crouched beside Ruth. "It's a date."

Ruth counted off on her fingers. "Eleven months ago. That must have been when he planted the tree."

But Helma wasn't so sure. And from her crouch she peered along the ground in the open meadow, the only spot near Meriwether's house where any sunshine reached the earth. "Look, Ruth. There are other mounds."

At first the mounds appeared to be piles of matted leaves from the surrounding big leaf maples, but by turning her head and taking in the shadows and pale sunshine, Helma noted the mounds were aligned in rows. She stood and walked to the next one.

This tree tube wasn't buried in dirt but only covered by the leaves. It, too, had writing on the side. "Twelve months ago," Ruth said, again counting on her fingers.

They continued uncovering the mounds, brushing away leaves, and unburying more tree tubes. All had dates, each a month apart.

"Why was he planting trees in the dead of winter?" Ruth mused, pointing to a tree tube with a January date. She brushed her hands on her pants and gazed around them at the twelve tree tubes they'd uncovered: spots of brilliant pink in the green and black forest. "Or was he?"

Helma moved around the clearing, taking in the slant

of the sun and, using skills she'd read about while helping a young student conduct research on Stonehenge, roughly calculated, the exposure of sun throughout the year.

"I never knew the guy suffered from a Johnny Appleseed complex," Ruth said doubtfully.

"Johnny Appleseed's name was actually John Chapman," Helma explained. "And some people believe his apple-planting was the catalyst of the hard cider industry in the early 1800s."

"My kind of guy."

"Meriwether set these tubes so they'd receive the most sun," Helma told her. "And notice how this meadow isn't naturally shaped. It's been *cleared* into an oval, oriented from east to west to take the most advantage of any sunlight."

"Isn't that what you do if you're planting trees in a gloomy place like this?"

"It is, but I don't believe he was planting trees."

"Helma, you never even met the guy; how do you know what he was doing? He was outdoorsy, played in the forest, frolicked in the trees, sat by his fire and carved little things out of wood."

"No. Think about this logically, Ruth. What we're looking for is what Meriwether the chain-saw artist and Vincent the chemistry instructor had in common."

Ruth rolled her eyes. "I thought it was obvious: late-night tree planters."

"What else?"

"Are we playing Sherlock Holmes and Watson here? Is this deductive reasoning? Or specious?"

"I don't play games. I'm thinking out loud with your assistance. What else did they have in common?"

"They were both men; they both adored me." Ruth ticked off her fingers. "They both fooled around in their garages. I painted both of them, at least my impressions. Oh yeah, and they're both dead."

"Plus," Helma continued, "they both were involved, in a way, in chemical concoctions."

"Oh yeah, the face cream and school experiments."

"And most of all they had the coral fuchsia tree tubes in common." When Ruth didn't respond except to gaze at her, Helma said. "I believe they were both experimenting on the tree tubes."

"Like how? To see if mice and moles can chew their way through to the tasty bark? Is that why some were buried?" Ruth nudged one of the tree tubes with her toe.

"Don't move those; they may be evidence. Brianna said one of their projects in Vincent's chemistry classes was photodegradation. Another was soil microbes."

"What's that mean?"

"I believe they're both factors in biodegradability. How long it takes, or even *whether*, materials will biodegrade when they're left in the elements: sunshine, wind, soil, changes in temperature, rain and snow."

"Gloom of night," Ruth added. She waved her hand around to encompass the rows of coral fuchsia tree tubes. "That was a useless exercise because these obviously aren't the degradable kind of tree tubes."

"That would be my estimation," Helma agreed.

Ruth frowned. "Oh. But aren't they *supposed* to melt away? Isn't that one of Ground Up!'s claims to environmental correctness? They plant the baby trees in conspicuous spots, drop on the even more conspicuous tree tubes, and claim they'll disappear within two years?"

Helma nodded, still gazing around at the tree tubes, each of them as freshly coral fuchsia colored as the next.

"Isn't regular plastic supposed to last about fifty billion years?"

"A plastic garbage bag lasts at least twenty years in a land-fill," Helma told her.

"So what Ground Up!'s been doing is *littering*?"

"Not the image they'd like to project, I'm sure."

"And Vincent and Meriwether figured it out so the Ground Up! mafia killed them. Let's go tell all our police friends."

"You don't want to do that," a man's voice warned from behind them.

Helma wasn't surprised to see Steward Arbor's sidekick, Richard, step out from behind a cedar tree. She glanced toward the shade, looking for Steward, but he wasn't in sight. She quickly scanned the trees, trying to discover his hiding place. She imagined him hunkered in the shadows of the denser forest, perhaps with a weapon, watching, waiting for a prearranged signal from Richard. To do what?

"Who're you?" Ruth asked. Then she snapped her fingers. "I know. You're Steward Arbor's little buddy. What are you, Ground Up!'s co-pooh-bah?"

In vulnerable situations Helma had learned to always keep a man's hands in sight, and Richard's left hand had slipped into the side pocket of his jacket.

"I don't think he's a member of Ground Up! at all," she told Ruth.

"Oh, haven't passed the initiation rites yet?" Ruth asked him. "Don't have your skill-at-night badge? Still an acolyte?"

The scarred eyebrow gave Richard a sardonic air. His eyes moved between Helma and Ruth.

Ruth was an excitable woman, unpredictable and, yes, emotionally overwrought. But during dangerous moments— and Helma judged this moment to have that potential—Ruth was prone to grow calm, casual, and, worst of all, to find the situation highly humorous.

"I know who he actually is," she said, deflecting Richard's dangerous attention from Ruth, buying time as she surreptitiously watched for Steward Arbor.

"And who's that?" he asked her. This time he meaningfully moved his left hand in his pocket.

Beside Helma, Ruth breathed a soft, "Uh-oh." If there

was an object in Richard's pocket, Helma doubted it was a GPS.

"You're the head of Earth's Sheath," Helma said, "manufacturer of these supposedly biodegradable tree tubes." She waved toward the rows of bright pink tubes, Meriwether's experiment.

He didn't falter. His left hand caressed the bulk in his pocket, and Helma noted the graze of wear on the left side of his jacket. Her heart sank; he truly was left-handed. "You think so?" he asked.

"I saw your picture on the Earth's Sheath's Web site. It's very difficult to be anonymous when people have access to the Internet. You claimed your tree tubes were biodegradable, but they're not."

"Are you a chemist?" he asked, his lip rising in a sneer.

"I'm a librarian. I can easily research local chemists who can assess the claims of your product."

"No need," he said. "Why don't we go for a little walk back to the house and shop so we can discuss this situation."

"I don't believe that's in our best interests," Helma told him, not moving.

"But it is in *mine*," he said.

The sound of a broken branch came from the woods. "Hey, what's going on?"

Steward Arbor emerged into the sunny little clearing, relaxed and smiling. "I thought we were meeting at the office first," he said to Richard. "I figured I must have missed you so I came out by myself." He gazed from Ruth to Helma. "You're the librarian. What're you doing out here?"

Helma nodded toward Richard, and Steward frowned at him. "What's going on?" he asked again.

She watched Steward's face closely and said, "What do you know about Earth's Sheath products?"

He looked back at her and shrugged. "They make the

biodegradable tree tubes we use when we plant our trees. Why?"

"What is Richard doing here?" she asked. "His company's in Illinois."

"Rich? He stops by every couple of months to be sure we're happy with the product. That's what I call service."

"That's what I call dumb as a stump," Ruth muttered.

"What?" Steward said to Ruth. "What did you say?"

"You two have become pals?" she asked.

"Partners, maybe," Steward said. "If we can put together the financing to buy this place."

"To develop it?" Helma asked, thinking of Douglas Bogelli.

"No, for a tree farm."

"I think sunshine is a necessity for all living things," Ruth told him, waving her hand around the clearing and then pointing upward toward the weak sunlight. "In this meadow you might eke out a whole half acre of sunshine to hover over your seedlings. Might grow an inch a year, the little blunted babies."

Richard stood easily, hand still in pocket, watching and listening.

"There's an open bench further back on the property, raped by loggers a few years ago," Steward said. "And we might take out a few trees here."

"You'll *remove* trees so you can *grow* trees?"

"Just a few of the big older ones so we can plant hundreds in their place."

"I get it," Ruth said. "The needs of the many outweigh the needs of the few, or the one."

"It's one of our most noble ideals," Steward said, actually raising his hand to his heart.

"Your ideals come from Mr. Spock in a *Star Trek* movie?" Ruth asked

"Steward," Helma said quietly. "When did you begin using Earth's Sheath tree tubes?"

"About a year or so ago, right after I founded Ground Up! Why?"

"And you investigated their products?"

"Definitely. We studied their scientific reports. Earth's Sheath is a new company, so they gave us an exceptional deal. Plus, they're getting ready to sign a multi-million-dollar deal with the National Conservation Consortium."

"Bingo," Ruth said, exactly what Helma was thinking.

"So Earth's Sheath stands to become a very profitable company," Helma said.

"At least successful," Richard said, taking a step closer to Steward. "Profitable is a relative term."

"So what are you all standing around out here for?" Steward asked.

Richard nodded back toward the house. "I was just suggesting that we chat back by the buildings instead of out here."

"I like it here," Ruth blurted.

"Steward," Helma said to the evidently puzzled and even more obviously unobservant man. "Do you see all these tree tubes?"

Steward looked at the rows of brilliantly colored tree tubes. He frowned. "Meriwether must have been doing a little tree planting himself."

"No, he was—"

"That's enough." Richard pulled his hand from his pocket and waved it toward Helma. The sun glinted from the barrel of a small handgun.

"A gun," Steward said, taking a step back and raising his hands as if the gun had been pointed at him. "What in hell's going on?"

"How many times are you going to ask that?" Ruth said in an irritated voice. "Your partner's a crook and a litter bug. Open your eyes."

"What'd he do?" Steward asked.

"You tell him," Ruth said, rolling her eyes. "He needs

somebody who explains things in a slow and thorough manner."

"Ruth is right," Helma told Steward as she watched Richard, who had a small smile on his lips. "Richard's cover is . . . blown. Two men, both now dead, figured out the tree tubes are not biodegradable. Richard killed them."

"They're not biodegradable?" Steward turned to Richard. "That god-awful color is *permanent*?"

"I love it when a man sees the light," Ruth said.

"No more talking," Richard told them. He waved the gun toward the path. "Back to the shop."

"Rich," Steward said. "Is this for real?"

"Get going. You." He pointed at Ruth. "You go first."

She pulled herself taller, straightening her shoulders until she gazed downward at Richard from the bottom of her eyes. Helma could see Ruth was about to balk. Not just because she resented being ordered to do anything, but because she was calculating the size and intent of Richard against the size and speed of herself.

"Go ahead, Ruth," Helma said, deciding from the look in Richard's eyes that pulling a trigger wouldn't require much forethought.

Ruth made a face, but turned and led the way toward the house and Meriwether's shop. Helma followed and then Steward, his hands still raised, a dazed look on his face.

Only Helma's car sat in Meriwether's driveway. "Where's your car?" she asked Steward.

"Back off the two-track." He shrugged sheepishly. "I don't know how to get here any other way."

"Be quiet. Inside," Richard ordered them when they reached the shop.

"I don't like this," Ruth said.

"But the tests said that within two years they'd disappear," Steward said.

"Scientific tests can be altered," Helma told him as she

entered Meriwether's shop followed by Ruth and Steward. "It's always worthwhile to have important tests independently verified, especially when you purchase items over the Internet."

They stood inside, at the rear of the building, as Richard put his shoulder against the stubborn door, then finished pulling it shut from inside.

"That's why you took the calendar," Helma said to Richard, glancing toward the lighter rectangle of wood where it had hung. "What I took to be daily temperature records was part of Meriwether's experimentation on the tree tubes."

"All gone now," Richard said cheerfully as he backed out the side door, closing it behind him.

Realizing what was about to happen, Helma had closed her eyes, giving herself time to adjust to darkness. When she heard the scrape and thump of the latch being dropped, she opened them, gaining a head start on distinguishing their surroundings. Lines of light outlined the double doors. A single pale ray shone through a crack in the wall.

There was a thump and Ruth said, "Ouch,"

"Stand still until your eyes adjust," Helma told her.

"Did you see that movie where all the settlers were locked in a church and then the bad guys burned down the church?" Ruth asked.

"That isn't helpful, Ruth," Helma warned.

"He's going to set the place on fire?" Steward asked.

"Certainly not," Helma said.

"Yeah, it would be too obvious: three people burned up in a locked building," Ruth said. "Even Carter Houston would realize that was suspicious."

"Actually," Helma corrected, "I believe Carter Houston is a very credible detective."

"Can we debate that another time? Right now let's figure out how to get out of here."

"We should wait." Steward's voice came from closer to the front of the garage. Helma made out his outline as he crossed in front of the double doors. "He's not going to hurt us if we stay here; he said so."

A guffaw came from Ruth's direction. "Yeah, just like he told you your precious tree tubes were biodegradable. Did he advise you to plant weeping willows to replace big leaf maples on Fourteenth Street?"

"We had a surplus of willows available," Steward said defensively. "Why would Richard have killed two guys, anyway?"

"Either Vincent or Meriwether must have confronted Richard with the proof that his tubes weren't biodegradable," Helma surmised. She'd felt along the wall until she touched the small door's knob, but that was locked, too. There was no give when she pushed on it.

"Probably Meriwether," Ruth said. "He was the compulsive type."

"And," Helma added, "Brianna said Vincent encouraged his students to defend their findings. So Vincent might have as well. Both men, either separately or together."

"So Richard flew out to our little kingdom to erase their findings," Ruth said. Helma made out her motioning as if she were erasing a chalk board.

"When airline records are checked, they'll match the times of both men's deaths," Helma said. "And when Richard returned to Bellehaven this time, he must have heard about your paintings."

"What's that got to do with it?" Ruth asked her.

"You *have* named names," Helma reminded her. "Richard had to make sure you hadn't left a clue for the police."

"Heck, even *I* heard about them," Steward said, "and I didn't even know who you were."

"Marketing's always been one of my better skills," Ruth acknowledged.

Chapter 30

A Question of Fire

"Well, I *know* Richard wouldn't kill us," Steward said without a shred of doubt in his voice.

"Oh yeah?" Ruth said. "Then what's that smell?"

Helma sniffed. Smoke. And charcoal lighter. "We will now move forward to the doors to this building," she told them. "Toward that strip of light."

"I think that's where the smell's coming from," Ruth said.

"That is also the only reasonable exit. Join hands, please."

After a fumbling and bumping of bodies, they found each other's hands.

"Forward, one step at a time," Helma said. "But first, Ruth you're facing the wrong direction."

Ruth pulled her hand from Helma's and then gave it back. Helma stood on the end, Ruth in the middle. Helma counted off their steps. "One, two, three, four, five, six. We're there."

The smoke and smell was stronger at the doors. "Stay low," Helma advised. "Hold your breaths and breathe shallowly."

"And pat your head while you rub your stomach," Ruth countered.

"We need to push together as a team to open this door," Helma said.

"We're going to die," Ruth said.

"Not if we work together. Form a huddle."

They wrapped their arms around each other, with Ruth in the middle. "Don't try anything funny," she warned Steward, and began coughing from the smoke. Helma counted off, "One, two, go," and they lunged against the door. It bowed but held. "Again."

Two more times they tried, and then fell back to catch their breath.

"Shouldn't there be a fan in here so we could clear out the smoke?" Ruth said. She sneezed.

"The power's off," Helma reminded her.

"Besides," Steward added. "It would create a draw and the place would burn down in thirty seconds."

"Instead of forty-five?" Ruth asked.

"This time we'll run at it," Helma said. The pinpoint of light flickered, and she thought she heard the crackle of flames. There was no time to waste. "Right foot first. One, two, go."

Holding each other, they ran across the floor and banged into the door. Pain shot through Helma's shoulder but she felt the door give, not where the two doors met but along the hinges on the right side.

"Here," she said, coughing, her eyes burning. "Push here."

They did, and the hinges screeched as the screws pulled from the wood, leaving enough space so they tumbled into the daylight one after the other. Helma expected Richard to be standing at the ready, gun trained on them, and she tried to get her bearings so that she could roll out of range, but she saw no sign of him. He was gone.

They caught their breath, gratefully inhaling the cool air, hacking out the smoke from their lungs. Flames crawled up the building, blooming and licking at the old wood. The shop wouldn't last long. Any evidence that might have been hidden inside was now destroyed.

"Look," Steward cried, barely able to speak. "The house." He lay down on the grass and gulped deep breaths of air.

It, too, was aflame, the fire already reaching the roof.

They heard the racing sound of an engine coming toward them from the road, and Ruth said in a raspy voice, "Somebody saw the fire."

But it was a police car that emerged from the trees and onto Meriwether's driveway, with Carter Houston at the wheel. He spoke into his radio as he threw open his door and jumped out. It was unusual to see the controlled detective moving with such urgency, but he raced toward them, his hand beneath his jacket.

"Are you injured?" he asked at the same time his eyes flashed toward the burning house, the forest. "Is everybody safe?"

"We are, but he got away," Helma told him.

"Who?" Carter asked her.

"His name is Richard and he's the owner of Earth's Sheath, the makers of bogus biodegradable tree tubes."

"What was he driving?"

She looked at Steward, who still lay on the grass, coughing.

"I suspect it was a dark car I saw him get into at the library."

"Make and model?" Carter asked.

She closed her eyes and remembered. "Birds."

"I beg your pardon?" Carter asked

Ruth and Carter stared at her as if she weren't thinking clearly. Steward uncovered his eyes.

"Birds," she repeated. "It's a self test I frequently engage in with license plate numbers. His license plate number is 598, the Dewey decimal number for birds. And the letters were FOH, which I turned into Flying Over Head to correlate it to the subject of birds."

Carter gave her a curt nod and said, "I'll call it in right now."

It was a testimony to the efficiency of public services that the fire department arrived within seven minutes, even if the buildings were already a complete loss. The firemen still set up their hoses and sprayed the surrounding grass and trees, protecting them from the flames. A few lookers drove in but Carter had placed his car so no one could drive past it. He handed Ruth, Helma, and Steward bottles of water from his trunk.

"Carter," Ruth said in dead seriousness, even smiling at the detective. "I was glad to see you pull in. Thanks."

He stared at her, silent, no doubt waiting, Helma thought, for the barb that usually followed, but Ruth raised her water bottle to him and took a swig. He had the look of a man about to shuffle his feet, but then straightened and said stiffly, "You're welcome."

"How did you know we were here?" Helma asked.

"I overheard you mention the coral fuchsia in Ruth's strip of paint. When I looked at it, I recognized that distinctive shade."

"You did?" Ruth asked, nudging Helma. "See, Carter has an eye for color. You should paint, Carter."

Carter looked down at his shoes. Ruth's mouth fell open.

"But how did seeing the pink lead you here?" Helma persisted.

Carter answered in a rush, as if to change the subject. "It was a hunch. I knew about Meriwether's face creams."

"You did?"

He nodded. "We had a batch analyzed after his death." He shook his head. "They were harmless. Useless, too. A little tree sap and ground plants mixed into a cheap petroleum-based lotion, but I recalled seeing a tree tube on his workbench. I didn't connect it at the time."

"Where's the chief of police?" Ruth asked.

He answered as if Helma had asked, not Ruth, looking straight at her. "He's on his way." And opening his notebook, he turned to Steward, "Can we talk?"

From a safe distance, they watched the buildings burn. There was a fascination with fire, that violent destruction. Nothing from something. Helma herself could barely take her eyes from the conflagration.

"Helma," Ruth said, wiping at her eyes with the corner of her shirt. "Wouldn't you call matching license-plate numbers to Dewey decimal numbers playing a *game*."

"Not at all. It's simply reinforcing my knowledge," she told Ruth as she finally looked away from the fire to see Wayne Gallant's plain car brake on the other side of Carter's.

Chapter 31

Maneuvers Worthy of a Champion

"You're familiar with the Ali-Foreman fight," Wayne Gallant said as he opened the door of Goodwin's Gym for Helma.

"Only the results," she told him. "I read about Ali's rope-a-dope strategy."

"The Rumble in the Jungle in Zaire. Don't expect anything so dramatic here," the chief told her with a small laugh. "TNT and I will spar a couple of rounds and then let's go for a walk along the boardwalk."

Helma nodded. She'd finally run out of polite excuses to decline TNT's invitations to watch him spar, as well as Wayne's assertions that she should witness the retired boxer in action.

Goodwin's Gym filled a remodeled grocery store. Mirrors lined the walls, images bouncing off images. Men and women of every age worked out on various sleek machines. Televisions played above some. On others, people in every variety of gym outfit read or listened to music—maybe books—on headsets. And in still another corner, a group of women exercised on colorful mats.

A row of folding chairs was set up close to the roped square of the boxing ring, and Wayne beckoned her to sit down, then sat beside her. "TNT should be here any minute. Are you warm enough?"

"It *is* cool in here," she agreed, "but I'm fine, thanks."

"Good temperature for exercise. You sure you feel up to this?"

"Of course," Helma told him. "I wasn't hurt, and my shoulder's definitely less sore."

"That's good. You thought fast in a deadly situation."

Thanks to Helma supplying the police with Richard's license-plate number, he'd been picked up long before he reached the Canadian border. He now resided in the Belle-haven jail pending his murder trial. "What about Steward Arbor?" she asked. "Will he be charged?"

Wayne shook his head. "Don't know yet. His greatest crime, besides trespassing, was gullibility. Right now he's removing all the pink tree tubes. That'll keep him busy for a while."

"Ruth said the color was coral fuchsia."

He laughed. "That's what Carter called it, too. Whoever thought those two would agree on something that obscure?" Wayne's smile softened. "Have you thought any more about our discussion about . . . us?"

He leaned closer to her, his arm against hers. Through their clothing, she felt the firmness of his triceps.

"I have been considering your suggestions," she told him, carefully choosing her words. "And—"

"Hey, Chief. I see you brought the audience." It was TNT, dressed in his usual gray sweats and carrying a gym bag. "Hi, Helma." His smile beamed. "You came to watch this old dog take it like a man, eh?" He danced on his toes and jabbed his fist in her general direction.

Beside her, Wayne whispered, "Nod for me. Just nod."

"Wayne says you're evenly matched," Helma said to TNT, at the same time she nodded her head toward Wayne. He squeezed her hand, his smile wide.

"Hah! What a guy. Did you hear the news?"

"Which news?"

"Somebody's buying the Bayside Arms. Walter told me the new owner doesn't plan to change a thing. No condos, no big remodel for megabuck rent. Isn't that great?"

"Who bought it?" Wayne asked.

Helma smoothed the fabric of her new slacks, her head down.

TNT shrugged. "Not even Walter knows. It's being handled by a hotshot woman Realtor from Faber. De la something. She told him it was a 'confidential party' looking for an investment. Some rich guy, I guess."

Helma looked up, cleared her throat and said, "Have a good sparring session, gentlemen."

Wayne released Helma's hand and picked up his gym bag. "No catcalls or boos," he warned her.

"I wouldn't consider such rudeness," Helma assured him, and he laughed.

The two men disappeared into the men's locker room, and Helma pulled out a book she was reading, *Color Theory.* She studied the color wheel on the front page, trying to figure out exactly *why* some colors simply should never be seen together. Behind her the gym sounds melded together and created a cacophony that reminded her of one of her father's bonfires, when he'd gathered the family—aunts and uncles and cousins—and tried to lead them in rounds of "Row, Row, Row Your Boat," only in Lithuanian.

The men's locker-room door opened. TNT and Wayne, in shorts and towels over their shoulders, entered the ring. They both wore boxing gloves: TNT's were red with his name emblazoned on the wrists; the chief's were plain brown. They also both wore padded helmets and mouth guards.

The two men retreated to opposite corners of the ring and dropped their towels. Bare-chested, they faced off in the center and a young man raised his hand, counted off, and said, loudly, "Ding!"

"This is one of the best parts."

Helma's mother sat down in the chair beside her. She wore sweatpants and a zippered sweatshirt. Helma spotted a hint of blue spandex peeking past the zipper.

"What are you doing here, Mother?" Helma asked. Wayne swung at TNT and the older man danced away from the jab.

"Yoga class. I told you." She waved toward the ring. "Go, TNT. You can KO that kid." TNT waved back, his smile visible even through his helmet and mouthpiece. Wayne took advantage of his distraction and landed a blow on TNT's shoulder.

Suddenly it made sense. "Mother, are you and TNT—"

"Not yet, but he certainly looks like he's capable, doesn't he?"

They sat next to each other, watching the two men clash in the ring. The chief's arms were longer. TNT was faster. The muscles in Wayne's back rippled with each lunge, the tendons in his thighs tautened.

He was surprisingly light on his feet for such a big man. Perspiration shone on his chest in a satiny gloss and darkened his trunks at his hips.

Helma slipped off her jacket. The gym manager must have turned up the heat. Lillian unzipped her sweatshirt. Yes, it was blue spandex.

"Very nice," Lillian said, nodding as TNT's fist connected with Wayne's chin. She picked up Helma's book and fanned her face, then turned to Helma and winked.

Investigate the Hottest New Mysteries!

Sign up for the FREE HarperCollins monthly mystery newsletter,

The Scene of the Crime,

and get to know your favorite authors, win free books, and be the first to learn about the best new mysteries going on sale.

To register, simply go to www.HarperCollins.com, visit our mystery channel page, and at the bottom of the page, enter your email address where it states "Sign up for our mystery newsletter." Then you can tap into monthly Hot Reads, check out our award nominees, sneak a peek at upcoming titles, and discover the best whodunits each and every month.

Get to know the magnificent mystery authors of HarperCollins and sign up today!